The
BAKLAVA
CLUB

JASON GOODWIN

SARAH CRICHTON BOOKS

FARRAR, STRAUS AND GIROUX

NEW YORK

Sarah Crichton Books
Farrar, Straus and Giroux
18 West 18th Street, New York 10011

Printed in the United States of America
First edition, 2014

Library of Congress Cataloging-in-Publication Data
Goodwin, Jason, 1964–
    The Baklava Club / Jason Goodwin. — First edition.
        pages   cm. — (Investigator Yashim ; 5)
    ISBN 978-0-374-29437-3 (hardback) — ISBN 978-1-4299-4955-2 (ebook)
    1. Yashim (Fictitious character : Goodwin)—Fiction.   2. Princes—Fiction.
3. Eunuchs—Fiction.   4. Istanbul (Turkey)—History—19th century—Fiction.
I. Title.
PR6107.O663B35 2014
823'.92—dc23
                                                                        2013048038

Designed by Abby Kagan

Farrar, Straus and Giroux books may be purchased for educational, business, or
promotional use. For information on bulk purchases, please contact the Macmillan
Corporate and Premium Sales Department at 1-800-221-7945, extension 5442,
or write to specialmarkets@macmillan.com.

www.fsgbooks.com
www.twitter.com/fsgbooks • www.facebook.com/fsgbooks

1   3   5   7   9   10   8   6   4   2

FOR ANNA

I could be bounded in a nutshell, and count
myself a king of infinite space—were it not that
I have bad dreams.

—HAMLET

The
BAKLAVA
CLUB

1

THE man lives, or the man dies. It is a matter of the weather.

Tonight he will live: because the sea is smooth like watered silk beneath a crescent moon, the ship's wake fanning out like a tear. The ship makes little sound: it is a still Mediterranean evening, and the timbers barely creak. A sailor in the fo'c'sle coughs; overhead a sail flaps and spanks the mast.

The man leans at the rail, looking out to sea; and the assassin stands back a little, also watching the wake of the ship as it slowly widens and ripples and disappears toward the empty horizon. He watches the incessant production of the wake, and scarcely glances at the man he has come to kill. La Piuma, "The Feather."

It would be easy tonight, the assassin thinks. A murmured conversation at the stern rail, a quick blow to the head. Man overboard. Then the assassin might raise the alarm.

But that won't do. The Committee wants La Piuma to simply disappear.

Better to wait for a wind. Cloud cover, more noise, the pitch and roll of the ship.

La Piuma can sleep in peace another night. He will eat another meal of fish, boiled chicken, and fruit with cheese, and drink his wine. Coffee will be served in the morning, if that's what he wants.

Would he fight for this day's grace? the assassin wonders, moving away along the deck. La Piuma was as good as dead as soon as the ship set sail from Bari to Istanbul. Would he be grateful to live even for one more dull, eventless day at sea?

He would, the assassin considers; yet he cannot answer why.

2

LONG October shadows were drawn across the yard as Yashim made his way to the Polish ambassador's residence in Pera, the European quarter of Istanbul. He passed the rusted iron gates bearing the faded coat of arms of a vanished country, and mounted the steps to the front door.

At the end of a long, hot summer the wood was dry. The door opened easily under Yashim's hand and he stepped into the gloom of the hall-way. A figure was coming slowly down the great stairs.

"Good morning, Marta. Is the ambassador at home?"

"The lord is in the pantry."

From her tone, Marta did not seem to think much of the lord's presence in the pantry.

The residency had been built on a generous scale in the days when a Polish ambassador was a figure of substance in Istanbul, representing a vast commonwealth that stretched from the Baltic to the Black Sea, its borders marching with those of the Ottoman Empire for hundreds of miles over marsh, black earth, rivers, and hills; a lively border distinguished by the exchange of fire, or amber for spice, as occasion required. Polish delegations to Istanbul, capital of the Ottoman Empire, had been magnificent affairs. One seventeenth-century pasha, viewing the Polish ambassador's arrival, had drily remarked that he'd brought too many people to sign a peace, and too few to fight a war. Those days had vanished, like Poland itself. By 1842, Stanislaw Palewski still maintained, on Ottoman sufferance, the diplomatic status of his forebears: but

Marta was his only retinue. His retinue liked to keep the pantry for herself.

"I'll go through," Yashim said.

The pantry was lit by a sash window that reached from floor to ceiling and overlooked the unkempt gardens at the back of the house. Palewski, in shirtsleeves and braces, was bent over a bench, fiddling with an assembly of rods and tubes. He had a rag in his hand and a smear of oil on his forehead.

Yashim stood in the doorway, watching his friend.

"Hullo, Yashim." Palewski glanced up. "Has Marta sent you to clear me out?"

"Not yet. Mechanics?"

"Or art, Yashim. Just look at this."

He tossed a dull metal tube across to Yashim, who caught it and turned it to the light.

"It's a gun." Yashim turned the barrel between his fingers, observing the damascene work beneath the tarnish. "Quite a piece."

"Better, Yash. Can you read the gunmaker's name?"

He hummed tunelessly while Yashim inspected the barrel more closely.

"Paris . . . Drouet?"

Palewski reached for the barrel and began rubbing it furiously with a rag. "Boutet, the finest gunmaker in France. Fowling piece. A three-foot barrel, and exceptionally light, no? Boutet's genius. I don't believe he made more than a dozen of these and I've found two here. If you don't mind getting your hands dirty, you can polish up the other one. Truth is, I'd forgotten all about them. Seen enough guns by 1812 to think they were worth avoiding, I suppose."

"And now?"

"Now, thanks to Midhat Pasha's invitation, Yashim, I've discovered these beauties. Look at that dolphin on the trigger guard!"

"Midhat Pasha's invitation?"

"Duck. Snipe. Sure you won't take a rag?"

"Midhat Pasha has asked you to go shooting?"

"We call it wildfowling. I was about to send him my regrets when I remembered the old gun cupboard in the cellar. Marta produced the key."

"And when you opened the cupboard—"

"When I opened the cupboard I found this sublime pair. Someone has left them in a shocking state. There's rust and fouling in the breech of this one, and of course the stocks need oiling."

Yashim picked up one of the wooden stocks, slim and fine-curled, almost like a bird in flight.

"There are a couple of good gunsmiths in the arms bazaar."

"I'll see how I do first." Palewski squinted down the barrel. "This one's barrel seems perfect, but there's something wrong with the lock."

Yashim nodded. "I know the feeling."

Palewski laughed. Yashim had something wrong with his firing mechanism, too. He was a decade younger than his friend, well built, dark, with curious gray eyes and a face that lit up with a smile: but Yashim was a eunuch.

"Let's have tea." Palewski threw down his rag. "Marta!"

Upstairs, in the more familiar surroundings of Palewski's drawing room, Yashim took a window seat and gazed out through the wisteria.

"Tea!" exclaimed Palewski, rubbing his hands. "You know, Yashim, I'm really looking forward to this shoot. It's thirty years since I went fowling. Almost forty since I did it for love."

He approached his bookcases and began to rummage across the spines. "My father gave me my first gun when I was ten years old. It was a German muzzle-loader. He used to take me out really early in the morning, still dark, in the frost. We went for duck on the ponds, mostly, with an English retriever. Once I shot a red kite, which made him furious. I had to draw it until my arm ached. We used the feathers to make flies for fishing—and I caught a trout."

He smiled at the memory. "He wanted me to understand nature, not just kill it. Those early starts, they were a sort of communion. William Paley says that's the way to approach God, seeing the world as its creator had made it. Learning its secrets. Nature's innocent," he added, gesturing at the books. "But these represent the world we've made out of our ambitions and our lies. All man's clever, devious things."

He darted on a book, and then another.

"Izaak Walton." He laid a book on the window seat. "*The Compleat Angler.* Cornerstone of Anglicanism. And this—private printing, Saint Petersburg. Sergei Aksakov."

"A Russian?"

"Of course. Anglican, Russian, aborigine—they feel the same. I believe in that God, Yashim, who made ducks fly at their hour, and the birds fall silent just before light, and the water and what lies beneath it. The God I used to see when I was ten years old, lying in the dark in a punt with my father, waiting for the dawn."

"And you want to see Him again? With the pasha."

Palewski ran his fingers through his hair. "Odd, isn't it? But yes. Midhat Pasha's invitation brought it back to me. And then the guns showing up like that. I'd forgotten we had 'em. Made me feel like a boy again—no, that's not it. Just gives me the feeling I had once, when I was a boy. It's in the smell of those old fowling pieces, too. Grease and metal." He flicked through the books. "As if everything fits again."

Yashim looked out through the window. Could he, he wondered, feel like a boy felt ever again? Like the boy he had been? He rubbed his leg, as if the twinge of jealousy he'd felt had surfaced there.

"You should get the guns looked over." He stood up. "I should go. You're expecting people."

Palewski cast him a quizzical look. "Do stay, Yashim. How the devil did you know?"

Yashim laughed. "My dear friend, at this hour you would usually offer me a little something—a digestif?—and instead you ask Marta to bring this excellent tea, which leads me to suppose that you are saving yourself. You're covered in soot and oil, but you have made no preparations for a bath. I see no tub by the fire, no hot water. Therefore it seems unlikely you mean to go out."

Palewski arched his eyebrows. Yashim placed his fingertips together. "So, you are receiving. But not an Ottoman—like your new hunting companion, Midhat Pasha. He may deal with foreign affairs but he remains an Ottoman gentleman. He'd take your appearance as a gross insult. So not him, or one of his kind. And not dinner. Even Marta would not have allowed you to take over her pantry had you asked someone to dine here. I saw no more evidence of cooking than of preparation for a bath. If not an Ottoman, then what? A Frank, or Franks. But they are either not quite *bon ton*, as the French say, or—"

He paused, in thought. "Or they are young," he said finally. "Yes, that would explain the lack of formality."

"A lady, perhaps?"

Yashim shook his head. "You would not have suggested I stay. No young lady."

Palewski leaned back against the sideboard, and crossed his legs carelessly. "As it happens, you're wrong. I think it very likely that there will be a young lady."

"Hmm. But not alone. Which demonstrates beyond doubt that your party will be composed of Franks, like yourself. Students? They will excuse your informality, even the oil on your face, because you can offer them an evening of wine, and song."

"Why would I want such a thing?"

Yashim smiled, and lowered his eyes. "Because, my dear old friend, you have been thinking of the past. Of your own youth, with the guns, shooting duck and all that. You are in that sort of mood."

"Ouf." Palewski left the window and went to the sideboard. "Let's have that digestif, Yashim."

3

IT seemed to Yashim that there were six of them, at least, after the front door banged and the young people raged upstairs and surged into Palewski's drawing room, making a noise like porters with iron-shod trolleys on the cobbles of Galata Hill.

"*Ciao, Palewski! Fratello! Conte Palewski! Permesso?*"

Then Palewski was surrounded, shaking hands, bowing at the young lady, and welcoming a tall fair youth who carried half a dozen bottles of champagne.

When the hubbub had abated, Yashim was surprised to count only four visitors in the room.

"Miss Lund, may I present my esteemed friend Yashim? Yashim, Miss Lund."

The men had not noticed that Palewski already had a visitor. Miss Lund sank a graceful curtsy and smiled at Yashim with enormous blue eyes. She was a very pretty girl, with almost white blond hair held up in a bun, her shoulders covered with lace.

"It is a pleasure, Signor Yashim," she said, in an accent Yashim could not quite place. Only, the accent did not matter, for Yashim could place her immediately, instinctively, the way a sipahi cavalryman judged horseflesh, or Palewski knew his guns.

"We brought you some baklava, Count Palewski." A flat box swung from her finger by a loop of raffia. "Giancarlo says it goes well with champagne! I think these are the best sort—but perhaps you will judge, Signor Yashim?"

Yashim smiled. He was an intimate of the harem, and he knew women. When he saw the inclination of the plump shoulder, the trace of laziness around the bright blue eyes, he had recognized something in Miss Lund's ease that reminded him of the *gözde*.

A *gözde*: yes, he would swear she was that. No door was closed to Yashim, as it was to half the population of the city, screened by tradition and law into discrete spaces. Selamlik was the man's world, at the gate; harem, the sanctuary. In the imperial harem lived many women who as slaves of the sultan's formed the sultan's private household. Some of them the sultan barely knew by sight, and some more he would know by name; but they all served him, in their way. They washed his shirts, arranged his kaftans, played him music, and blushed at his approach. A few—a very privileged few—would have the honor of amusing him in bed. These girls were *in his eye*, as the saying went: the *gözde*, whose particular task was to bear the sultan a child—a son—and so ensure the continuation of the House of Osman, which had ruled the empire now for six centuries, making it the oldest royal line in Europe, and perhaps the world.

If Miss Lund was the *gözde*, it did not take Yashim long to guess who, in this room, performed the duties of a sultan.

Palewski introduced his friends in turn. Giancarlo was the tall one, who would turn heads in an Istanbul street: fair-haired and broad-shouldered, he looked well-fed and well-bred, with a high forehead and prominent cheekbones. His nose was big and his teeth flashed very white when he laughed. He laughed often, and then his eyes went to Miss Lund as though they shared a secret joke of their own.

Rafael looked older, but probably wasn't: maybe it was the spectacles, or the short, dark hair that was already thinning a little. He shook Yashim's hand and looked to the ground with a smile.

Fabrizio was a head shorter than Giancarlo but beautifully formed on a small scale, with a head of glossy black curls and a neatly waxed mustache. He was impeccably dressed. He had flung off a cape when he entered the room, to reveal a shirt of dazzling whiteness and trousers creased like knives.

Yashim inclined to them all, and smiled: they were the very group he had predicted, young, foreign, and eager for an evening of champagne.

Giancarlo flung himself into an armchair and let his long legs fly upward. "*Allora!* I am not in love with the ladies of Pera, Palewski!"

"Indeed." Palewski took some glasses from the sideboard and set them up.

"Very ugly, and their mustaches bigger than the men's. You haven't noticed?"

"As you may know, Pera was a Genoese colony before the conquest," Palewski observed. "The ladies you object to are descended, in the main part, from the original colonists. Your compatriots."

Fabrizio smiled, showing a fine row of little white teeth. "Giancarlo is all for Italian unity, in principle. But the Genoese? When you get down to it, Giancarlo's Italy barely stretches from Lucca to Viareggio, by the sea. It excludes a village near Carrara, and even certain houses in Lucca, I believe."

They burst out laughing, Giancarlo laughing hardest of them all. Yashim listened, mystified by their private jokes. Carrara? Some houses in Lucca?

Palewski popped a cork and filled the glasses. "I feel just the opposite. When Poland rises from the ashes, I want her to reunite with Lithuania, and have East Prussia thrown in for good measure. All or nothing!"

"To the great Commonwealth of Poland Lithuania!" cried Giancarlo, raising his glass.

"To a united Italy!" Palewski rejoined.

"Death to tyrants!"

"Down with the Inquisition!"

Miss Lund settled quietly beside Yashim on the window seat. She took a sip of champagne and glanced over the rim of her glass.

"Politics," she murmured. "The *boys* find it exciting." She had very pretty little ears, Yashim noticed, decorated with bouncing corkscrew curls. She blinked. "And you, Signor Yashim, are you a passionate politician, too?"

Yashim thought of Palewski with his new toy and his memories of punts and ducks on the Polish lakes, and of these youths, with their noisy enthusiasms. It was all boys, and boyhoods, this evening. "Perhaps," he said, "I was never quite young enough."

Miss Lund chuckled. "The ambassador is not—so young."

Palewski was leaning against the mantelpiece, glass raised, expounding something to the young men.

"Enthusiasm for his cause may keep him young, all the same. Politics."

It was Miss Lund's turn to pull a face. Yashim gave her a sympathetic smile: "United Italy?"

"Oh yes, in spite of what Fabrizio says. They're all mad for it, Giancarlo most of all. That's why we've come to Istanbul."

"To unite Italy? You seem to be a long way from home."

She misunderstood him. "I'm Danish," she said. "You can call me Birgit. Don't forget that my ancestors probably sailed up here a thousand years ago, to do business with the Byzantine emperor."

"Or to join the Varangian Guard."

"The Varang—? Remind me, please."

Yashim told her about the Viking warriors who had formed the imperial bodyguard in Byzantine times. "But Palewski knows much more about it than me. Fair-haired giants, he says, with double-edged axes."

"Hmm. Do you think Giancarlo could be a Varangian, Signor Yashim?"

"I'm sure—you at least could rely on him, Miss Lund."

She glanced away, with a pleased smile.

"And you, signor?"

"I suppose you could say," Yashim replied thoughtfully, "that I am a sort of nineteenth-century Varangian."

She laughed. "And who do you guard, Signor Yashim?"

He would have said that his role was to protect the sultan's household and his empire; but then a cork popped, and a boy was shouting across the room.

"Birgit! Drink up and have another!" Giancarlo sprang from the armchair and took up the bottle.

Rafael laid a hand on his arm. "She doesn't need—"

Giancarlo shook him off with an impatient shrug. "Birgit's all right. These northerners can drink—eh, Palewski? Fabrizio's the one we ought to watch." He stood behind Fabrizio's chair and circled his shiny curls with the bottle. "Sicilian blood."

Fabrizio glanced up, his exquisite little face a perfect mask. Giancarlo swung the bottle toward the window and advanced on Birgit.

Yashim stood up, smiling. "Your friend was saying that you are in Istanbul to unite Italy? You'll forgive me, we Ottomans are sometimes out of touch . . ."

"Of course." Giancarlo hesitated, then lowered the bottle. "Birgit— Signor Yashim—some champagne?"

Birgit shook her lovely head, and laid a hand on her glass. "But I see you have opened the baklava, Giancarlo?"

"Baklava? Of course. Forgive me." He returned with the box. "I like the green ones best!"

"They are pistachio, no?" Birgit's hand hovered over the honeyed treats. "Will you explain, Signor Yashim?"

He glanced into the box. "These are pistachio, and these are made with walnut. This one is made with the same thin dough, as fine as a rose petal, shredded first and then baked. They smell very good. Where did you get them?"

"Not very far from here." She gave some directions and Yashim nodded. "He's very good."

"I love the way he picks them out, in sheets, with his knife. And this one," she added, taking a bite, "is my favorite."

Giancarlo nodded. "Italy is divided, Signor Yashim. It's time that Italy belonged to her people, the Italians. Not Austria. Not Piedmont or the two Sicilies. And first we have to deal with the Pope."

"The Pope?"

"I am—or was—a Catholic, Signor Yashim. The Pope should be a man of God but not a despot. He cannot serve two masters."

"These boys, Yashim, think the Pope is in a fix," Palewski said. "On one hand, he's the vicar of Christ, the conscience of the church, our Holy

Father—a sort of Catholic Grand Mufti, whose fatwas are called encyclicals. On the other hand—"

"The other hand is dyed in the blood of the people!" Fabrizio burst out.

"Well, certainly. On the other hand he is the temporal ruler of that swath of Italy known as the Papal States, consisting of Rome, naturally, and lands to the north of Rome, and Giancarlo's beloved Tuscany, or parts of it. Whatever his virtues as a priest, Yashim, as a ruler he is a reactionary idiot." Palewski drained his glass. "After the 1830 uprising, when the Poles fought against the Russian occupation, we looked to Gregory for support. A word would have carried weight. Yet Gregory was the first to condemn us. Our Holy Father took the side of the Orthodox oppressors against the Catholic Poles, and blamed the insurrectionists for 'disturbing the peace.'"

"Gregory is a tyrant!" Fabrizio said. "He is ruthless—but weak. And being weak, he relies on the Austrians to enforce his rule."

Rafael, the shy one, nodded. "We stand against arbitrary oppression and the corruption of power."

Yashim spread his hands: "Why Istanbul?"

It was Giancarlo who answered. "Don't you see? We're free men here. Italy crawls with papal spies—it's the same in France. Superstitious clerics, credulous informers. Russia? Habsburg territories? They scent revolution, and they all work together, signor. When a continent is poisoned by lies, truth must be an exile," he added, waving his hand dramatically. "So we come east, for freedom. Where else could we go?"

"You could have tried England," Yashim pointed out. "As Voltaire did."

Giancarlo looked blank. "England? Why, yes . . ."

Rafael butted in: "It's just another system—"

To Yashim's surprise, Birgit spoke up from the window seat. "It's too cold for them, Signor Yashim. If a cloud enters the sky their mothers make them wear a scarf!" She laughed, daring them to contradict her. "And none of the Italians in England have class. They are organ-grinders or dancing masters. They sell gelati," she added, drawing out the word as if it appealed to her.

Giancarlo flushed. "That's not true, Birgit. We don't care if a man is a crossing sweeper or a duke, as long as he's with the people."

"Aha." Birgit yawned lazily. "But I'm right about the weather."

"There are no spies here," Giancarlo said, appealing to Yashim. "Nobody in Istanbul cares about the Pope. We breathe free air, beyond the reach of the Inquisition."

"And what will you do from here, to deal with the Inquisition?"

Giancarlo caught a glance from Rafael, and returned him a dismissive shrug. "We have to change people's ideas, and break through this—this crust of feudalism that has formed across the country. My country."

Birgit ambled across to the sofa and lay down.

"And our voices have to be heard," Rafael added. His eyes shone. "That's why we have to stay free."

"It reminds me of that old joke," Palewski put in. "The drunken man who searches for his wallet, under a lamppost."

They all looked at him, expectantly.

"They ask him if he remembers dropping it here, and he says no, he dropped it somewhere farther down the road. So they ask him, 'Why are you searching here?' And he says, 'Because the light is better under the lamppost.'"

Everyone laughed. Only Birgit was silent. Her eyelashes fluttered and her chest gave a slight heave.

She had fallen asleep.

4

THEY made quite a row, of course, going back to their flat through the silent streets, waking up dogs, puzzling the night watchmen. Their landlord, Leandros Ghika, heard them banging up the stairs, and scowled.

Fabrizio raised a fist. "That Palewski—he is one of us!"

"A splendid fellow, Fabrizio, I heartily concur. He likes freedom."

"He likes champagne."

"Champagne is freedom! We should liberate it all!"

They burst into the flat. Giancarlo flung himself onto the divan, Fabrizio plucked out a bottle, Rafael lit a lamp. Birgit settled down and let Giancarlo slide an arm around her shoulders.

"And that Yashim—he's what?" Rafael fiddled with his glasses and sat down on the only chair.

Giancarlo laughed, showing his strong white teeth. "A man like Farinelli, Rafael. Without the voice."

"A castrato?" Rafael's eyes were round.

Fabrizio flicked up his hand as if it held a knife. "*Toc!* They come in all kinds. Only our Pope likes the ones who sing too high."

"The Pope takes them young," Giancarlo said. "He cuts off their balls to sing 'Ave Maria'—in a sweet voice," he added, falsetto. "Pah! He cuts off their balls to stop them becoming men. It's symbolic, no?"

"Of—?" Rafael looked stubborn.

Giancarlo waved a hand. "Political emasculation. He turns men into women and so he rules. What chance do we men have in Italy?"

"But Yashim doesn't sound like a castrato."

Fabrizio grinned. "No. And I know a man from Catania who was just the same. When his house collapsed in an earthquake, he was crushed down there, like that. He had five children already but after the accident that was it. No more. Poor man."

"Poor man," Giancarlo echoed.

Fabrizio wagged a finger and laughed. "Not so poor, because you know what? His wife was happy ever after—and so were all the beautiful virgins of Catania!"

"You mean he stopped pestering them?"

"Pestering? Are you out of your mind? He had them all! One by one, these lovely virgins came to him to be deflowered! They wished to discover the art of love, without any unfortunate consequences. They called him Dell'alba, the man of the dawn. The same as the fisherman who always takes his boat out first after the storm, to test the wind."

Giancarlo laughed. "But the other men—why didn't they kill Dell'alba?"

Fabrizio gave him a look of exaggerated surprise. "Kill him? They asked for his advice ever after—does she squeal? Is she clean? He knew every girl in Catania."

Giancarlo leaned forward. "So when he was crushed—this accident. He lost his balls but he kept, you know, the other part?"

"Certainly. Just not in his trousers!"

Everyone laughed. Birgit chuckled and stood up. "I'm going to bed," she said. "Don't overdo it." She stretched and yawned. "That Yashim—he's a man, anyway."

"Should I be jealous?" Giancarlo let her hand go.

"That depends," she said lazily. "On how long you mean to stay up. Good night, all."

She waved, and they chorused their good nights, and sat about smiling, like good friends.

5

YASHIM and Palewski dined together on Thursdays.

Yashim heard a tread on the stairs as he was dusting the pilaf with pepper and a sprinkling of finely chopped coriander.

"You've come alone?"

He had spent the afternoon preparing their ritual supper almost without thinking, like a participant at mass.

At the beginning, when Palewski had suggested that they take turns on Thursdays, Yashim had arrived at the residency to discover Marta exhausted and almost in tears, while the mahogany table in Palewski's sepulchral dining room was spread with a feast fit for a conclave of Byzantine despots.

After that, by tacit agreement, Palewski came to Yashim.

Yashim enjoyed the preparations. On Thursdays he went early to market, and bought the finest ingredients his friend George could bring to his stall: tiny eggplants, peppers as long and curled as Turkish slippers, fresh white onions, okra, beans. Later, Palewski would come into the room, sniffing the air, surprising Yashim by his knack for guessing what he'd made for dinner. A chicken, perhaps, Persian style with walnuts and pomegranate juice; mackerel stuffed with nuts and fruits, and grilled; a succession of little mezes, soups, dolmas, or aromatic rice. Once he had brought a Frenchman to dine with them, too, and as a consequence a man had died—and Stanislaw Palewski had saved Yashim's life.

"Alone?" Palewski echoed. He put a bottle of champagne on the table in Yashim's tiny kitchen. "Certainly. Youth's all right, but it never knows when to stop. Salvaged this one from the wreckage."

"I assumed they would stay late."

"In the end I went to bed. Marta tells me they were still at it in the small hours. I rather think she encouraged them to go."

"Marta?"

"She doesn't mind my reading at all hours, thinks it goes with being a kyrie. Noisy boys are another matter. Marta doesn't like Birgit much, either."

"She's not Italian, like the others."

"She's a Dane. A beautiful, sleepy Dane, Yashim. Something of a rarity in these parts."

He twisted the wire off the bottle; Yashim slid two tea glasses toward him.

"Of course, I was much the same in Cracow at their age. Up all night talking about revolution, emancipating the serfs, giving power to the people, all that old stuff. In my day it was Saint Simon and Locke. Now it's some Jew in London, Marx, good journalist—and Owen." The cork popped and Palewski poured the wine. "The boys raised a row loud enough to get them kicked out of the Papal States. Or maybe they just took a warning and ran. Papal agents lurking in every café and hiding in boudoirs. It's a rotten little country, and the Pope's just as bad as they say. Fiercely reactionary, like all of Metternich's creatures."

"The Habsburg minister? He's behind the Pope?" Yashim thought: we Ottomans allow ourselves to get out of touch.

"Metternich was the architect of the Congress of Vienna in 1814, Yashim: present—the tsar, the Austrian emperor, the German princes, and Frederick of Prussia, a lot of frightened old men getting together to put a stop to the next Napoleon—and to keep the lid on revolution. All reactionary and afraid. Pope Gregory is their father confessor. Can't stand change. Instead of *chemin de fer* he calls railways *chemin d'enfer*—the road of the devil. Won't have any railway lines in his little Papal States."

"Your Italian friends, Giancarlo and the others—they want to abolish them, do they?"

"They want to dissolve the Papal States, unite the Italian kingdoms, and create a constitutional monarchy. It should keep them pretty busy." Palewski laid his head on one side. "I can't say I blame them. I'm an ally, naturally, as a thorn in the side of the Metternich system, still holding out for Poland. With the help of you Ottomans." He raised his glass. "Thank you very much.

"But whether they have the steel, I don't know. It takes more guts to be an exile than you might guess. More than they know yet. And to keep to an idea—well. It isn't easy. The champagne runs out, after a while."

"So for them it's just a game?"

Palewski blew out his cheeks. "For them it's like a club, with honey and pistachios. The baklava club—they'll probably end up making their peace and going home. In twenty years they'll have joined the civil service and be judges on the bench, with paunches and ambitious wives, and this will be an interlude they'll scarcely be able to remember. Giancarlo, the tall one, will come into his estates and settle down as quiet as any Tuscan gentleman. He pretends to be a man of the people but he's an aristocrat, obviously."

"And Birgit?"

"Oh, Birgit will be all right. She goes along but she doesn't have much time for all their nonsense, as you must have noticed. Maybe she'll stick with that Giancarlo—but I wouldn't bet on it. She'll smile at someone and before you know it she'll be married to a fat little councillor and have four children, all in her sleep."

"So you don't think they're dangerous, at all?"

"Here, in Istanbul? No more than a crate of puppies."

Yashim smiled and nodded. The street dogs of Istanbul pupped quietly in corners, in doorways and stairwells; someone usually found them, and fed them, and put the puppies in a box, where they lay scratching their fleas and nipping at one another's tails.

6

PALEWSKI did not stay late. He was up again in the dark, grabbing the satchel Marta had made up for him. It contained, among other things, the Polish sausage he liked, and a package of baklava. He attended to the contents of his flask himself, with a mixture of brandy, sugar, and water.

He made his way by starlight to the Ortaköy quayside, and was on the water before the muezzins called the morning prayer. The low chants keened across the Bosphorus as he sat huddled in the caïque, cradling the good Boutet wrapped in an oilcloth.

He had been up for hours and already had bagged three mallards by the time Yashim emerged from the café on Kara Davut. Dressed formally in a fresh turban, a brown cloak, white chemise, loose breeches, and a pair of soft leather boots, he carried an invitation that had been brought to his door by an imperial *chaush* the previous afternoon. The formality of the invitation had surprised him. He was on easy visiting terms with the valide; he had wondered for a moment if, perhaps, her mind was wandering. He made his way to the waterfront and took a caïque down the Golden Horn.

At the Eminönü stage he tipped the caïquejee and started uphill, past the Mosque of the Valide: another valide, another sultan's mother, who had built the mosque on the water's edge with money she received from harbor dues at Piraeus. The reigning valide had not yet endowed a mosque. Perhaps it was time to speak to her about this: she was not young, after all.

At the top of the hill he washed his eyes at the Fountain of Ahmet III before entering Topkapi Palace. The First Court, open to the public, was empty at this hour; he walked past the great planes to the High Gate, Topkapi, which had given its name to the whole sprawling complex of courts and kiosks, wrapped one within the other like so many Russian dolls, until they subsided down the far side of Seraglio Point and into the sea.

At the gate, two Halberdiers of the Tresses stepped forward. He knew them both by sight.

"Yashim, for the valide," he murmured, drawing out the paper with a vermilion ribbon attached.

The men stood back; he passed through to the Second Court.

It was—or rather, had been—the court of imperial business, screened from the hubbub of the populace in the outer court, for as one approached the inner sanctum, the home of the sultan, the courts became exclusive. The Second Court was reserved for ministers of state—the pashas and viziers; only the sultan and his grand vizier were permitted to enter on horseback. To Yashim's right stood the great kitchens, built by Sinan, massive tents of brick around their twenty central chimneys; only one smoked now. To his left lay the Hall of the Viziers, shuttered and still since the business of state had removed itself to the Sublime Porte.

The palace was almost empty. The young sultan had taken his household off to Beşiktaş, where the viziers attended him in a room hung with heavy drapery and stuffed with French furniture, fragile gilded chairs, and a European rosewood table. In Yashim's early days, Topkapi had hummed with the sound of running feet, messengers, scullions, page boys: through the murmur—which should never rise beyond the sound of wind in the grass, by imperial tradition—came those imperturbable pashas, for whom calm was an indication of rank; and formidably armed janissaries stood around the walls of the courts like statues, moving nothing but their eyes.

All gone now. Only weeds growing in the paths, and birds nesting in

Sinan's chimneys. The Ottomans were unsentimental. In the nomadic spirit, Yashim reflected, Topkapi had been struck like a tent and the caravan moved on.

Except, of course, for the valide, mother of the last sultan. She had no intention of leaving—alive.

He found her in her apartments in the Court of the Valide. A checkerboard of sunshine drifted through the fretted wooden blinds and spilled across the flagstone floor. Yashim took off his shoes and crossed to the carpet.

The valide was reclining on the divan that filled the window embrasure. She put down her coffee cup, and nodded.

"*Très bien*, Yashim. Ask the girl to bring my writing box. And some coffee, if you like."

The valide's handmaiden appeared in the doorway. Yashim asked for coffee, politely, and suggested the girl fetch the valide's writing box.

"Autumn," the valide murmured, "I never liked it much. People say the color is good, but to me it speaks of death." She gave an elegant shrug. "On Martinique it never troubled us."

Martinique, that tropical speck on the atlas, was where the valide had grown up.

"But people died there, all the same," Yashim reminded her.

"*Mais oui*, Yashim. All the time. So, bring it to me."

She gestured to the girl for the box. It was a shallow rectangle, painted russet, and decorated with garlands; the valide laid it on her lap, and tilted the lid.

She took a pair of silver spectacles from the box and put them on.

Yashim mastered an urge to look inside the box. From here, he supposed, the valide managed her affairs, and wrote to her Parisian bookseller; for the valide, like any successful woman in the harem, possessed far more than jewelry and fine clothes. Sultan Abdülhamid, her sultan, had long since died; but in his lifetime he had vested his favorite with innumerable sources of revenue—bridge tolls and shop rents, the income from provincial farms, obscure taxes. As far as Yashim could remember, with the independence of Greece the valide had lost several useful taxes levied in Athens; she had protested in the strongest possible terms to her son, then Sultan Mahmut, who had made up the loss with a sizable interest in attar of roses from the Rhodopes.

The valide took out a packet of letters done up in vermilion silk ribbon, and closed the lid sharply.

"*Et voilà.*" She untied the ribbon, and spread the letters out on her box before selecting one. Not for the first time, Yashim found himself thinking that the valide would have made an excellent administrator. "This will interest you, I think," she said. "Natasha Borisova. Her French is impeccable."

The name sounded familiar, but he couldn't place it.

The valide sighed. "And yet, Yashim, it is a kind of miracle that she writes good French. Natasha has never been to France. She was brought up in Siberia. Where it is always cold, and not at all *à la mode.*"

She tapped the letter with her fingertip.

"You were young when these events occurred, Yashim. Sergei Borisov was one of the conspirators who wanted to prevent Tsar Nicholas's coronation in 1826. They knew that Nicholas was an autocrat, and they believed that Constantine, his older brother, would be a liberal tsar. So at the coronation they brought the people out onto the square in Saint Petersburg and demanded Constantine instead. They shouted '*Constantine and Constitution!*'"

"I remember."

"I am told the common people thought Constitution was the name of Constantine's wife," the valide added with a smile. "However, the coup failed and Nicholas, as we know, became tsar. The ringleaders were hanged. Borisov and the others were condemned to death but their sentence was commuted to exile."

"The Decembrists." He remembered now: the coup had been launched in December. "And Borisov?"

"To Siberia, like the others." She looked at Yashim over her spectacles. "Some have died, and some have received a pardon. But Borisov is still living in Siberia. Natasha is his daughter."

Yashim glanced at the letters on the writing box. "She—she has opened a correspondence with you, hanum?"

The valide hesitated. "I was able to be of some assistance to an acquaintance of her mother's," she admitted. "The girl has written to me several times these last few years."

"What does she write about?"

"Oh, Yashim—always the investigation!" The valide gave a tinkling laugh. "She writes what an intelligent young woman thinks will interest a sultan's widow. I have not traveled, Yashim—at least, not since I was younger than Natasha."

At sixteen, Aimée Dubucq de Rivery had left her home on the tiny Caribbean island of Martinique to go to Paris, like many girls of her age and class. The Dubucq de Rivery were minor nobility, living as planters on their Caribbean estates. It was no place for a girl to find a well-connected husband. The expectation was that she would learn polite accomplishments in Paris and find a man; which, in a sense, she did. But she never went to Paris: her ship was captured by Algerian pirates and the young Aimée Dubucq du Rivery, with her fair hair and dazzling white skin, was sent to the sultan in Istanbul. Topkapi had been her home ever since.

"She writes about Siberia," the valide said. "The snow. The cold. Her mother's death. She tells me about the natives who believe in spirits and never eat vegetables. *Incroyable!* She draws, too. Quite lovely little pictures."

And what, Yashim wanted to ask, does the valide write back?

"In return, Yashim," the valide said, unnervingly, "I tell her something about life."

She patted the letter, and closed her eyes.

"To tell the truth, Yashim, I am actually a little nervous. At my age! But of course, I have been much alone."

"Nervous, hanum efendi?"

"Like a debutante. It is not just the irregularity. She is young, Yashim. There is a difference in our experience."

"I don't understand."

"*Tiens*, Yashim. Didn't I say? Natasha will arrive this week."

Yashim almost choked on his coffee. "Arrive—here?"

"Why not? She is twenty-one, old enough to do as she likes. I invited her to stay."

"But hanum—the daughter of an exile? The consequences—"

The valide was not quite frowning, but her expression had tightened.

"You think I am unaware that my invitation might have consequences? Do you forget who I am? A valide's acts always have consequences!"

She placed her hands on the writing box, and drew back her shoulders.

"I was a politician before you were born, Yashim, I would have you remember that. Natasha Borisova is looking for a pardon for her father. Others have had it. I intend that the tsar should grant him one."

Yashim opened his mouth to speak, but the valide silenced him with an upraised hand.

"If you think the girl asked me for this, you're wrong. Not in so many words. But I wish to meet her, and form my own opinion."

A visitor in the harem? It was normal for foreign ladies, the wives of ambassadors, an Egyptian begum, perhaps, to visit and pay their respects to the sultan's ladies. They would come for a few hours, talk stiffly over coffee, examine one another's dresses and jewels, and then graciously depart.

But to have a visitor! A foreign woman—as a sort of houseguest? It was unprecedented.

"How long will she stay, hanum efendi? Where will she live?"

The valide waved a careless hand. The bangles tinkled. "Oh, a few weeks, I don't know. Perhaps I will be better able to judge once we have met her." She took off her spectacles. "I rely on you, Yashim. For once, I hope you have no gruesome murders to occupy your time . . . ? But of course the dead can wait. For a young woman, the harem has some fascination, no doubt; but after a few days she will be strangled by ennui. The old ladies," she added pointedly. "They will devour her."

Ever since the unmarried ladies of her late son's household had been permitted to retire to Topkapi, the valide had complained of being beset by old women. "Like children, Yashim," she had remarked. "Like very, very old children."

Some were barely half the valide's age, as they both well knew.

"You wish me to—?" Yashim left the sentence half-finished, unable to conjecture what, exactly, the valide would wish.

"Don't be stuffy. Entertain the girl, Yashim. She's not a Muslim, nor a slave. If Mademoiselle Borisova wishes to go out, then you must be her chaperone. Show her interesting things—the bazaar. Ayasofya. Caïques. Justinian's Pedestal, or whatever it is."

Yashim inclined his head. "Justinian's Pedestal" was a confection of the valide's. She had, of course, no experience of the city in which she had lived for so many years. Topkapi was her home, and the walls of the palace framed her horizon; at most she would have been taken for an outing on the Bosphorus, to the sweet waters of Asia or Europe, to picnic on the grass.

"As I have seen so few of these things, Yashim, Natasha can act as my eyes. She writes well about Siberia, as I mentioned. Now, when she arrives I want you to collect her from the ship. Bring her here, *avec ses bagages.*"

She spoke with a certain relish: in some respects the valide was not so unlike her companions. She, too, would want to examine the *bagages.*

"A young person will do me good. The girls here are all so dull—or they wish to murder me," she added, referring to a recent episode from which she had made a perfect recovery.* "Never, I find, both together."

"Inshallah," Yashim responded. He hoped that Natasha Borisova would not be one of those intelligent women who wound up wanting to murder the valide.

She gathered up the letters, knocked them together against the lid of the box, and tied them up with the ribbon.

"Enough planning, Yashim. You can see to the rest of it." She put the packet of letters back into the box and pushed it aside. "Now," she said, "I will have a little sleep. It is all quite an excitement, *n'est-ce pas?*"

* See *An Evil Eye.*

7

L E A N D R O S Ghika listened to the tramp of feet on the stairs outside and smiled, a little sourly, in the near dark. The feet meant lodgers, and lodgers meant money. But it also meant damage and repairs, which cost; and worry.

He passed his hand across the ulcer in his stomach; then he put another sunflower seed into his mouth and cracked it between his teeth.

The woman had been a mistake. Three men was enough, and the woman was a complication even if she was married to one of them. He spat the shell onto the floor. And that was by no means certain, was it? Ghika had not thought, when they took the place, to look for a ring; but he was fairly sure he had not noticed one; and Ghika was a man to notice things.

He put out his hand and mechanically retrieved another seed from the bowl.

For the woman, they paid extra. Three men with a woman—it wasn't right. And they'd paid up, too—so they knew that as well as he did.

His ulcer twinged: he should have asked for more. They would have paid. He had looked them over, and seen at once that they could afford to pay. Well-made, well-fed boys, and the girl—well; plump as a partridge, and pink and blond like something from a sultan's harem, like the women he could dimly remember when there had been money at home and his mother took him visiting in the neighborhood. He had spent hours playing with buttons on stiff-backed chairs while soft and beautiful wives with starched coiffures and necklaces of lucky coins received them in rooms draped with figured silks and decorated with icons. The women smoked *chibouks* scented with applewood. Another life, before his father died.

The Frankish woman was soft, like them. A different creature from the women he knew best now, those bundles of bones and sores and stinking mouths he resorted to when he felt the urge.

And when he had the money. Well, he had the money now. But had also, he discovered, lost the urge.

He listened. There was a woman's laughter coming down the stairs. It made him wince just to think of it, the attention it attracted. Priests, imams—and always someone to run off and complain. The ulcer flared, as he knew it would. It wasn't worth the money. What was it that the Jew who lived on the corner used to say? What was money if you didn't have your health. Your health, and your family.

Ghika rubbed his nose. Perhaps the Jew was wrong. If you had a pain in the stomach, and no one to run around for you—then you did need the money. Money, most of all.

He waited for the sharp, slicing pain below his ribs to subside, then he got to his feet and opened the door to the stairs. He'd go up and have a word with the rich boys—and have a look at that woman, too.

See if she really wore a ring.

Have another look at her white blond hair.

8

THE cart that had met Palewski at the waterfront rolled to a halt by the bridge, and Palewski climbed down stiffly, cradling his Boutet, to stamp his feet on the solid earth.

To the east, the dawn made a thin pale rim against the black land. The cart moved off, creaking, across the bridge, and Palewski leaned on the parapet, wondering how long he would have to wait, listening to the gurgling of frogs in the reeds below. It was a sound that, like the feel of the narrow fowling piece, carried him off to another time in another country, and he had drifted into a reverie when a hand took him by the shoulder, and he jumped.

"*Salaam alaikum,*" a voice murmured.

"*Salaam alaikum.* You surprised me."

A low chuckle. "We hunters have to move quietly, am I right? Come, the punt's below."

Palewski followed his near-invisible companion off the bridge and into the reeds. The punt showed as a dark length jutting into the water, on which the faintest glow was just visible. It wobbled as the two men climbed aboard. A third man Palewski had not seen pushed off: a small hunched figure in the bow, stealthily laying a paddle over the side.

Palewski sat behind his companion as the boat glided silently out over the water. A mist lay over the surface, scarcely a foot high, and Palewski had the odd impression that he was gliding through time as well as space, into some region of the mind where all the lakes and creeks he had ever shot—the ice-bound chasms of the Lithuanian forests, the great soft-edged lakes of Podolia, the marsh flats of the Baltic coast—glinted mysteriously in the early dawn.

Above them loomed the dark span of the bridge, across which Ottoman armies had marched each year into Europe, a thick black line against the bluer darkness of the western sky.

"And so, Ambassador?" The voice in his ear was very low.

Palewski shifted his length, and eased his gun out of its wrapper. "He's coming, Midhat Pasha efendi," he murmured, scarcely moving his lips. "I have had word that he has already left Paris."

"Marseille?"

"Brindisi."

A ripple trickled along the hull, so close to Palewski's ear that he almost shivered. In spite of his clothing he felt the cold; he squeezed his fingers.

"Everyone will know."

"He's taken every precaution. In Marseille he would be watched, but in Brindisi? Even their resources are limited."

The pasha grunted. The punt nudged against the reeds, and the boatman rested his paddle on his knees. In the stillness, Palewski heard the familiar whir of wings overhead: two mallards, he thought. There was a splash as they settled on the lake.

"His coming here is still a risk." Midhat Pasha was looking along his gun. "I have heard of the committee they still maintain, the 1814 Committee. Like it or not, they have kept the peace—among themselves."

"*Solitudinem faciunt, pacem appellant,*" Palewski murmured. "They make a desert and they call it peace. Tacitus."

"Hmm?"

"The Committee's job is to protect its members," Palewski whispered. The sky had lightened almost imperceptibly. "It has done you no good. Since 1814 you have lost Serbia and Greece, and nobody lifted a finger. Then Algeria, and Egypt, of course. Your empire is fraying at the edges, pasha."

"We make reforms, to treat Christians the same as Muslims. They will bind us together, inshallah."

The pasha had moved and the punt rocked slightly.

"Not unless it's accompanied by a more active foreign policy. You can't just sit and wait."

Three black spots appeared against the dark sky: they curved around the edge of the lake and then began to descend. Palewski's gun cracked, and a bird spun down into the water.

"Good shot!" Midhat whispered. "Go, Aslan."

The dog was already in the water, making a V on the surface with its nose. It took the duck gently between its jaws.

A drake. Midhat took the feathered corpse and laid it in the bottom of the punt. Palewski reloaded.

"It's a mistake to leave the balance of power in Europe in the hands of others, my pasha."

"The Committee again?"

"The Committee. But also the English and the French. When the Powers talk, the Ottomans must be there to talk, too. Conferences and congresses are all the rage—but you do need something to say."

"I hope our visitor will give us some ideas," the pasha said dubiously.

"He will," Palewski replied, ruffling the feathers of the dead bird. It was, he had to admit, a good clean shot. "Certainly he will."

9

YASHIM went up slowly to his apartment. It was a top-floor flat in a tenement in Balat, reached through a doorway that had sunk lower and lower below the street as the centuries slipped by: Palewski had conjectured that the ground floor, at least, was a relic of Byzantine times—stone-built, with a vaulted hall, and the faint impress of a decorative frieze around the doorway. The Greek key, Palewski called the motif, turning in and out like the winding of a river, or the master key to a labyrinth.

"Highly suitable for your line of work, Yashim," he had suggested once. "Complexities made plain: inquire within."

The stairs creaked as Yashim climbed: the wooden upper stories swelled and contracted with the seasons, dry as tinder after a long summer. Lately there had been fewer fires, Alhamdulillah. Maybe the firemen no longer started them, as they did in the bad old days.

Yashim did not climb the stairs alone; not quite. Once he stopped and looked back down the dark stairwell, the hairs prickling on the back of his neck, an odd taste in his mouth—but whatever he was looking for had no shape and made no sound as it rose stealthily from floor to floor.

Brave as he was, Yashim felt himself break into a sweat. It took him an effort to turn, and climb; to push the door at the top, and go inside; and though he shut the door carefully behind him, his dark follower slippèd in, too.

He made for the window like a bird, leaning his head against the glass and looking down into the street.

Laundry fluttered on a line between two houses. Below him the lattices were up. A man with a bundle over his shoulder was trudging toward Kara Davut, maybe hoping for a sale, and the yellow bitch who had pupped in August followed him with her eyes as her puppies sneezed and pawed one another on the dusty road. The broken pavement was full of holes; they would grow in the rain and fill with icy water, until a gang came with a cart of rubble to fill them in, the way they had filled them in before. As if nothing changed, or might ever change for another hundred years: the lattice or the laundry, or the whelping pups, or the holes in the street, filling and draining across the years.

Yashim pressed his hands against the jamb and then, with a look of amazement, whirled around: there was no one there, but something had changed in the atmosphere of the room.

He touched his head to the glass again. There had always been schemers in Istanbul; that was the nature of an imperial capital to which petitioners, delegations, zealots, and hustlers were all drawn, involved in the endless negotiation that maintained Ottoman imperial power across many lands and many faiths. But Palewski's Italians weren't interested in the Ottomans, or in making the Grand Tour. They meant to overthrow the Pope! Running here, as if Istanbul with its cliques and concealed zones and careful compartments diligently maintained were a city like London, or Paris. As if it were just another port, another place to drop bales, unload grain, pick up tobacco.

Even the valide seemed to have caught the new mood, entertaining a houseguest as if Topkapi were a château on the Loire. Writing to the tsar at that box of hers, suggesting he pardon an errant subject: one ruler to another, fiddling with each other's affairs.

She had summoned Yashim to keep the visitor safe while they toured the sights. To be a—what? A cicerone—like a man in Venice he'd once met, batting off beggars and organizing shawls and sherbet.

He knocked his head gently against the window, where his dark shadow met him—knowing all Yashim's holds in advance, infiltrating his defenses, turning his strengths. For months he had eluded him, never quite daring to stop, lest the pity settle around him like a cloak.

He put out a hand to touch the glass, pushing it with his fingertips until they whitened. The glass surrounded him. Beyond the glass the faintly stirring laundry on the line, the dog with her pups, the man walking down the road, the valide, those boys, Palewski: they were all outside, moving and alive in the easy air.

It wasn't the way things changed that he resented: change was the only constant. *Chemin d'enfer*, indeed! The unease he felt was more personal. The boys with their girl, perhaps; and the valide's assumption that he had nothing better to do than wait on her Russian guest. Or was it Palewski, retracing his boyhood with an ease Yashim could only dream of?

I hope you don't have a murder, the valide had said. Attend to the living, Yashim: the dead can wait.

He took a lungful of air and turned away from the window.

The dead, in Yashim's experience, could never wait. The shock of murder penetrated glass, and betrayal shattered stone. And death brought Yashim across the border of men's lives.

Right now, he thought savagely, a murder would suit him very well.

10

MARTA nudged the door with a hip and backed into Palewski's bedroom, carrying a tray with a pot of tea.

She laid the tray on the side table and drew the curtains. Sunlight spilled into the room and the white counterpane convulsed, screwing itself tighter around Palewski's head.

"Nine o'clock, kyrie," Marta suggested, gently. "It is Sunday."

When Palewski drank, or overslept, or fell asleep in his clothes, or rang for her in the middle of the night, Marta bore it with loving patience, for these, she understood, were the ways of a scholar. The kyrie served his books, she felt, as she served the kyrie, with steadfast devotion.

When the bedclothes did not move, she called out. "Kyrie? The tea is hot, and it is nine o'clock."

A reluctant head appeared above the sheets.

Marta's concern for her lord extended to his immortal soul. Marta herself was going to church. It had never occurred to her not to go to church, any more than it occurred to her to wear pantaloons; church, for the Greeks of Istanbul, was as inevitable as pleated skirts or a knowledge of the sea.

The lord had his church, of course, which was sadly different from hers: probably ineffective, possibly dangerous, she bore it for him all the same as a misfortune of his birth. It never occurred to her that Palewski might not want to attend mass. He was a Frank, and on Sunday the Franks heard mass.

So she waited, patiently, until Palewski put out a bare arm and took the tea.

Two hours later, Palewski stood in his pew at the French embassy chapel, listening to the priest intone the introit. The French ambassador and his family occupied the pews in front, with various secretaries and attachés, and beside Palewski stood the Sardinian consul, breathing out a pungent whiff of onions. To his left, one of the nuns who had recently arrived in Istanbul to run a sailors' hospital listened with her eyes closed. Palewski examined her face covertly: she was very young, and quite pretty.

"Eructavit cor meum verbum bonum: dico ego opera mea Regi."

Palewski's eyes wandered over the blue vaulted ceiling, spangled with silver stars, and down the fluted stone columns, past the Virgin Mary holding her baby with an expression of tender idiocy, past the plain oak confessionals, and over the congregation of nuns who filled the pews across the aisle. A priest stood with them, a small, round fellow with tidy black hair turning white and a pair of very blue eyes. Palewski wondered who he was, and as he did so the priest turned slightly. Their eyes met, and the priest winked.

Surprised, even a little shocked, Palewski returned his attention to the altar. He thought perhaps he had been mistaken: the wink had been a trick of the light, streaming through the stained-glass windows.

"Audi, filia, et vide, et inclina aurem tuam: quia concupivit Rex speciem tuam."

At the end of the service, Palewski found himself leaving the chapel with the unfamiliar priest, whose blue eyes twinkled with amusement.

"The Feast of Our Lady of the Rosary!" With a happy smile the priest patted Palewski's shoulder. "Known in centuries past as Our Lady of the Victory. I take it as an augury, sir. Wouldn't you say so?"

Palewski hesitated. The phrase echoed in his mind, but he could not quite recall its significance.

"Regina sacratissimi rosarii," the priest confided. "Battle of Lepanto! Tactless to mention it out of doors, as it were, but here we're all friends together, am I right? Father Doherty, from County Cork—by way of Rome," he added, lowering his voice a trifle.

"Palewski." He extended a hand. "Ambassador to the Porte."

The twinkling eyes creased with intelligence. "Delighted to make your acquaintance, Excellency. Delighted. Now, would you say it was Pius the Fifth who introduced the beautiful Feast of the Rosary to the missal? Or not exactly, you might say—I seem to recall that it was Clement, his successor, who named it so."

"You have the advantage of me, Father," Palewski murmured.

"Aha, aha," Father Doherty returned complacently. "Saint Pius set the form for the Missal, to be sure. Not be deviated from under any circumstances!" he added genially, wagging a finger. "Bar a few minor confessions and congregations who were allowed their own variants. The Mozarabs of Toledo, now, they had exemption—but then they had a very different tradition, after all? He saw fit to add the Feast of our Lady of Victory to the mass, his own self, in celebration of a great Christian victory over the infidels. A saint's prerogative, no doubt."

Palewski glanced about in desperation, and caught the French ambassador avoiding his eye. The Sardinian consul swam into view, and Palewski hailed him before he could sidle past.

"Signor Ramberti, Father Doherty. We were just discussing the missal."

The consul shook hands, and shrugged. "The missal?"

"People are apt to forget, signor, that today marks the anniversary of the Turks' defeat at Lepanto, in 1571. Pius the Fifth ascribed that victory to Our Lady."

"In my country, Ambassador, we ascribe every victory to Our Lady," the consul returned suavely.

"But not every victory is commemorated in the mass," Doherty pointed out. "It's a remarkable thing. It's just arrived that I am, and my first mass is a commemoration of Christian victory. I take it as an augury."

"You are here to convert the infidel?"

Father Doherty spread his fingers. "And a wonderful thing it would be, to be sure. Sadly, martyrdom and glory are not my style. I'm merely a humble ecclesiastical pedant, and boring you both with my talk of rosaries and saints." He bent forward and whispered confidentially: "D'ye think they'll be serving champagne?"

Palewski found himself smiling. "You're going on to the residency?"

"Are you not? What's the form, Your Excellency? You'll forgive me, I'm sure, I'm apt to forget the niceties in the wider world. In Clonakilty, now, a man could work up something of a thirst in church. But your diplomatic world's a long way from my own. Of dust," he added, "and palimpsests."

The word seemed to have an effect on the Sardinian consul, who promptly bowed and moved away. On Palewski the effect was different.

"Palimpsests?" he echoed, considering whether he might invite the pedant for a light refreshment at his own, rather shabbier, residency.

Father Doherty sighed, and beamed. "The saintly Pius is a little too modern for me, I'm afraid. I approve of the encyclical, of course, the content. But I'd be lying if I didn't say the Latin is a little racy for my blood. Saint Anthony, now. The Vitae Patrum. Crude carpentry Latin, with all the vigor of the living tongue."

"I'll tell you what, Father," said Palewski, linking his arm through the cleric's rather lower one, "I can't offer you champagne, but—" He stopped, and checked himself. "Indeed, I can. By happy chance, I can."

"Chance has nothing to do with it," Father Doherty replied. "I called it an augury, and I'll be martyred and glorified if an augury is not exactly what it is. Lead on!"

And arm in arm, to the stupefaction of the Sardinian consul, the ambassador and the Irish priest sallied out together into the street.

11

"*E H bien*, Yashim?" The valide was almost eager. "So you received her on the quay? And all went well?"

"Perfectly well, hanum efendi. She took a caïque ashore. I had no trouble in recognizing her."

Mademoiselle Borisova had sat very stiff in the frail caïque, holding her skirts against the wind. Her trunk had traveled in a second boat.

Yashim reached out to take her hand as she stepped out. The boat wobbled and she landed with a yelp, as Yashim caught her firmly around the waist. She sidestepped smartly, her head averted so that Yashim could not see her face behind her bonnet.

"The little boat—" She made a gesture. She wore a dark woolen redingote over a brown dress, and when she raised her head Yashim glimpsed a face that was unmistakably Russian lurking in the depths of her bonnet, with pale lips, dark brows, and slanting eyes. She smoothed her dress and shrugged her shoulders, so that her shawl dropped a little.

"Mademoiselle Borisova. My name is Yashim, and the valide has sent me to bring you to the palace." He sensed her shiver. "The caïques take a little practice. I don't think they were designed for European skirts."

"No."

"Please, this way."

He held out his arm toward the waiting fiacre, and she climbed aboard with a little cast of her hooped skirts, and settled herself on the seat. Yashim saw to her trunk, stepped up, and ordered the driver to Topkapi.

Brought to her apartment, Natasha had unpinned her bonnet. Her straight black hair was neatly parted in the center and tied into a bun at the back. "It's so strange," she said, looking curiously around the room. She ran her hands over the tiled walls and plumped down on the divan, putting her eye to the lattice. "I was never in a palace before," she added, unsmiling, leaning back on her hands.

"It's not like other palaces, perhaps," Yashim explained. He told her something of its history, of how the harem quarters had been built up slowly, over the centuries, while kiosks and pavilions were added to the seraglio, the private quarters of the sultan. "He doesn't live here anymore. He moved to a Frankish palace, along the Bosphorus."

"A Frankish palace! I like this one."

A maidservant had come in, bowing. Yashim introduced her, and explained that she knew a few words of Russian. She was a Circassian: Natasha's eyes had narrowed slightly.

"Well, she was the best I could find," the valide commented when Yashim had finished telling her about her guest's arrival. "I've forgotten her name, but she's been here some years already. And what did you discuss?"

"The weather, her journey." Her replies had been brief; he had supposed, among other things, that she was tired. "And you a little, of course, hanum efendi."

"You thought she needed to be *prévenu, hein*?"

"I sensed that she was interested, hanum efendi," Yashim answered carefully.

"And you said I was old and bored, and wanted company? That I was charming, but could still bite?"

Yashim had not, in fact, said quite as much. He laughed. "I brought her to the apartment, to settle in and rest."

The valide's brows arched. "And the old women—did they crowd around?"

"I told them that your guest needed to rest." Even they had wilted slightly before Natasha's stare.

"I doubt that will put them off, Yashim. They will pull her *bagages* to pieces, and insist that she disrobe to show off her stays. I do not entirely blame them. In my day, even European fashions were more free. After the revolution in France, I understand, the girls wore white chemises. *Charmante!* You will bring her to me in the morning, and we shall discuss everything."

She dismissed Yashim by closing her eyes and leaning back into her cushions.

Outside in the court, he wondered if he should look in on Natasha Borisova once more; but he remembered her cool expression and decided that Mademoiselle Borisova would have no need of his help this evening.

There was time before dark to see Palewski, if he hurried.

12

"It's not a collection you have, Palewski. It's a disease."

The priest patted one of Palewski's bookcases.

"I recognize the symptoms myself, by way of being a fellow sufferer, somewhat. I palliate the torment, Palewski, by a strict diet of incunabula and manuscript, the latter preferably illuminated. A regimen of perpetual Latin, classical where I can find it, but church Latin still does for me. I recommend the practice, sir."

Palewski chuckled. "Just the approach my own father took. Of course we lost it all after the Partition, and I didn't have the heart to start afresh. You'd have appreciated the collection."

Doherty lowered his head. "Speaking as a friend, if I may, I sympathize with your loss—although to be perfectly honest nothing excites the collector in me more than the thought of a library being broken up." He took a sip of champagne and licked his lips. "But that's as may be. What have we here?"

He took down a commentary on Juvenal. It had been written some seventy years ago, by a relative of Palewski's, and before long they were discussing the value of commentaries, the merits of early Venetian typefaces, the translation work done in Toledo in the thirteenth century, and the influence of Arab thinkers on Thomas Aquinas. Since neither Palewski nor his guest saw any good reason to shy from considering how many angels might dance on the head of a pin, the hours flew by comfortably.

Palewski was delighted to discover that Father Doherty was working in the Patriarchal Archives, poring over thousand-year-old deeds, scriptures, and texts with a view to drawing up a comparative register. The Vatican Library, to which Father Doherty had privileged access, was famously well stocked, but a huge amount of material—especially material relating to the early history of the popes—was evidently missing.

"We know it, Palewski. Everything at the Vatican points to the existence of documents somewhere else. A correspondence, for example, of which only one side remains. A trail of reference that goes cold, a chain that falls apart, some document of which only fragmentary quotations survive. I'll not deny you, there's more in the Vatican itself than any man knows, and yet—the burning of the library at Alexandria! The wretched conflagration of parchment and vellum that attended the sack of Constantinople in 1204! Not to mention the Viking raids, in my own country, and the rest of the Isles—Dublin and Lindisfarne, Glasgow and Iona! It makes my flesh creep to think of it all."

"But it brings you to Istanbul?"

Doherty nodded, and poured another glass. There were still various important papers and manuscripts, he explained, which might—just might, at that—be found to have survived in the Patriarchal Archives. As recently as 1453, when the Turks seized the city, an Orthodox bishop had borne some priceless manuscripts away to Rome, and left hints about the treasures that he'd left behind. Finally, almost for the first time in centuries, Vatican officials had reached an agreement with their Orthodox counterparts, and Doherty had been sent by the Vatican librarians to take a look.

"Not that it's easy to do so, Palewski. There's Brother Agapios, for one thing."

"Brother Agapios?"

"The very same." The Irishman took a stand next to Palewski's bookshelves and announced: "Brother Agapios!" He stooped, folded his hands, and slowly allowed his head to revolve, suspiciously, along the spines. *A chained library? We don't need a chained library here. My name, schismatic, is Agapios.*"

He straightened up, grinning. Palewski nodded, uneasily.

"To be sure, to be sure. I like the man!" Father Doherty pulled out a handkerchief, and mopped his forehead. "Admire him." He swayed slightly beside the shelves. "I understand him, to tell the truth."

"It has been four centuries, and a little more, since the Ottoman conquest of Istanbul, Father. Not always easy for the Patriarch—or his librarians—to steer a safe course. At times sultans would have cast them all to the flames, and their books, too."

"Four centuries, and a little more," Doherty echoed. "And a Brother Agapios every generation, I've no doubt."

He came over and sat on the chair Yashim liked, and stared at the ceiling.

"You're young at this, man."

"Young?" Palewski lowered his feet to the floor. "Young at what?"

"Endurance."

Palewski bent forward and tilted his glass until the champagne touched the brim. "Poland, you mean?"

Doherty meant Poland, but it was Ireland he spoke about.

"Will you endure when they've driven you to the marshes? When they desecrate your churches, will you endure? When your professors and your priests have been driven from pillar to post, starved, beaten, and deprived of a living? Tell me how you think about endurance when your children take instruction in the hedgerows, and the wisest man in Leinster gathers his audiences in a ditch—a ditch! With a boy to be peeping out for the redcoats! Say it again, my friend, when you see the language beaten out of them, afraid to speak to their own sires in their own tongue."

Palewski bowed his head. "Even if it comes to that."

He watched the bubbles rise in his glass. There was a speech he could make, too, but instead he said: "We have greater hopes than you might imagine."

Doherty was silent.

"Ireland is isolated—but the whole continent of Europe is poised for change."

Doherty blew out his cheeks. "That's what they said about Napoleon— but he didn't pull Poland's chestnuts out of the fire, man."

"No—I don't look to the French. They follow their own interests."

"But you'll not have change without them," Doherty said. "That's what history tells us. Who else is there?"

Palewski swung the bottle and refilled the glasses. "Credit where it's due—at least the French gave us champagne! Tell me more about the Patriarchal Archives."

Doherty gave an enormous sigh, and began to describe the stacks, loaded with ancient books. "Very much in my line, Your Excellency, for there's barely a printed book of any worth among them. My Greek's a little rusty, to tell the truth, but I can see that their Greek texts are a pretty crude affair, neither well made (they send to Venice for the better sort), nor interesting from a theological point of view. But it's a rare treasure trove of manuscripts—some bound, some loose, organized by the devil himself, I take it. That's what makes Brother Agapios so indispensable—he's the only one who knows where the things are. And he does it all by touch."

"By touch?"

"God's truth. The man's blind as a bat."

Palewski leaned back in his armchair, smiling. Every now and then he got the urge to reshelve his own voluminous collection of books, according to some new principle that had occurred to him: size, perhaps, or subject, or author. But touch—that was a new one. He turned the idea over in his mind, and was still musing when the front door banged and the sound of footsteps rang busily on the staircase outside.

"*Ciao, Palewski! Sta bene?* Here we are again, and—ah!"

Giancarlo swiveled to the little priest, who inclined his head politely.

Palewski's first thought, when he heard the familiar rumpus on the stairs, was that the timing was poor; but he had underestimated the priest's affability and the Italians' natural good manners. When Doherty finally understood why the boys were in Istanbul, he only smiled and cocked his head, and observed that modern politics were not in his line.

"By modern, now, I mean anything that occurred after the Schism of 1054," he added, with a twinkle in his eye. "No doubt about it, that's why

I get along so well with my Orthodox brethren. After all, I am only a parish priest," he reminded them, "with the soul of a librarian."

Giancarlo laughed. "We have no argument with libraries!"

"But they should be open for the people," Rafael added, solemnly. "Even at the Vatican."

"Especially there," Giancarlo retorted. He glanced at Birgit but she was smiling out the window.

"Mary and Joseph!" Father Doherty cried. "But you touch me on the raw, my dear fellows! I'm all for the people, love them and bless them. But"—he wagged a finger—"but it's not to say I want a library at the very mercy of all the dust, dirt, and sneezes of Christendom! My dear fellows, just consider the mayhem and the destruction that would ensue, should all the world's scholars and wasters descend in a body on those priceless documents and books! I speak as a scholar, not as a politician, of course." He half-turned to Palewski. "The ambassador has the old disease, as well as me. Bibliomania!"

"Incurably," Palewski murmured.

"There's manuscripts in the Vatican that would fall apart if you so much as breathed on 'em! It's not a library—it's a record of civilization itself!"

"A part of one civilization," Rafael corrected him, holding up a finger.

"Oh, my darlin' boy—you'd find stuff from all your other civilizations in there, too. To whom, might I ask, did the Great Cham write, when he wanted to speak to Christendom? To whom did the sultan here in Istanbul address himself—or the Great Mogul, or the Khans of Bulgaria? There's letters in that Vatican Library, let me tell you, written in scripts that are dead and forgotten everywhere else—written on bark and in blood, dear men, letters from vanished civilizations, testaments to worlds and lands that are buried beneath the desert sands, or deluged beneath the waves for their iniquities, no doubt. How—how did the great Charlemagne sign his name, do you know?"

Giancarlo shrugged. Palewski bent forward: "With an *X*."

"That's right! With an *X*. It's on the deeds, preserved in that great library! Not a library at all, but a hidden world, a preserved testament to the history of mankind in Europe—and beyond! I'll have another glass, yes, why not. I'm enjoying myself." Father Doherty twinkled as the wine flowed, and even Rafael, dark and solemn, could not resist a smile. He was not quite ready to give up the fight, though.

"What about the Index? The books His Holiness thinks are too dangerous, that we are too weak to read?"

Father Doherty gave one of his cheerful winks. "Oooh, now, the Index. I'll tell you something about it, if you like. There's books in there that would make your flesh creep, and books that would make you laugh, and nine out of ten aren't worth the paper they're printed on, God's honest truth. Drivel, flattery of princes, praise of the Seven Sins, the production of weak and disordered minds."

"Galileo Galilei? Dante? Savonarola?"

But Doherty wasn't having that. "And who's to stop you reading them, if you've a mind to do it? There, you're an educated man, and you've read these books, no doubt . . ."

Palewski's eyes wandered toward the window, where Birgit sat and gazed pensively at the wisteria that drifted up the wall. He joined her, leaving the others still talking around the fireplace. She turned her head toward him, smiling her slow Danish smile.

"I thought Istanbul would be—different," she said. "But really, it's the same. A priest, the boys talking, champagne. The ambassador."

"The ambassador's not different?"

Her eyes flickered. "Maybe. Unusual."

"Istanbul has become more unusual since you came," Palewski said.

"How do—oh!" She took his meaning, and blushed. "I wear a headscarf in the street."

Palewski shook his head. "If it were only your hair . . ."

Birgit gave a low laugh. "That I am traveling with these boys? Is that what you mean?"

It was Palewski's turn to blush. "I didn't mean—that is, it's something else about you, unknown in Istanbul. An independence, perhaps."

She gave him a mocking smile. "Independence? It's not my most obvious quality."

"Oh, that. *Ce n'est qu'une façon de vivre.*" He dismissed it with a wave, as just a way of life. "In yourself, you're independent. I daresay it's the Baltic air."

"Our sea. Yours and mine." She leaned her chin on her fist. "The Baltic seems a long way off. In experience, I suppose. Not miles."

They were silent then. Ever since the pasha's invitation to shoot, Palewski had spoken to his father in dreams; sniffed the air of early morning; recalled the boy that was. He thought it was age but perhaps he was wrong: the distance was experience, as Birgit said.

She turned from the wisteria and his heart thumped. Her eyes were blue like childhood seas. The sound in his chest was so loud that he leaned back and folded his arms; he was hardly surprised to see someone detach himself from the group around the fireplace.

"Forgive me, Palewski. Your clerical friend confuses me." It was Fabrizio: he glanced at Birgit. "Are you all right?"

She smiled. "The ambassador needs champagne." She took Palewski's glass; her fingers brushed against his and his heart jumped.

"Gentlemen," he muttered, rising to his feet. "Some more champagne!"

He felt boorish; his feet were heavy. He went to the door, opened it, and stepped onto the landing.

Closing the door behind him, he paused, leaning against the wall with his eyes closed.

"Kyrie? You look pale." Marta stood with her hands crossed at the wrists.

"Yes, Marta. I think I'll go upstairs." He turned, not to see the expression in her face.

13

To Yashim's surprise, Marta opened the door just as he was about to push the handle.

"Yashim efendi! I'm so glad it's you," she said, wringing her hands. "Those Franks are in the drawing room, and the kyrie has gone to bed."

"To bed?"

"He looked so pale, I am worried about him. There is a new visitor here, too, a priest of the kyrie's church. The kyrie brought him home from the French embassy."

Yashim shook his head. "Perhaps I had better go home myself."

"Oh no, efendi, please! The men are drinking wine. The woman is there, also."

Yashim grasped Marta's predicament. "Very well. I'll talk to the kyrie, and then we'll see."

"But he is asleep."

Yashim felt a flash of irritation with Palewski. "All the more reason, Marta. I'll dig him out."

Marta still looked doubtful as he climbed the stairs. Passing the door to the drawing room, he paused to listen to an unfamiliar voice, a high, bluff voice that resounded through the thick panels.

"You'll not get me to admit that! You'll not take me along on that line!"

Yashim continued up the stairs, knocked at Palewski's door, and went in without waiting.

His friend was not asleep: instead, he leaped from the bed as the door opened.

"Oh, it's you!"

Yashim looked at him curiously. "Marta told me you were looking pale."

Palewski ran a hand through his hair. "Yes. Poor Marta. I felt—I felt odd. Are they still here?"

Yashim came into the room and closed the door. "You're ill?"

Palewski sank down onto the bed and rubbed his forehead. "I don't know. I had—well, a sort of shock. A surprise." His hand dropped and he looked up at Yashim. "I think I fell in love."

Yashim leaned his back against the door. "Go on."

Palewski gave a weak laugh. "I'm trying to recover, Yash. She's half my age, and spoken for. I had to get away."

"Shall I encourage them to leave?"

"No—yes, that would be best."

"I'll say you're feeling unwell."

"Don't—that is, don't put it like that. Tell them I've got something— an appointment."

"At this hour?"

He left Palewski sitting on the bed, his face buried in his hands. Downstairs he found the Italians in the drawing room, and the priest scribbling at Palewski's escritoire.

"Signor Yashim!"

There were several empty bottles on the sideboard, and one had rolled close to the window seat where Birgit still sat with her hands folded and a slight smile on her face. Giancarlo was sitting beside her, Rafael at the bookshelves. Fabrizio was bent into an armchair, like a spring, cleaning his nails with a thin knife.

"My apologies, gentlemen, and mademoiselle. I'm afraid that I have detained the ambassador on some government business—he sends his apologies with mine."

The priest got up from the desk. He bowed slightly and touched his forehead. "Father Doherty," he said.

"Yashim. I'm an old friend of the ambassador's."

"A privilege. I've enjoyed Count Palewski's company since mass today, and am delighted to make the acquaintance of any friend of his. I had an inkling that the ambassador was detained, so I have taken the liberty of writing him a note." He gestured to the escritoire.

"Of course. I'll see he gets it."

"It's been quite a day!" The priest's eyes twinkled as he took his leave. "I've enjoyed our discussion, Giancarlo, all you young people . . . well, a pleasure. A very great pleasure."

When he had gone, Giancarlo asked if Palewski would be coming back. "No? Then we should not disturb him any longer. Come on, boys and girls."

"But I am comfortable," Fabrizio protested. "The ambassador doesn't mind."

"I say we go."

The girl at the window seat looked from one to the other, and arched her eyebrows.

"You go if you like," Fabrizio retorted, lowering his eyelids. His face was slightly flushed. "I want to stay."

"If it helps, I'm going, too," Yashim said peaceably. "It's dark already."

Birgit got to her feet and picked up her shawl. Giancarlo and Rafael were at the door.

"We're leaving." Giancarlo stood looking at Fabrizio.

Fabrizio made a slight movement and something whirred through the air to strike the doorjamb with a soft thud. It happened so quickly that Yashim was not sure what it was.

Giancarlo was the first to move. "You bloody idiot," he hissed. He reached out and yanked a small knife from the wood. "You could have killed someone."

Fabrizio smiled. "I wasn't aiming to kill anyone. It was only a joke."

Giancarlo glanced at Yashim, awkwardly, his face set. He pressed the knife between his fingers and the blade disappeared; he slipped it into his pocket. "I'm sorry, Signor Yashim." He lowered his voice. "Fabrizio can be like this when he's had a bit too much to drink."

Yashim responded with a murmur; Fabrizio got to his feet.

"*Va bene.*"

They stood aside to let him pass, then followed down the stairs.

At the door, Yashim gave a sigh of impatience. "I was meant to fetch some papers. You go on."

They said their farewells. When they had gone, Yashim went upstairs to find Palewski already coming down.

"You got them to go? Thank you."

"Father Doherty left you a note."

Palewski took a glass of brandy to the escritoire, and picked up the note. "*Dear Palewski*, blah blah, *great pleasure* . . . blah blah . . . *your young friends . . . unexpected treat . . . Father Doherty.* Hmm. Wonder why he bothered, really."

"Feeling better?"

"Not so mad, at any rate. I suppose it'll pass. It was just—such a jolt, Yashim. Must have been something in the air, God knows."

"Hmm. Not the only thing in the air this evening." Yashim told Palewski about the knife-throwing incident. "Your pretty Dane again, I suspect."

Palewski took a sip of brandy. "Now you're making me jealous. Girls like that shouldn't be let out," he added. "We should adopt Ottoman practice, keep 'em in the harem."

Yashim laughed, thinking of Natasha Borisova with the valide at Topkapi. "We seem to have got it the wrong way around today. The beauties running around Istanbul, and the solemn ones in the harem."

"What d'you mean?"

"A very solemn Russian girl arrived today as the valide's guest. Natasha Borisova."

Palewski almost choked on his brandy. "She what? Who?"

"The daughter of Borisov, the Decembrist. He's in Siberian exile, but she's elected to travel. While you've been drinking with priests and shooting duck with the pasha, I've been getting ready to escort Mademoiselle Borisova around the city. I thought I could bring her here, if you'd like."

"Here?" Palewski glanced around. "Well, why not? Borisov was a good egg, poor fellow. What's she like?"

Yashim shrugged. "Tired from the journey. She wasn't very communicative."

"Pah! Russians don't tire easily. I expect she's keeping her mouth shut and her eyes open. I don't understand why she's here."

"She hopes the valide will persuade the sultan to intercede with the tsar on her father's behalf. He's been in Siberia for fifteen years or more."

"That's nothing."

"She's lived there most of her life."

Palewski looked thoughtful. "It's strange, her wanting a favor. Last year I'd almost given up on you Ottomans. You remember? Egypt biting your neck, the Russians acting like your big brother, France and England sharpening their knives. And now, it seems, everyone's turning to the sultan for support."

"It's only one woman, hoping to save her father."

"Of course. It's only that." Palewski took his glass to the sideboard. "Brandy?"

Yashim gave him a narrow-eyed look. "There's something you're not telling me."

Palewski made a business of stooping to fetch the bottle from the cupboard. "A boyish infatuation," he said, not looking around. "Perfectly absurd."

"I meant shooting duck with Midhat Pasha."

Palewski set the bottle on the sideboard, and fiddled with the cork. After a moment he sighed. "All right, Yashim. But I can't tell you much. Not yet, at least."

Yashim dropped into Palewski's comfortable armchair. "So it would seem. You don't trust me?"

Palewski snorted. "It isn't about trust. Forgive me—it's something, I don't know . . ." He hesitated, then poured himself a drink. "I'm sorry, Yash. Call it a superstition, if you like. Afraid if I put something into words, it won't happen."

"Something you want badly."

"Badly."

"Mime it."

Palewski smiled. "No, it's too complicated. Too exciting, maybe. It's just—well, I'm expecting a visitor."

Yashim waited for him to go on, and when he did not, he prompted: "Someone connected to these Italians?"

"The Italians?" Palewski looked surprised. "Good Lord, no. Rather a big wheel, in my world. Completely different. At least, a difference in scale."

Yashim shook his head. "You've lost me. What scale?"

Palewski came and sat forward in the other armchair, dangling his glass between his knees. "I mean the scale of change, Yashim. The Italians—they want to shift things around in Italy. Good luck to them, I say—though Doherty's right. They are just babes in arms, really. My business is bigger, and I've waited a long time. Keeping the faith, or something like that."

"So—Poland?"

Palewski tilted his glass and stared for a few moments at the golden liquid. "Europe, perhaps. A feeling exists, Yashim, that the balance of power in Europe is too heavily weighted in one direction. We may have reached a moment that gives us the opportunity to, ah"—he proceeded slowly, choosing his words with elaborate circumlocution—"to attempt some sort of redress. Of the balance. There."

"And the sultan?" Yashim stared at his friend. "Your big wheel is coming to see him?"

Palewski nodded. He did not need to urge Yashim to secrecy: the trust they had spoken of was absolute.

Yashim blinked. Any change to the balance of European power would have to involve Poland, if Palewski was involved. That affected Russia, and Prussia and the Austro-Hungarian Empire, three highly reactionary regimes that had taken their slice of Palewski's homeland. He thought of Giancarlo and Rafael, railing against a pope who could not abide a railway line.

"But those boys aren't involved?"

"Boys? What boys?"

"A moment ago they were your rivals in love. Those boys."

Palewski started. "The baklava club? Good God, no. This isn't politics for puppies, Yashim. God forbid they should ever get an inkling . . ."

"That's a relief." Yashim nodded. "As long as you haven't mimed anything for them, at any rate. They've been in and out of here all week."

Palewski glanced up and smiled uncertainly. "You're right. They have been around too much. My fault. Reached a stage in life when I see only the people who invite themselves. I don't mean you," he added hastily. "The Baklava Club. I can't seem to stop them."

"Perhaps you should discourage them while you're—busy."

"You're right. I must. I need some seclusion."

He looked flustered. Yashim bit his lip, frowning. "You'll call on me, if you need help?"

"Of course."

Yashim nodded again: Palewski would not know he needed help until it was too late. Yashim rubbed his chin. He appeared to be on escort duty for some Russian girl, while larger business was afoot between Palewski and Midhat Pasha. He drew his feet up into the armchair to cover a stab of wounded pride. The management of secret affairs of state was his job, practically. He was the sultan's ears and eyes, his *tebdil khasseky*, or confidential agent: his Varangian Guard, as he had almost explained to the beautiful Dane, Birgit.

There'd been a time when only Yashim—and a willowy librarian— had stood against a madman who meant to bring down the House of Osman. He once saved the valide's life, and on another occasion he saved the young sultan from disgrace. He had thwarted plots against the empire and its rulers. But the palace had not called on him this time.

Of course, the affair involved Midhat Pasha, and there was history between them, not of Yashim's own making. The Ottoman state was like any family, riven by unseen currents of friendship and patronage, sympathy and mistrust. Midhat Pasha had not chosen to call on him: well, it was no disgrace. But still it hurt, and he was anxious for Palewski.

"Mehmet the Conqueror," he said, slowly, "was once asked where his army was headed, as they passed through the Edirne gate toward the

Balkans. 'If one hair of my beard knew our destination,' he replied, 'I would pluck it out.'"

"I know the story. But nobody knows about this business, I can assure you."

"Hmm. I know a little now. Midhat Pasha knows, and your visitor, of course. I suppose he has servants? His valet will know. Fellow passengers, if he takes a ship. And the docks are full of informants." The docks of Istanbul were full of men of all nationalities, and none.

He got up to study Palewski's portrait of Jan Sobieski, the Polish king who had saved the Austrians at the walls of Vienna.

"And whatever you're about," he murmured, "the balance of power has not come about by sheer accident. It has to be maintained, like a clock."

"It has been," Palewski responded gloomily. "For more than twenty-five years, since the Congress of Vienna. They have a secret committee devoted to it."

Yashim blew out his cheeks. "Sometimes secrets are revealed because people involved only see the secret, and forget that all the avenues that lead to it may be watched. A paper tossed into a basket. A regular appointment canceled. I've known secrets exposed by an inappropriate smile."

Palewski held his glass to the light. "What do you take me for?"

Yashim laid his hand on Palewski's shoulder. "Secrets are awkward bundles, and they can shift unexpectedly. I'll go home now. I have an appointment with Mademoiselle Borisova tomorrow."

At the door he looked back. Palewski had the glass pressed against his forehead, and Yashim felt a surge of affection for him. "Keep it all in your head," he said.

And with that, he was gone.

14

IF Istanbul seemed to Yashim to have grown commonplace, another stop on the circuit of cities that ringed the Mediterranean, his day negotiating the streets with Mademoiselle Borisova should have taught him otherwise.

It was not, really, a city for visitors. Even in the heyday of the Grand Tour, when English milords completed their education by traipsing around the sights of Europe, painting, botanizing, scrutinizing architecture, and haggling for artworks to adorn their country seats, Istanbul was considered a far reach. The milords had no friends there, no letters of introduction; no painting masters would step forward eagerly to teach them the rudiments of perspective, no pashas opened their houses to them, no cicerones offered them sisters or daughters—and there was nothing to drink.

The sights themselves were hard to get at, if they were worth visiting at all. From the city walls to the Ayasofya, the former capital of the Byzantine empire was truffled with antiquities—but the western gentlemen had all read Gibbon's *Decline and Fall of the Roman Empire*, which maintained that Byzantine architecture, like the civilization it represented, was effete, artificial, and corrupt. Gibbon's judgment had prevailed over European opinion for a hundred years.

The milords wanted public spaces to stroll about in—those squares and *places* and piazzas, furnished with arcades and cafés, promenades and palm trees, that claimed to be the drawing room of Europe, or the Rotten Row of Italy, or the forums of the ancient world. Other cities called themselves the Paris of the East, or the Venice of the North, but no comparison, how-ever well intentioned, could be offered to Istanbul. In the eyes of its inhab-itants, Greek, Turkish, or Armenian, it was simply the center of the world.

But Natasha had the Orthodox Russian's kinship with Byzantium, and its arts: she was Orthodox, and Istanbul remained the seat of Ortho-doxy. Unlike the milords, she had one friend, and one powerfully placed. The valide sent her out with Yashim, making her promise to tell her about everything she did and saw, and providing Yashim with a firman that would act as a laissez-passer to palaces and mosques.

The milords avoided Istanbul, because there was no society and they wished to see and be seen. Mademoiselle Borisova certainly did not wish to be seen—she shrank from the sideways glances of the porters and the shopkeepers, or the franker stares of the Greeks; but Yashim was not sure that she wished to see very much, either. She walked through the Grand Bazaar without once turning her head, blinkered by her bonnet, and holding her parasol very firmly by its ivory handle, tightly furled, as if she meant to assassinate someone with it. Ayasofya she declared to be very big, which seemed scant reward for the difficulty of persuading the guardian—who did not read—to obey the valide's firman when Yashim waved it under his nose. The Blue Mosque of Ahmet III brought her out in an attack of shivering; she complained that it was too cold. She, a child of Siberian winters!

He took her to see the new bridge across the Golden Horn: it reminded her of bridges she had crossed in Russia. He took her to the Galata Tower, and though Yashim admired her strength and fitness as she ran up the seven hundred steps to the top, she did not seem to admire the tower so very much, and responded to Yashim's evocation of the Genoese city that had stood here once with something like a grunt. She exclaimed over the view, however, as Yashim pointed out the silhouetted mosques, and the outline of Topkapi Palace, where she was lodging; and she admitted that the effect of all the roofs, cascading down to the water's edge on the Stamboul side, was pretty.

It was not easy, because of the wings of her bonnet, but every so often he would catch a glimpse of her face, lips compressed, her eyes dark and unrevealing, her chin tilted in a way that echoed the angle of her parasol.

He debated whether to take her to a pudding shop or to the French patisserie on the Grande Rue, and decided that she might be more comfortable in a Frankish setting. Once seated, she removed her bonnet, and began to make small circles on the table with her fingertip. Yashim gave his order, and waited for her to speak.

"Your people seem to live very well," she said at length. "In the Grand Bazaar I saw—so many interesting things. So many cloths, and jewels, and pretty shoes."

The remark surprised him: he had felt, at the time, that nothing interested her at all, that she saw nothing.

"You must tell me what you like, and I will buy it for you," he said. The valide had slipped him a purse of gold coins and told him to spend it.

She moved uneasily on her chair.

"The bazaar is like a world of its own," he said. "Everything in our empire is made there, or traded there. It has its own mosque, of course, and two bathhouses." This was dull information, for a young woman; he tried again. "I used to go there for books, especially. The bookseller was a Greek, with one eye: he couldn't read, but he knew just how much to charge. In the end he was murdered."

That had caught her attention.

"Murdered? But why?"

Yashim leaned forward and began to tell a story, about a book that should have never been sold; about an archaeologist who came from France, and a corpse whose face was eaten by dogs as it lay in the street.*

She gazed at the table as he spoke, like a schoolchild trying to understand a lesson; but when he thought she was bored, she said: Go on. So he told her also about the old sultan, who died, and about the cisterns and tun-

* See *The Snake Stone*.

nels beneath their feet, and how he had once searched for treasure there. It was a long story.

"But in the end—you found it?"

"Yes, I found it. But it was not where I thought it was, and it was not what I thought it would be."

His coffee grounds had dried in the cup.

"That was an interesting story," she said. "I will not tell it to the valide."

"Why not? She knows most of it, anyway."

"She knows? But she—she . . ."

"She enjoys a good story. In fact—"

At that moment someone loomed over their table, and Yashim glanced up to see Compston of the British embassy, fingering his fair mustache.

"I say, Yashim efendi, what? Your coffee's gone cold, haw haw."

Yashim got to his feet and presented the newcomer: "Mr. Compston, Mademoiselle Borisova." Natasha nodded and looked away.

"I gather your friend Palewski's taken up shooting duck, efendi."

Yashim gave a start.

"They're rather in my line, ducks," Compston explained. "We're a Norfolk family," he added, turning to Natasha. "Plenty of good shooting out there on the flats. I'd like to ask Palewski if I could join him some morning. I shouldn't think he'd mind, do you, Yashim efendi? What sort of gun does he shoot?"

Out of the whir of thoughts racing through his head, Yashim brought out a name. "Boutet."

Compston whistled. "Must be beauties. Heard about 'em, never seen one fired in anger, so to speak. Pater left me his Purdeys."

Yashim recalled the make: the valide had once, to his astonishment, scored a bull's-eye with one of a pair of Purdey pistols given to her by Sultan Abdülhamid.

"Along with his Hunter?"

"Here it is, and all thanks to you." Compston fished the watch from his pocket, flipped it open, and snapped it shut again. "Well, must run! I don't forget a good turn, Yashim efendi. Mademoiselle."

He was gone, with a short bow.

"Who was that?" She didn't sound very interested, and anyway, Yashim was thinking back to the warning he had given Palewski the previous night, and wondering what else Compston knew about. Wondering who else might know about it, too.

15

GIANCARLO, Rafael, and Fabrizio left the apartment in the afternoon. Birgit stayed at home, pleading a headache.

When they had gone, she loosened her stays and began to brush her hair at the mirror, putting one finger down on a book on the dressing table to keep it open. The book was a new one, written by a Dane named Søren Kierkegaard, and it seemed to be about the effect of religious convention on religious faith. It was called *On the Concept of Irony*.

Birgit found parts of it rather hard to follow, but she didn't mind. She wanted to read a book in a language that none of the boys could understand and talk to her about—talk *at* her, perhaps, being the better term, for they were of an age, and sex, that made them recite their opinions, rather than discuss them. Søren Kierkegaard was her secret, her private friend. She found that he had a tendency to recite his opinions, too, but he did it in a language only she could understand.

There were parts of *On the Concept of Irony* she did not follow, but she accepted that as a sort of irony, too, and it made her smile. "People understand me so little," Søren had written, "that they do not even understand me when I complain of being misunderstood." She thought of him as Søren.

Birgit did not actually have a headache, but she craved a few hours of solitude, and she liked to brush her hair and read her book. Now and then she found herself wondering what Søren was like. She imagined him with flaming red hair, a long, beaky nose, and spectacles.

It was rather hot, and her stays stuck to her skin where she had loosened them, plucking at her stickily as she shifted on the chair and followed the cascade of yellow hair with firm downstrokes of the brush. The feeling grew into an irritation, until she stood up, slipped out of her dress, and released the fastenings one by one. She tossed corset and dress onto the divan, and went on brushing her hair, standing with Søren's book between the fingers of her left hand.

It was warm enough to go naked. She glanced briefly at the window, but the latticed shutters were firmly closed.

"Der ligger i den hele nyere Udvikling en stor Tilbøielighed til—langtfra med Taknemmelighed at erindre sig de Kampe og Besværligheder, Verden har udstaaet for at blive til det, den er—om muligt endog at forglemme de Resultater, den i sit Ansigts Sved har erhvervet, for paany at begynde forfra, og i ængstende Forudfølelse af."

There was nobody about to hear, and it felt nice to hear Søren speaking their language in the deep, scholarly voice she gave him, as best she could.

"Efter disse almindeligere Betragtninger, hvis inderligere organiske Forhold til vort Forehavende paa sit Sted vil, saa haabe vi, vorde Læserne klart."

As for Ghika, the landlord, he didn't care if the woman spoke Sanskrit or Irish—though he would have preferred to hear her speaking in a higher, more girlish tone. It wasn't really her voice he cared about, as he congratulated himself on taking the trouble to put his eye to the keyhole of the apartment.

What he could see exceeded all his hopes and expectations: a young woman with breasts that quivered with every stroke of the brush, every stroke of the brush that caressed her long blond hair.

She was quite alone now. Those men had gone.

And the door, evidently, was unlocked.

He put out his tongue to wet his lips, breathing heavily at the door.

16

"I wonder," said the valide, touching her hair, "if we did quite right to ask her?"

"We, hanum efendi?" It was a bit of a jump, even for Yashim, who knew how the valide's mind could work.

"Such a homely little thing. A real hen."

"Hanum efendi?"

"So reticent," she said. "I expected, from her letters, more *joie de vivre*. A little wit."

"This evening you will present Natasha to the ladies?"

"You needn't stay. It will be an undignified affair, *sans doute*. Old women clacking at her underwear and pinching her cheeks. In spite of everything, Yashim, I don't think of you as—well, at least, it is not your place. But you may tell her that I will be ready to receive her in an hour."

He found Natasha in her apartment, sitting on the divan and still in her outdoor clothes. Only the bonnet lay beside her, its ribbons dangling.

"Then I must dress," she said wearily. "She wants entertainment—but I don't dance the troika."

"At her age," Yashim said quietly, "the valide has seen a great deal of the hot and cold of fate. Now, I think, she wishes to avoid melancholy."

Natasha tilted her head to one side. "If you say so." Her voice was flat, bored. Why, it was as if Natasha Borisova had come all this way to turn the empire over in her mind, like a piece of china in the bazaar.

"You have come with an object, I understand that," he said, "but you are also the valide's guest. Her first foreign guest, I believe. Perhaps you didn't know that?"

Natasha said nothing.

"I just want you to understand that the valide has done something quite unusual. Of course she's being watched by—everyone. The other ladies. The eunuchs. The gossips. That's the nature of palace life. And you can make it easier for her to help you. I hope you don't think I am being too crude."

She gazed at him levelly, for the first time. "It's what we Russians understand," she said heavily.

She put out a hand and groped for the ribbons of her bonnet on the bed.

Yashim took a step forward. "Mademoiselle Borisova—I'm so sorry. I didn't mean . . . Please don't cry."

The tears had sprung from beneath her closed eyes. "Oh, Monsieur Yashim, oh, oh, oh!"

He spotted a pile of lace handkerchiefs and passed her one.

"Forgive me. I thought—" He was about to say he thought she was dissatisfied, and that Istanbul gave her no pleasure, but she broke in first, wiping her tears away with her fingers.

"I can't dance!" She hiccuped through her tears, shaking her head. "Can't sing! I know I am plain, and not elegant, and everyone wants me to be a beautiful princess who knows how to sing and be witty and I don't know how . . . I don't know . . . oh!"

She went to the window and stood there, covering her face with her hands, her shoulders heaving.

Yashim bowed his head. "Among the Ottomans, Natasha," he said, "princesses, like pashas, are not only born: they are made. It's not like Russia or France, where everyone defers to ancient families. The only ancient family in the whole Ottoman Empire is the family of Osman bey, the founder of the dynasty. The greatest princess that ever lived was Roxelana, the wife of Suleyman the Magnificent. She was Russian like you, captured in some raid across the Don. No aristocrat by birth, and she certainly spoke no French."

She shrugged miserably.

"And you don't have to win a sultan's heart, either."

She pulled a rueful face. "It's just as well."

Without her bonnet, now that Yashim could see her face properly, she was not bad-looking, with those sloping eyes and high cheekbones.

"Who knows? In another age . . ." he said gently, and smiled. She glanced around and blinked.

"The valide asked you here, Natasha, because she liked the girl who wrote her those letters. Not some princess poised to wield her charms: women like that, remember, have surrounded the valide all her life. She saw through them all, long ago. Your letters are clever, and funny. You draw beautifully. You wrote to her in your own voice, not with the affected lisp of some Circassian beauty."

"Are they so affected, then?" She almost smiled.

"Terribly. Lisping is the fashion, and mincing, and speaking in a sort of high-pitched trill. And a lot of malice underneath, believe me. Flint, beneath the honey."

He drew her down onto the divan, to sit beside him, and held her hand.

"I wrote to no one else," she said, with a sharp intake of breath. "It was Prince Volkonsky's idea."

"Prince Volkonsky?"

"He was one of those who came to Siberia with us. I was very young then—too young to remember life before, really. To begin with, my father had to work in the mines. We lived in the mine village, twenty-seven of us. I didn't see him very often. My mother cared for all the children, with an old Siberian woman who lived there. My little brother died when he was five. I wanted to explain to the tsar what had happened, but we were not allowed to write to the tsar, or the tsarina, of course. So Uncle Sergei—Prince Volkonsky—said I should write a letter to the Ottoman sultana instead."

"Why the sultana?"

"In the stories, you see, it is always a tsar and a sultan. Moscow and Constantinople."

"Yes. In our stories, it is the same. A tsar, a sultan, and a wise fool, like Mullah Nasreddin."

"Everyone used to tell those stories. My father came back very weak from the mines. We were all sent to live at Irkutsk then. Some of the families were rich, so they built an opera house, and had soirees. The governor used to come. We all spoke French to confuse the spies and the soldiers—and for the sake of my mother and her friends. I wrote to the sultana—the valide—in French, and did those drawings for her."

"And she wrote back."

"Oh yes! At Christmas she sent boxes of *lokum*, and when I was fifteen she began to send me shawls, and flowery material for making a dress. I make my own dresses," she added, with a touch of artless pride.

"And your mother?"

"It was very hard for her. She could have stayed in Saint Petersburg, you see. We all could—except Father. But she came with him, and she and some of the other wives signed documents that declared them officially dead because they chose voluntary exile in Siberia. When Igor died . . ." She blinked. "And she died four years ago. A real death. She told me to take care of my father. Many others have been pardoned, Monsieur Yashim. But I fear the tsar has forgotten us."

Yashim squeezed her hand. He had treated her exactly as she described—as a rare Russian princess, representing everything that he, as an Ottoman, feared and admired about the old Russian enemy. When he showed her the sights, she hardly knew whether to be impressed or even interested: she supposed that a sophisticated princess would have seen it all before.

"Remember, the valide has promised to do what she can, so there is nothing you need to do or worry about while you are here."

They sat in silence for a moment. "Sometimes I wish I'd never written those letters." She turned her head. "I'd better dress," she said. "Do I look awful? All horrid and red?"

He shook his head. "You look better, Natasha. You should go out in a while and meet the ladies. It will be very correct and rather formal, no doubt, although I warn you, they'll want to examine every detail of your wardrobe, down to your stays. But soon we'll have a picnic, out in the country. No more city sights, just sun and the open air. How's that?"

17

FABRIZIO drummed his fingers nervously on the table.

"It can't go on," he murmured at last. "Waiting, waiting, not a word. I don't have money." He flushed.

Giancarlo shrugged. "It is like the ambassador said: patience."

"All right for you," Fabrizio pointed out. "You have funds, and a woman. You can stay here as long as you like. What I don't understand is why we hear nothing. Maybe our friends have been jailed? Why don't they write?"

"We agreed that correspondence should be kept to a minimum, Fabrizio. You know that. When La Piuma has instructions—"

"Every day we come and drink coffee, and jump when the waiter nods at us. I'm sick of it."

Rafael frowned. "You would rather be sitting in a papal cell, crumbling a little bread? No? Come on, Fabrizio. Here you are a free man, and when our people need us, they will call. Then, perhaps, you will find life too exciting."

"Are you saying I'm a coward?"

"No more of that," Giancarlo said sharply. "Rafael is simply saying the truth—that the moment will come, and we shall all be tested. We should be prepared."

Fabrizio flashed him a look of concentrated scorn, but he kept his mouth shut and his hand reappeared on the table.

"Let's play backgammon."

They played for an hour or so. Giancarlo won two games, Rafael won another. Fabrizio lost to both of them and sat with his arms folded, scowling at the board.

Finally they signaled to the waiter. Giancarlo put some coins on the table.

"For you," the waiter said as he swept them up. He dropped a note onto the table and went away.

Giancarlo glanced about and covered the note with his hand. His heart thumped.

"So."

Fabrizio had sat up; Rafael looked from Giancarlo to the paper.

"We'll leave now," Giancarlo said. "As if nothing has happened."

Each of the young men stood up, feeling the weight of everyone's eyes. Now that it had arrived, they each felt clumsy and conspicuous. Giancarlo felt the ground heave as he crumpled the note and put it into his pocket.

They walked in solemn silence to the end of the street, where Giancarlo reached into his pocket and drew out the note.

"Aha! The young revolutionaries!"

They all started. Around the corner had come the most astonishing figure they had seen all day, as out of the melee of men in turbans, robes, frock coats, and fezzes came the Irish priest, Doherty, beaming in his black saturno hat, cape, and dog collar, and clutching a pile of books.

"Will you look out for me now, lads! These books are beginning to go!"

Fabrizio was the first to recover his wits. He grabbed at Father Doherty's pile of books and spooned them back toward the priest's chest.

"Ouf! I thought you might actually take them from me, young man! Maybe spare a fellow the rigor mortis that dusty old tomes generally induce," he added, with cheerful outrage.

"Of course, Father." Fabrizio let the pile slide into his arms.

Giancarlo gave him an exasperated look. "We're in a bit of a hurry, Father, forgive us."

Father Doherty was waving his arms and flexing his fingers, and did not appear to have heard.

"It's my Calvary, if I might make so bold, and to be sure, I'd not blaspheme." He turned to Giancarlo. "I find a stack of books to be a wonderful protection for a man walking abroad in this city. Idolaters and infidels they may be, but the meanest beggar of the Balkans has respect for the written word. And when I say respect, I mean only to say that these books—treatises and whatnot, written by pious men, and pious women, too, I don't doubt, for let's not forget the holy ladies, gentlemen, moved by a passion for Christ like Teresa of Avila, bless her and keep her—that these books, I say, might prove to be singularly unenlightening, were the aforementioned beggar to lay his hands upon them, God forbid, and attempt the reading of them. And for why?"

It was a rhetorical question, for which he put out his hands and adopted an expression of absurd surprise. Giancarlo and Rafael stood as if turned to stone: only little Fabrizio wheeled slightly under his burden.

"For the fact that they are all written in a language that strives for— nay, might have seemed to have—achieved universality, but which not one of them could possibly understand! Not a Greek, for sure, nor a Turk, neither. No, gentlemen, I make so bold as to asserver that in all Istanbul there may be no more than a handful of gentlemen like yourselves capable of comprehending the simplest Latin text."

He pulled out a handkerchief and began to mop his forehead. "And so, shall we move out of the street?"

"I'm afraid we've just left the café," Giancarlo explained. "And now, if you'll forgive us, we must be getting home."

"*Home*—there's a handsome word! Home! Manna! That's the thing— the very word falls like manna in the desert to a lonesome priest in a city of idolaters and infidels! Well, come on then!" he roared cheerfully, linking arms with the two men who had arms free. "Home it is! And I'll be thinking, my welcome lads, that it's none too far from here?"

It was a curious procession that wound up the road—the infuriated Fabrizio, weighted with his books, bringing up the rear; Father Doherty talking at the top of his voice and clasping two reluctant young men to his sides. Giancarlo's expression, on account of his height, was invisible to the priest.

Doherty was right that home was not far away. In five minutes they came to the door of Ghika's place, where they met Ghika himself coming down the stairs with a sly look on his face.

"Just took up a note for you, efendim," he said, rubbing his hands together. "Arrived just now. I wasn't aware that there was anybody home, so I took the liberty—"

"Birgit!" Giancarlo exclaimed involuntarily. "Why, *diabolo*, my wife's up there!"

"I didn't disturb her, that's sure." Ghika felt an urge to prolong the conversation: the newcomer was a priest of some sort, and he wanted to look closer.

"Disturb her?" Giancarlo felt cold: he dashed past the priest and took the stairs three at a time.

"Birgit? You're asleep?"

He raced into their room and saw Birgit asleep, seminaked on the bed. He dragged at the note in his pocket, and tore it open.

Alea iacta est. The Rubicon is crossed. The time is coming. Be prepared. There will—

Cursing as he heard the rest of them enter the apartment, he crumpled the note into his fist and thrust it back into his pocket.

Birgit was lying very still—and very alluring, with her neck thrown back, her breasts exposed to the slatted sunshine that fell low through the lattice.

Alea iacta est. The Rubicon is crossed. The time is coming!

He felt a rush of blood: he wanted to leap at the bed, rip up her petticoats, and plunge himself into Birgit's warm, yielding body. The Rubicon! Somewhere in his mind he saw her as a sleeping Europe, pale and full of love, tender and directionless: he as a Hannibal, a dark avenger, a liberator— bruising her with his merciless attack, his thighs between hers—

But then, there was the priest.

He dragged the door closed, shoulders drooping, and turned back to the unwelcome guest.

18

"Please," Doherty said. "You've had a note."

Giancarlo jumped. "A note—what?"

"The letter your man delivered just now? I know just how important these things are, when you're abroad and far from home. Don't let me stop you from reading it, while I take the weight from my feet." Doherty sank onto the divan and removed his saturno. "Please, don't trouble to make tea now. That's the weight taken off, there." He patted the cushions happily. "But what can a man do to take the weight off his mind, at the end of a long, hard day, now? Heh-heh!"

Giancarlo scanned the apartment for the note that Ghika had delivered, and found it propped up against the fireplace.

"I expect you're all dying to know what's in it," he declared, with a sort of vicious sarcasm that was lost on the priest. "Shall I open it? Very well. Now," he said, tearing the envelope, "the Rubicon is crossed."

He gave Rafael a significant look.

"My, my, the Rubicon, is it? Who knows but what it might be merely a tailor's bill, Giancarlo, or is it an invitation?"

Doherty chuckled amiably, waving a hand as though it should hold a glass. Giancarlo glanced through the note, and laid it aside.

"Oh, oh! A bill!"

"It's not a bill. It's an invitation, to a picnic lunch."

"Who from?" Fabrizio asked, and bit his tongue.

"Yashim."

"The ambassador's friend?" Doherty suggested, while Giancarlo scowled at Fabrizio.

"Any friend of the ambassador's must be a good man," the priest declared. "The ambassador is a very good man, himself, a gentleman and a scholar. Am I right, young Rafael? He gives his friends fine hospitality, in a dry country."

"Well, would you care for a drink?" Giancarlo's politeness was instinctive.

"I won't lie to you, a little splash might have a splendid medicinal effect. Lay the dust, so to speak. I work with dust, sir."

Fabrizio fetched the bottle, and poured Father Doherty a glass.

He talked, and had another.

"I'm afraid it's all gone," Rafael butted in, when Doherty waved the empty glass again in Giancarlo's direction. "We must go back to the Belgian wine merchant tomorrow."

But Father Doherty's face was a little flushed; it had been a hard day at the library, as he had observed, several times. He wagged his finger amiably at Rafael: "Would it be that you've gone solemn on me now?" His blue eyes flashed. "Could it be that"—he lunged forward—"you're *hiding* something from me?"

His eyes narrowed: they were watery and slightly red, and he held up his empty glass.

Giancarlo actually groaned. "Come, Father. We'd planned to go to the ambassador's tomorrow, but this fellow Yashim has invited us out instead. No doubt the ambassador will be there—why don't you join us? I'll send a note to let him know. In the meantime," he added rather desperately, "we all need an early night."

"Early night." Father Doherty grumbled. "Early night. Well, I daresay you're right. It doesn't do to be abroad late in this city."

Everyone got to their feet. It was as if, after pushing for ages against a heavy stone, it had suddenly rolled away. Fabrizio almost staggered.

"Good night! Good night!" They thumped the priest on the back in their eagerness to see him off. "*A domani! À demain!* Goodbye!"

He was out the door, and Giancarlo had begun to close it behind him, when he stuck his bleary head around it again: "The lady! I should give my respects to the lady!"

"Don't worry," Giancarlo said smoothly. "I'll see she gets them. *She's fast asleep*," he whispered, as if speaking to a child.

"Heh-heh! The sleep of the just. Then I'll be away!"

"That's right! Good night!"

They listened to the priest's heavy footsteps descending the stairs, and eyed one another.

"My God!" Fabrizio breathed. "I could have killed him."

Giancarlo closed the door. "For once, Fabrizio, I couldn't agree with you more."

"You didn't have to carry his books!"

"When he asked for the second bottle?"

"My God, let's have it at last!"

Even Rafael broke into a smile.

There was a thump on the door and Giancarlo leaped away as if it were red hot.

"I'm afraid I left my books," said Father Doherty, blinking. He crossed the room and gathered them up from a chair. Nobody spoke.

Father Doherty nodded. "I'll be off, then."

Giancarlo offered to see him down, but Father Doherty waved him off.

"He was there," Rafael said, finally, when they had held their breath for what seemed like minutes, and heard a door slam far away. "He heard us."

Giancarlo looked worried. "I don't know. It doesn't matter. We were only complaining how he drank too much."

"He must have heard we had another bottle."

"Where *is* Birgit?" Fabrizio glanced at the bedroom door.

"She's asleep."

"Very well." Fabrizio pulled the cork from the bottle. Rafael fetched glasses.

Giancarlo felt that a rite had to be observed and waited until the wine was poured.

"The Rubicon is crossed," he said meaningfully, pulling the note from his pocket and smoothing it on his knee.

"Go on."

Giancarlo's voice trembled slightly as he read.

"It—it's in Latin. *The Rubicon is crossed. The time is coming. Be prepared. There will be shocks but you will know your duty, to the people and to the sacred cause of freedom! Be forewarned—and be forearmed. Vale, La Piuma.*"

"He's here," Rafael whispered. His eyes shone. "We are being called."

"That's it! I felt sure something would happen today!" Fabrizio bent forward. "That fucking priest!"

Rafael giggled. "I couldn't believe it."

"The revolutionaries!" Giancarlo threw out his arms, swaying like Father Doherty. "Home! Onward! Drink!" He started to laugh, showing his gums.

Fabrizio waved his arm. "The note!" he spluttered. "Let's see the note!"

Rafael's shoulders shook. Giancarlo began to whoop with laughter.

"Carry these, young man!" Fabrizio crowed, rolling about on the divan. "The whole fucking Patriarchal Library!"

Their laughter rolled to and fro. "Heh-heh!" Giancarlo wiped his eyes.

"I should like to pay my respects to the lady!"

"The lady!"

"Ha ha ha!"

Giancarlo stumbled to his feet, tossing off a glass of wine.

"The lady!" he caroled, through tears of laughter. "And where is the lady, by all that's holy? Birgit!"

He darted to the bedroom door and slid inside.

Rafael looked at Fabrizio, and they burst into uncontrollable giggles.

19

YASHIM felt the sunlight on his arm and awoke, blinking, wondering what time it was. The street, always quiet, was silent.

He rolled from the divan, opened the door, and retrieved the jug of water that his landlady had left for him. He washed and began to dress. Finally he tucked his feet into a pair of slippers, took a basket from a nail on the wall, and went downstairs.

A few minutes later he arrived at the café on Kara Davut, where the proprietor put a pan on the coals to make his coffee, medium sweet. Yashim ate a *corek*, drank his coffee, and left the coins on the table.

Every year, when the city grew hot and sultry in the autumn sun, parties of Stambouliots would take to caïques and go up the Golden Horn to spend the day at the Sweet Waters of Europe, or cross the Bosphorus to enjoy the shade and the peace of the Sweet Waters of Asia, for the Turks were always great lovers of nature.

These outings could be tumultuous family affairs, with preparations laid in harem kitchens weeks or days in advance. They could be undertaken by a small party of medrese students, perhaps, for reading and poetry, with simple meze, cheese, and fresh fruits. But they were generally constructed around food: and in the provision of food, as in so much else, the bazaars and markets of Istanbul excelled.

Behind ziggurats of vegetables, George was paring the leaves from artichokes with a small knife, and dropping the hearts into a bowl. Now and then he looked up and called out: "Zucchini-beans-arugula! Zucchini-beans-arugula!" in a singsong voice. He caught sight of Yashim and nodded.

"Yous early today, Yashim efendi!" he boomed, and added "Zucchini-beans-arugula!" without breaking stride. "Many peoples?"

"Four or five," Yashim replied. He wasn't sure if Palewski would join the party. "I'll take an *oka* of the artichokes."

George had trimmed and hollowed the hearts, leaving them with a tender stem that reminded Yashim of the domed roofs of the imperial kitchens at Topkapi, each with their massive central chimney. He wondered if the architect Sinan had shared the same thought.

He bought onions, big and small, and a dozen long slipper-shaped peppers which George slid from a dazzling display arranged on a barrelhead like the spokes of a wheel; he bought a few big knobbly lemons, red and green chilies, an *oka* of long purple carrots, a large celeriac, and a couple of pounds of zucchini, small and firm with dark glossy skins and rumpled orange flowers. He chose thin green cucumbers, a melon, a pound of Smyrna figs, purple and fat, and plenty of apricots and pomegranates.

When he picked out enormous bunches of mint, coriander, and flat-leafed parsley, George folded them over and crammed them into the basket. "This is a present," he explained.

Yashim did not protest. For months now, George had been trying to give him vegetables for nothing, because Yashim had saved his life.* His largesse had been threatening to become a burden, to the point where Yashim almost considered buying his vegetables somewhere else, so the gift of mere herbs, generous in itself, came as a relief.

He left the basket with George while he visited the butcher and the cheesemonger, and then he took his shopping home.

He thought about the Russian girl while he unpacked his basket. He wondered whether her confidence had returned, so that she could be happy

---

* See *The Snake Stone.*

with the valide and her ladies. Today would be hot: a good day to take to the water, and into the woods.

Before he left for the palace he dropped the artichokes into a bowl of water with lemon juice, grated the zucchini into a colander, and sprinkled them with salt, to sweat.

The valide was wearing a crocheted jacket and a pair of silk pantaloons. She sat with one elegant wrist resting on her drawn-up knee.

"I understand, Yashim, you have proposed a picnic! *Charmante!* I have not been on a picnic for many years. Sultan Abdülhamid adored them, and so did I. It always does the sultan's girls good, to get them out of doors. It's how they were raised, after all, on their mountains. *Au naturel.* Yes, a picnic will be great fun."

"That's what I hoped," Yashim replied cautiously. Was the valide planning to come as well? *Great fun?* A nightmare for him! A royal progress—he'd have to redouble the food, find caïques, servants . . .

"Of course, it will all be rather rough," he added.

"Mais, c'est ça!" The valide clapped her hands. "A little rough—how perfect."

Yashim was quite sure that the valide's idea of rough did not extend to sitting on the ground, or carrying a basket.

"There's the question of food," he said slowly.

"But you are a good cook, Yashim. It's famous!"

"And of course I asked the Italians to come. You might find them rather, well, boyish, Valide hanum."

"It doesn't matter what I think," she said. She thought for a moment and raised an interrogative eyebrow. "Goodness, Yashim, you didn't imagine that I would come on your picnic, did you?"

Yashim looked embarrassed, while the valide laughed.

"Hee hee! Oh, Yashim!" She wiped her eyes. "What an idea! I am valide—how could I possibly condescend? A picnic, with Franks—and men! *Pas de chance!*" She waved him away. *"Pas—de—chance.* The idea!"

He found Natasha dressed and waiting for him in the Court of the Favorites.

"Did they pull you apart last night?" he asked; but she only smiled and shook her head.

"The valide was very kind."

Yashim suggested taking a sedan chair to the water, but she assured him that she preferred to walk.

"Too much luxury will make me fat," she said.

He took her arm. Already, as they passed through the First Court, he observed a change in her. She seemed to have grown by inches. When they passed under the great gate she did not flinch—and her bonnet bobbed from side to side. As they made their way through the crowded streets, eliciting glances from the Turks and franker curiosity from the Greeks, she turned to him and laughed.

"Round, tall, flat, square—I've never seen so many different hats!"

At the back of the Mosque of the Valide they plunged into a rabble of men and goods around the quayside, maneuvering their wares into the Egyptian bazaar.

"Where is this?" She lifted her head and sniffed the air. "Spices!"

"Come." This was something he wanted to show her, a halt on the great caravan that summoned scents from the four corners of the world. He thought of Natasha raised in Siberia on a ribbon of forbidden road, at the far end of which lay Saint Petersburg and the tsar, and the dimly pictured world of quadrilles, braid, carriages, and shoulders under fur, and the lights sparkling in the snow. There was, he imagined, no in-between: only the place of exile and the lost Eden, back to back.

Which meant, of course, that Eden had a secret door that all the dancing feet and swirling skirts of Saint Petersburg could not entirely disguise: a door that dropped you suddenly to the lonely road, left you thousands of miles away in the howling blackness of a Siberian winter.

He took her arm, and they plunged into the spice bazaar.

Natasha's eyes grew round as they made their way up the cavernous arcade. On either side, baskets and barrels were heaped with spices, mounds of every color—powders, leaves, twisted roots, long strings of dried vegetables, boxes of dates, of dried plums, raisins, figs. She stopped in front of a huge basket crammed with little black berries.

"Is this pepper?"

"Black pepper. There's green there, and red. That's white pepper." Yashim spoke to the spice merchant. "It's Sumatran. He says it's the best quality. They bring it to the Red Sea and then overland, through Egypt. Most of these spices—"

He broke off. Natasha's eyes were sparkling, and he realized she had tears standing in them.

"I've never seen anything like it." She tried to smile. "In Siberia— pepper! It's like money. We carry it in little screws of paper." She gestured to the piles of colored spice. "We know salt. Only salt, and some berries."

Yashim nodded, and guided her onward. "Here you see the world under one roof. And we're buying stuff for our picnic."

She glanced at him inquiringly.

"Some Italians are coming—they are young, like you, and seem to be in some sort of exile themselves. The valide has given me her permission to invite you. For an awful moment I thought she meant to come along as well. I'd have had to hire elephants."

Natasha laughed. "No elephants? You disappoint me. I thought every Ottoman picnic had at least one, to carry the musicians!"

"First I must go home to prepare the food," Yashim said. He hesitated. "If you like, we could go home and cook together."

"I can make soup. And pancakes."

"I'll cook. But I'd like your company."

She pressed her hands together. "Oh, I'll come! Just don't tell me that you live in a palace, too."

"I think, Natasha, you're in for a shock. And now we will take a caïque, as I promised. It's always cooler on the water."

20

SHE untied the ribbons of her bonnet and reached up to take it off.

"This is where you live?"

She knelt on the divan, and looked out of the window. "I—I have never been so high up. In a house."

The juice of the grated zucchini looked like jade in the bowl. He lit a fire in the grate, sprinkled it with charcoal, and set a pan to boil. With a sharp knife he peeled the celeriac, chopped it into small cubes, and dropped the pieces into the water, with the artichokes.

The pan was boiling: he skinned a dozen small onions and blanched them.

"I like to watch you work," Natasha said.

He had almost forgotten her sitting on the divan.

"Tell me about Siberia. Tell me about your home."

He worked while she talked. He put carrots, onions, artichokes, and celeriac into a bigger saucepan, with a sprig of thyme and a bay leaf, and covered them all with stock.

"We used to pretend we were in Saint Petersburg. Uncle Sergei had money—they didn't confiscate his estates, I don't know why—and he had the opera house built in Irkutsk. We sewed our own clothes, but we threw proper balls, with an orchestra. Everyone always wanted to believe that we would go home."

Yashim broke two eggs into a bowl with a cup of flour and beat them together. He gave the zucchini a final squeeze and mixed them in. On the board he chopped onions with a handful of dill and parsley, and pounded some garlic in the mortar with a pinch of salt. He swept it all into the zucchini mixture and stirred it around. Finally he set an open pan on the heat, and threw in butter and olive oil.

"One by one, the families left. We used to give them a ball on the night of their departure. The boys who were leaving would ask the girls who were staying for the first dance . . ."

Her voice trailed off.

"Eventually the balls stopped happening, when everyone had gone."

"And your father?"

"He runs the school where I have been teaching. He paints. He is making a book of Siberian wildflowers. It's very beautiful, very detailed. I think he's the first person to really study Siberian plants."

She laughed a bit awkwardly. "His real problem is me."

The butter was bubbling. Yashim began to drop spoonfuls of the zucchini mix into the pan: they spread and blossomed as they fell.

"Why you?"

"I think he feels he's let me down. There's no society. He feels that."

"No one to marry, you mean?"

Natasha blushed. "I suppose so. Oh, Anton the miller is rich, but he thinks only about trees. And there's a furrier who sends furs all over the world, and spends the winters in Moscow, but he's old and has a mustache that gets into his soup. My father says he was a sort of criminal once. I can't marry him."

Yashim slid the zucchini fritters from the pan, then started to make some more. "No, I see that."

"Do you? It sounds silly, perhaps. But I think it would break my father's heart if I married one of the mujiks. As it is, he has very little heart left to break—it's been broken so many times already."

"But you've come here to get him out of Siberia." The vegetables were done. He fished them out of the broth and laid them on a platter.

Natasha was so silent that Yashim looked around.

"He has his school and his flowers," she said, thoughtfully. "My mother is buried there, too."

"And you?"

"Me? I'd stay with him."

Yashim cocked his head. "Then—" He waved a spoon. "What are you looking for?"

"A pardon. I want the tsar's forgiveness, for my father. He was so young when he joined the Decembrists. I would like to see him as a free man, not a prisoner. It is how he would wish to be seen."

Yashim nodded. He chopped a larger onion into shreds, and began to soften it in a pan with butter and garlic. He threw in a handful of pine nuts, and then a cup of rice, pushing the grains against the pan, feeling them stick and move reluctantly.

He reached into the stockpot, tore off a piece of chicken breast, and laid it steaming on the board. He chopped it quite fine, stirred it into the rice, added currants, sugar, cinnamon, allspice, and a pinch of salt, then poured in some stock. The pan hissed and steam rose into the air.

"You like this—cooking?"

The question surprised him. "Yes. Why not?"

Natasha shrugged. "In Russia, it's a job for old women."

Yashim let the stock liberate the rice, and settled the pan to a low simmer on the edge of the stove. "You know *L'Avare*? The Molière play?"

She smiled. *"You should eat to live, not live to eat."*

"I think the truth is somewhere between the two."

"In Russia we have bread, butter, and cheese. We eat a lot of soup."

"Soup's good. I make soup in winter."

"I suppose you have many things to choose from in Istanbul."

Yashim chopped a clove of garlic with salt, and stirred it into a bowl of yogurt. "Try this, see if you like it." He put a fritter on a plate, added a dollop of yogurt, and offered it to her.

"What is it?"

Yashim smiled, and explained.

"Eggs. Of course, we have eggs, too," she said hastily.

Yashim was rolling the peppers on a board, shaking out the seeds. He lifted the lid of the rice, which was almost done, and squeezed some lemon juice over it, with a twist of pepper from the mill.

"It's delicious," she said, handing him back the plate.

"Would you like a job? It's easy. Just spoon this rice into the peppers, like this."

She held one, green and waxy, between her fingers, and took a teaspoon. "Ow! It's hot!"

"Leave a little room at the top—the rice expands. Then, like this—put the lid on again, and lay it in the pan."

They stood side by side, working the rice into the peppers. When they were all done, Yashim poured some more stock over them and covered them with a plate.

"Now they can lie quiet," he said. "And we can go out again."

He led her downstairs, and out onto the street. At Kara Davut he shepherded her to the café. "I'll show you how we drink coffee in Istanbul," he said. "I think you should try it sweet."

When the coffee came, black and thick and small and strong enough almost to stand without a cup, she tried it gingerly.

"Just sip it," he warned her. "And then—like this."

He drank the coffee, set the saucer on top, flipped it, and laid it on the table.

"Why?"

"Because you can read your fortune in the shapes the grounds make in the cup. The bottom of the cup is the past, and the sides tell the future. What's left on the saucer—that tells you about your home. Let me see."

A shadow fell across the table and a man clamped his hand over Natasha's cup. She pulled back in alarm: he was a wild-looking fellow, with long mustaches and ill-kempt gray hair tied back with a dirty ribbon; the nails of his hand were chipped and rimmed with black.

"I will read the cup for the Frankish lady," he said.

Yashim and Natasha exchanged glances. "Very well," Yashim said. Sufi or beggar, it was polite to let him go on.

The man squatted down by the table, and when he drew the coffee cup and saucer toward him Yashim noticed he put a coin on the cup—perhaps to encourage them to pay him afterward, perhaps to avert bad omens.

He turned the cup over and peered into it silently. He looked so serious and intent that Natasha suppressed a smile. "What does it say?"

"The lady has no family?"

"She has a father."

"Hmm. But not here. She has come a long way by sea."

Yashim gave Natasha an amused glance.

"There is something here she very much wants." The fortune-teller shook his head slowly. "Different paths may lead to her goal, but it will not be easy for her to decide which one to take. The quickest route is not the best. It is unsafe. Dangerous. But the other route is slow and seems hard, so she will be tempted. I am afraid when she realizes, it will be too late."

Yashim frowned, but translated faithfully what the fortune-teller said. "How is she to recognize the path of danger?"

"Because a man will offer it to her, but—" The man frowned, and cocked his head. "He is a man and not a man. I don't understand it." He leaned sideways and laid a hand on Yashim's arm. "I see death, efendi. Death and punishment," he added, looking at him with yellow eyes.

"A woman's death. I do not like this reading," the fortune-teller said, replacing the cup. "I had not expected such a fortune." He made a gesture with the flat of his hand, and stood up.

Natasha looked anxious. "But what's he saying?"

The man had left the table.

"He rambled, Natasha—many of these men are charlatans, beggars really. I am sorry."

"You think so? Why did he leave us with a coin?"

Yashim followed her pointing finger, and there, on the table between them, was a copper asper.

"Hey!" Yashim was half on his feet but the man was already gone.

Natasha looked pale. "He said something, didn't he? About my father?"

Yashim shook some money from his purse. "Come on, we'll get the other things we need, and then go back. I'll show you how we make an Ottoman picnic, without the elephants."

At the cheesemonger's stall they stopped for a block of salty white *beyaz peynir*, made of pure sheep's milk, and a block of stringy *dil peyniri*. They crossed the street to an old man with curved mustaches, whose wife's pickles were widely considered to be the best in the market.

"*Dil peyniri* is good to eat with your fingers. It's mild, and you pull it into strings and wrap the strings around a green pickled tomato and pop it into your mouth."

They hesitated over the jars of pickles, eventually choosing three of Yashim's favorites: *patlican tursusu*, made of stuffed eggplant; a jar of turnips, pickled in grape juice, with a sliver of beetroot thrown in, for the prettiness of its color; and some long green chilies.

The basket was almost full, and very heavy.

"We used to picnic on the Black Sea," Yashim remembered. "They made me carry a basket, and I always grumbled."

He smiled: he could see now that his parents had given him a little basket of his own to help him appreciate the coming feast. Of course, the real picnic was carried by porters and slaves. Hampers and hampers!

"Let's get *pastirmi*."

At the meat stall he bought a pound of the best from Kayseri, made from beef filet. He explained to Natasha how the meat was pressed, rubbed with *çemen* paste made of fenugreek, garlic, and chili, and then sun-dried.

"Fenugreek?"

"Smell it."

She did, and pulled a face. They bought a couple of horseshoe-shaped *sucuk*, a dried sausage made of lamb with garlic and cumin, and moved on to buy pistachios and fresh green chilies.

"Do you like caviar?"

"Yashim, you're joking . . ."

So he bought half a pound of Persian sturgeon's eggs, the black kind, lightly salted in their own purse. "Try it from the other side of the Caspian," he remarked. On their way out of the market, Yashim stopped a *simit* seller, and bought a dozen coils of the spiced dry bread from the tray the man carried on his head.

"I think the valide must be coming after all," she whispered.

He selected a tray of baklava: "I think you'll like this," he said, thinking of Palewski's joke. "The Italians love it." They watched the man lay his selection carefully between thin wooden boards. The man's young son bound the boards together with raffia ribbons, which he tied off and curled with a zip of his fingernail.

Finally, at the apothecary, he bought four ounces of China tea, wrapped in paper.

The basket was so heavy he engaged one of the porters who carried bales and boxes uphill on their backs, secured by a band across their foreheads. He was a stocky man with delicate hands, and he grunted with amusement when he saw Yashim's load.

21

YASHIM was surprised to find Father Doherty sitting on the stairs on the half landing, reading a book.

"Ah, Yashim efendi! I was afraid you'd never come." His blue eyes flickered over Yashim's shoulder and fastened on Natasha. "The boys tell me you're having a picnic—and invited me along as spiritual adviser. I came straight on."

"The door wasn't locked."

"Well, I saw that, of course, but I'd no wish to invade, sir."

"Not at all," Yashim said. "You're very welcome to join our picnic. Mademoiselle Borisova. Father Doherty."

Once the cooked dishes were packed, the sturdy hamal took the picnic baskets down the street to the Balat stage, where Yashim had to engage a second caïque for the priest. Father Doherty sat nervously erect and let out a muttered invocation whenever the delicate craft rocked too far for his taste.

At Eyüp, at the top of the Golden Horn, they found Birgit and the Italians taking coffee at a small café and admiring the distant view of the city from an unfamiliar angle. The sun shone, the water sparkled; it was an excellent day, they all agreed, for a trip into the countryside.

"Count Palewski will be joining us, I hope?"

"I'm afraid he has other engagements, Miss Lund. He sends his regrets."

Yashim engaged another porter to carry the baskets. Coffee taken, they set off through the village and past the shrine to the Companion of the Prophet, and up into the low wooded hills that surrounded them.

The porter proved quite incapable of giving directions; born and raised in the village, he had never left it, either.

"He's been to Istanbul, surely?" Giancarlo exclaimed. "Why, it's the view from his own bedroom window!"

The porter, it seemed, had always been happy to keep it there, too. "What do I want with all that trampin' up and down, efendi? Too many people, beggin' your pardon, and nowhere to sit."

They reached a hilltop, but there was no view through the trees.

"This is the way!" Birgit said gaily, pointing out a path that followed the hilltops; so they followed her, and came out above a shallow valley where the woods had been cleared, and a farmhouse nestled at the foot of the slope.

Everyone cast admiring glances at the view, attracted by the sight of a glittering pond just beyond the house. The walk had made everyone quite hot.

"This will be perfect," Yashim declared, and when Rafael looked dubious he pointed to the sagging roof. "There's no one here—look."

The farm had been recently abandoned. The grassy slope was dotted with juniper and thin beech saplings, as the woods encroached on the cleared land, and the farmhouse itself was enlaced in wild figs and thistles that grew luxuriantly in the rich soil of the yard.

The porter laid down the baskets, and they agreed to meet before sundown. He stumped off up the slope and disappeared into the woods.

Giancarlo produced wine from his haversack and buried it in the pool, while Yashim unrolled a rug and set up the picnic. Father Doherty sat on the rug, and ran a handkerchief over his face. Natasha and Birgit laid their bonnets aside and wandered off to pick flowers while the boys explored the ruined house, forcing open a door and rummaging inside for bits of broken pottery and an old tin jug with no bottom, little offerings which they brought back with the excitement of savants opening an Egyptian tomb.

Giancarlo made a fire.

"More sticks! Fabrizio, Rafael—go and look under the trees."

Father Doherty watched the boys go up the hill. "Leadership," he murmured, and winked at Yashim. "A regular platoon."

Natasha had found a long stick and was prodding the pool with it, chatting to Birgit. Yashim watched them together for a moment, the dark head and the blond bending together, and smiled.

Fabrizio returned with an armful of kindling and dropped it on the ground. "Ouf!" He brushed twigs and lichen off his shirtfront. Rafael came down the hill dragging a branch; Fabrizio laughed.

"Much too big, Rafael!"

"We can feed it into the fire," Rafael said.

"Natasha's peppers, stuffed with rice and chicken," Yashim announced, setting the glazed dish on the rug. He laid out the salad, and dishes piled high with fresh mint, arugula, and parsley, with the bread from the Libyan baker on Kara Davut, unwrapped from its linen coverings, still warm.

"Please, eat," he urged, dropping a spoon into the dish of artichokes.

There were sighs and exclamations of delight: the long walk had given them all an appetite. They drank the Italians' cold wine and ate *à l'Ottomane*, with their fingers, reclining like emperors and empresses on the grass.

"It's like home," Giancarlo said. "The grass, and the woods. It could be Tuscany."

"Really?" Birgit looked around. "It's like your home? Perhaps, one day—"

"Well, with the hills, too, and the figs. I don't know—it has a Tuscan feel. Italian, I should say. It's good to be out of the city."

Rafael said quietly, "I've always lived in Rome."

"And does Istanbul remind you of Rome, at all?" Yashim wondered.

"They call it the second Rome, with its seven hills."

"Both littered with ruins," Rafael agreed. "And domes, too, and sunken roads. A little. But Istanbul looks grandest from the water. You can't compare the Tiber to the Bosphorus."

"Istanbul's more like Palermo, anyway," Fabrizio said.

They waited for him to go on. He shrugged. "Blank walls. Alleyways. Palermo was Arabic, but they're Islamic cities, aren't they? Right on the water. Plenty of hills, and lots of steps. Up and down—and hot."

Yashim nodded. It was the longest speech he'd heard Fabrizio make.

"And all of them crumbling," Giancarlo pointed out. "Flaking stone and peeling paint. Rome is just the same."

"For the present," Rafael said. "When Rome is the capital of a united Italy—"

"Boys, boys." Doherty rolled his eyes. "Must you always be spoiling a good view with your politics? I appeal to you, Miss Lund—and to you, too, my dear! Just look about you. For the Lord thy God bringeth thee into a good land, a land of brooks of water, of fountains and depths that spring out of valleys and hills!" he declaimed, grabbing a tuft of grass and holding it aloft. "Deuteronomy, my friends. The good land!"

He raised his glass. "A land of wheat, and barley, and vines, and fig trees, and pomegranates," he recited. "A land of olive oil and honey, wherein thou shalt eat bread without scarceness, thou shalt not lack anything in it! Ay, it's the Irish lament, to be sure.

"When thou hast eaten and are full, then thou shalt bless the Lord thy God for the good land which he hath given thee."

"Amen," said Birgit.

The priest declared his intention of having a snooze. Rafael ate two pieces of baklava, and Birgit laughed at him affectionately.

One by one, slightly flushed, the boys stripped off and splashed about in the pond, slinging mud and shouting happily in Italian. They pretended to want to throw the girls in, but Birgit only smiled and waved them away. Giancarlo reached out for Natasha, who was gathering more flowers. He grabbed her arm.

"No!" She wheeled on him, her hand raised. "Let go!"

"A nice swim!" He swung on her arm, teasing.

"Let me go."

He began backing toward the pool, tugging Natasha along. She struggled. Giancarlo laughed.

"Oh!" He sprang back, his hand to his cheek. "I—I am sorry, mademoiselle. I didn't mean . . ." He glanced around, guiltily, and Yashim quickly looked away.

"I am sorry," Giancarlo repeated. "Your flowers—let me pick them up."

"I'll do it. It doesn't matter."

Giancarlo backed away, embarrassed, and joined the boys in the pool. Natasha crouched in the grass, collecting her flowers: Yashim thought he should go and help, but just as he decided to get up, she stood and walked away toward the farmhouse, her head bent.

He found her leaning on a wall behind the ruined farmhouse, where a spray of nettles had attracted a thousand blue butterflies. She looked around.

"Like the colors of the tiling in the mosque," she said. "I've never seen such butterflies. My father would love them."

"They are beautiful. Perhaps you should paint them for him?"

"I don't paint the way he can," she said. "I wonder why they don't get stung? I suppose they tread very lightly on the nettle leaves."

They watched the blue cloud lifting and falling.

"I'm sorry if I behaved badly," Natasha said at last. "I didn't mean to hurt him. Giancarlo. I just don't like being grabbed, like that."

"He won't mind. He shouldn't have panicked you."

"Panic—that's what it is." She smiled at him. "Shall we go back to the fire? I picked you some flowers."

Later, Birgit drifted down to the water wearing only her shift, and swam with her lover while the other boys picked over the remains of Yashim's feast. She emerged unself-consciously transparent, voluptuous in wet undergarments that clung to her pale nipples and revealed the contours of her body. Yashim spotted Doherty rearranging his hat over his eyes, and poked another stick into the fire. Birgit came and sat beside them, now and then holding out the hem of her skirt to catch its warmth.

She talked about the Danish summer, short but so warm that everyone went to the countryside if they could afford it, and swam, if they knew how. "We have picnics, too—but not so good. Herring and black bread. And you, Natasha? In Siberia?"

"In summer it's a bit the same—cheese and bread, with pickles. And smoked meat. Too many mosquitoes. I like the winter picnics best. Then someone digs a hole in the ice and catches fish—pike, and perch, and salmon, too. They make a good soup, and it's hot. But we start with stroganina."

"Stroganina?"

"Frozen fish. It's cut into long strips, and you eat it with salt and pepper. It's a very strong taste. I like it."

"Brrr!"

"I like these spices, too," Natasha admitted. She put the flowers she had picked in a patterned glass and set them in front of Yashim. He smiled at her.

"I'll show you how to use them," Yashim said.

Birgit chuckled. "Yashim efendi's School of Cookery—why not? I'm sure Natasha would enroll."

Seeing Natasha blush, Birgit changed the subject. She was reading a book by a young philosopher called Søren Kierkegaard, who would have liked it here, Birgit was sure. Yashim smiled. He liked her easy manner. She reminded him of those palace odalisques but she lacked their affectations—their lisps and piping insincerities.

She talked about Kierkegaard, and the conversation turned to the love of nature. Natasha mentioned Aksakov.

"Palewski was talking about him, too, just the other day," Yashim said. "Aksakov and an Englishman called Gilbert White."

"Oh yes," Natasha said. "Gilbert White of Selborne." She proceeded to give them a digest of White's nature writings. Yashim lay back and listened. She must make a very charming teacher in her father's school, he thought, impressing the little Siberians with her low and serious voice. After a while Birgit started to get dressed.

"White examined all the evidence," Natasha went on, "and he says that the little birds, in winter, hibernate by burying themselves in the mud of ponds, like this one. Do you think that's true?"

"White was an *Anglican* clergyman," Father Doherty murmured from under his hat, which had slipped sideways. "Very little he could say would be dependable. Aristotle, now, he'd tell you about the little birdies, so he would."

Natasha startled: she seemed to have forgotten Doherty's presence. "What brings you to Istanbul, Father?"

Doherty sat up and fanned himself with his hat.

"Philology, theology, divinity, and prayer! What do you think of that? Which is, of course, only a way of saying that I am a humble ant who toils in the dust of ages past! Vellum, my dear girl, and papyrus—isn't that the name for paper still, in Russian? Pappa-roos!"

Natasha was about to correct him but Father Doherty swept on, patting his forehead with a handkerchief.

"It's a battle, dear lady. On the one hand, libraries, archives, the accumulated lore of the millennia—and on the other, mites, worms, and natural decay. So many books, so many testaments—and we are so few."

Poor Doherty, Yashim thought. Nobody much liked him, and he was lonely.

Much later, when everyone had taken the slow caïques back down the Golden Horn, and said goodbye, Yashim took Natasha back to the palace.

"Those boys—they aren't really exiles," Natasha said. "Not like my father."

"They aren't prisoners, no."

Natasha shivered. "I didn't feel easy with—what was his name?"

"The priest? Doherty."

"No, the boy, the smaller one. Fabrizio. His eyes."

Yashim smiled. "Perhaps you were looking too beautiful."

"Don't say that. Birgit's the beautiful one. He looked at her in a funny way, all the time. And—well."

"Well?"

"Just, well."

The caïque dipped as it turned toward the shore. Lights burned at the Eminönü stage. He helped Natasha out of the boat.

"Do you feel safe here—at night?" she asked, breaking the silence as they walked slowly up the long street toward the palace.

"Just here, as safe as anywhere. There are some districts—the port, at Tophane, for one; some places around Pera—graveyards. But it's a safe city. Nobody goes out at night, except the watchmen."

"I had no idea it would be so big," Natasha admitted. They turned at the palace wall and began climbing the narrow alley behind Ayasofya. "Perhaps that's what frightens me, sometimes."

The slope leveled off, and they emerged at the Fountain of Ahmet III, whose enormous eaves puddled the ground in the shade of a waxing moon. Yashim took Natasha to the gate, where the guards saluted him, and walked her through to the little gate of the harem.

One of the elderly black eunuchs opened the door, yawning.

"It's not a caravansary for travelers," he said sniffily.

"Good night, Yashim."

Yashim touched her hand, and bowed. "Good night, Natasha. Thank you for coming."

22

PALEWSKI laid the letter on the desk and poured himself a brandy. He took the glass to the window and knelt on the seat, looking into the night through his own dim reflection in the glass. Somewhere a dog barked, hoarse and deep.

It was many years since he had undertaken a mission that could be compared with this, he thought. Commanding a troop, or riding to Moscow alone through the winter snows, he had felt the weight of empires on his shoulders.

His reflection shrugged back at him. It was a long time ago. Some of the empires had fallen, some of the hopes had died. Everyone had changed.

He closed his eyes. Palewski pictured Europe as a map tilted against the light, on which mountains rose and rivers flowed, and the names of countries were stamped out like the letters of a patent medicine. France was lit; England lit; Spain—it was too far away. But at the center of the map the light was dimmest, the borders bleeding into gray at the junction of three empires, obscuring the shadow lines of his own, dejected country.

Once an Austrian, drunk, had shouted at him: "Your Poland is nothing to the Committee!" Palewski had seen the sudden look of regret on his face, an almost comical shift from sneer to fear, and then the gray-clad officers had crowded around; it was hard, a few moments later, to be sure what the man had said. The Committee, yes, it existed: men with hands on the levers of power, their ears straining at every door, sustaining despots and emperors.

What if now, beneath his hand, the spirit of change could be awakened? Palewski saw the borders breaking up like ice floes on the Vistula or the Don. Light crept across the surface of his mental map—with Istanbul pulsing, like a lighthouse.

Of course the Porte was afraid. The Porte—the Ottoman government—took its name from the High Gate, leading to the offices of the grand vizier: it was a good name for it, a gateway. Each door opened to an opportunity. He would help to push that door, open it a crack to allow a beam of light to fly out across the enclosed and darkened lands of eastern Europe.

He felt a flutter of excitement. He was the only Polish diplomat in the world, the only ambassador accredited to a government that had as much to gain from change as Poland herself. The Ottomans were battered and uncertain but still a power. Perhaps it was for this he had waited all these years, maintaining the dignity of Poland as a name, carrying the idea, year in, year out, in the teeth of scheming and envious enemies.

Palewski squared his shoulders, unconsciously: he, at least, was not afraid.

He turned back to the desk and folded Midhat Pasha's letter. *We cannot send to the ship . . . communication must remain secret . . . note to the residency . . .*

Midhat had to be cautious. By agreeing to a secret meeting between the sultan and the Polish statesman, Prince Czartoryski, the Porte had put itself in Palewski's hands. If word were to escape! News of the meeting might bolster the Polish cause, but it could do the Porte unforeseeable harm. The autocrats of Europe would protest in the most vigorous terms. They would unleash threats, at the very least.

Palewski had given the pasha his word of honor.

He opened the drawer and took out the packet of correspondence, intending to slip this last communication in above the rest. For a moment he frowned—the letters were spilling from the packet. He must have jogged them as he drew them out of the drawer. Why couldn't he remember? His hands were trembling. Excitement again—or too much brandy!

Czartoryski, the old warhorse, the noble senator, was coming to Istanbul! They hadn't met in a quarter century, but he supposed he'd recognize him still. Connections of sympathy, affection, and even family: Czartoryski was a cousin on his mother's side. Exiled in Paris since the early thirties. Prince Czartoryski had money. The Palewskis had fared worse.

Istanbul. Paris. London. Polish émigrés were everywhere: all they needed was another lead, a sign, a powerful protector.

If Stanislaw Palewski had anything to do with it, a protector would be found, and very soon.

Funny, that Russian girl Yashim had spoken of, coming here on a similar errand. Odd chance they should coincide. He hoped her petition would not interfere with his. Poor old Borisov, driven out to Siberia and the mines.

He slipped the newest letter into the packet and sealed it carefully. Death to tyrants! He put the packet into the drawer and slid it shut.

Instead of flinging himself into a chair and taking up a book, as he was used to doing, the ambassador bent forward and almost tenderly blew out the candle.

Then, *mirabile dictu*, he went upstairs to bed.

23

N ATASHA saw a light was burning in the valide's hall, and she crept close and touched the door.

Through the crack she could see the serving girl, asleep on a low divan. An oil lamp burned on the marble floor. She was about to tiptoe away when she looked again and noticed that the lamp was guttering, a juddering black smoke rising from the mantle.

She slipped off her shoes and went in; the door creaked and the girl on the divan started up.

"Who—what's that?"

Natasha crouched down beside the lamp and lowered the wick. "The flame," she explained.

The girl got up rather testily, Natasha thought, as she pointed to the soot in the mantle and tut-tutted, to show what had happened.

"Mais qu'est-ce qui se passe?" The valide stood in the inner doorway, in a pair of loose pajamas.

Natasha jumped to her feet, while the slave girl scrambled to the floor.

"We were just checking the lamp," Natasha explained. "It was smoking."

"Hmm." The valide spoke rapidly to the girl, then turned with a gesture. "Come in, little one. I am not asleep."

Natasha followed her into the apartment. The valide climbed onto the divan and drew up her quilt.

"Eh bien. Yashim's party. Tell me about it."

"I helped him cook. I stuffed some peppers, Valide hanum."

The valide raised an elegant eyebrow. "A great honor, no doubt. Yashim is very particular about his cookery. Go on."

Natasha described Yashim's flat, the view out the windows, the little kitchen in the corner, the bookshelves. "It's quite high up, very light."

The valide drew up her knees under the quilt and closed her eyes. She was smiling faintly. "It's his lair," she murmured. "Who came?"

"First there was a priest, a Catholic."

"Mon dieu! I remember the type. Did he put a hand on your knee? No? Go on."

"Then three Italians, with a girl called Birgit. She was beautiful—blond, Valide!"

The valide's eyes opened. "I don't doubt it. Most of those girls are. A Circassian?"

"No, Valide. I think she was Danish, in fact."

"Danish?" The valide turned her head. "And tell me, what did she wear?"

Natasha had been very observant. Used to doing her own dressmaking, she was able to describe every article of Birgit's costume, and the careless elegance of the three Italians, to the valide's evident satisfaction.

"And which was the lover?"

"Giancarlo, the tall one. But the little one, Fabrizio, kept looking at Birgit in a strange way. Very intense."

"Hmm. It's extraordinary, how these Europeans persist in creating danger for themselves. Can you imagine? In our empire, Natasha, it's always about one man. One at a time, *au moins*."

She laughed, and Natasha found herself laughing, too.

"*Eh bien*, you have cheered me up. I'm very glad. I'd like to sleep now." She presented her cheek for a kiss.

Natasha kissed her and retired; the girl in the hall even smiled: the Russian girl had not given her away.

Natasha slept well, for the first time in Istanbul, dreaming of cooks and lovers and a priest wrapped in a quilt.

24

"REALLY, Benjamin might have warned me we'd be walking all morning. It's very hot, Mr. Compston." Eliza stopped to fan herself. "I suppose you do know where we're going?"

George Compston, who had lost all sense of direction ten minutes earlier, gave her a queasy smile. "Certainly, Miss Day. Know the old place pretty well, if I say so myself. Just a lot of infernal alleys—all look the same."

"It seems to me that this one is the same—I'm sure I remember those dogs."

"Ah, that's because the dogs are everywhere, all the same, just like the alleys." He looked around uneasily. "I'm afraid you can't avoid this sort of maze, if you want to get anywhere in town. Here's the street we want."

They descended the crooked street. Compston's plan was to keep going downhill: they would eventually hit either the Galata Tower or at the very least the bridge below it, over the Golden Horn.

Ben Fizerley, Eliza's cousin, was Compston's superior at the British embassy. A couple of years Compston's senior, he was an easygoing fellow whose family had decided to join him for a month after a successful tour of the Italian peninsula. Sir Garrard and Lady Fizerley were up at Therapia, where the embassy maintained its summer residence, and Compston had been called in to escort Eliza around the sights of Pera. He had been dismayed to find Eliza less easygoing than her cousin.

"Really, Mr. Compston, I am afraid you are lost. I saw the tower most plain at least an hour ago."

"Almost there now, I think." Compston mopped his forehead. If they came out, as he feared, on top of the bridge, he might pretend that he had brought her down to the water's edge to get cool. He regretted claiming to know the city so very well indeed.

"And that, Mr. Compston, is not the first time you have said so." Eliza pressed herself to the wall to avoid a team of porters, straining upward with loads on their backs. "Why do they wear a band around their foreheads? They seem to be carrying everything on their heads."

"Tradition," said Compston, who had no idea. "Everyone is in a guild here, you see, and they're very fierce about keeping up the traditions. These chaps—hamal, the Turks call 'em—always carry stuff about on their heads and backs, just like their fathers, and their fathers before them. Mind the steps."

They were at the top of a particularly steep alleyway between two enormous buildings that Compston could not remember having ever seen before.

"Steps? I don't believe these are steps at all. It looks to me like a pile of collapsed masonry." She began to advance cautiously, one hand to the wall, choosing her footing with care. A pretty girl, Compston thought, admiringly, as she hopped from one lump of stone to the next.

"That's the way here," he explained. "Roads always in a shocking state. Mules vanish into holes, that sort of thing. Steps worse."

"I suppose that's a tradition? Upheld by the worshipful company of Ottoman road menders?"

Compston could think of no reply to this. He was engaged in keeping his own balance.

Five minutes later, feeling sticky and irritable, they emerged onto flatter ground.

Eliza pointed with her finger. "Is this the Golden Horn? It's awfully wide."

Compston gazed, and frowned, and his mouth dropped open. He had no idea how it had happened, but they seemed to have emerged by the Bosphorus, instead.

"I—I thought we should come down to the water, to get a bit of breeze," he said.

"What about the Galata Tower? Or the bridge you talked about?"

"Better to cool down for a few moments, don't you think?"

"Where are we, exactly?"

"Exactly? Ah—" He peered around, trying to get his bearings. "I'm afraid we may have missed the tower."

"Missed it? It's unmissable, surely? I have read that the Galata Tower is over a hundred and fifty feet high. Do you mean to say we have to climb back there to reach it? I'm afraid you give a lady too much credit. I am not weak, but it is very hot, and I am certainly no Atalanta. What I should like now is a gelato and a cab. Or even a sedan chair."

Compston looked around wildly. Apart from the Grande Rue, on which most of the embassies stood, and some sections along the shore of the Bosphorus, the roads of Istanbul were mostly impassable for carriages.

"A cab. A cab," Compston muttered, looking up and down the road.

"My kingdom for a cab," concluded Eliza, pertly.

"I'm afraid—"

"What's that?"

And she pointed to a wan clump of trees close to the water's edge, where an emaciated horse was enjoying a bag of oats. The horse was in harness, and behind the harness stood a black carriage.

"That?"

"Looks decidedly like a cab, Mr. Compston."

25

THE matter of cabs had exercised Palewski, too. For several days he had been debating in his mind the best way to collect the prince from his ship. It would anchor at Tophane, and the prince could be alerted to come ashore at almost any time.

The best time, Palewski initially thought, would be under cover of night, when few people would see a passenger come ashore. Those few, however, might be the wrong few: Palewski knew that the Russians and the Austrians had a system of spies and informers scattered all across the continent.

He might ask the prince to travel in a sedan chair. Yet a sedan, even if it could be found at four a.m., would be noticeable at the dockside, obtrusive in town, and extraordinary at the gates of the residency, where news that a sedan chair had been brought up into Pera would spread like cholera. And a sedan chair had room for only a single traveler: Palewski would need either to secure a second or leave the prince to travel alone.

The prince was a man of seventy or more. No longer young, accustomed to a life of sedentary pleasures, it was hardly to be expected that he would relish an early morning hike through the uneven streets to the Polish residency.

It might be better, Palewski reasoned, to bring the prince ashore immediately, in daylight, trusting the hubbub of the port to mask the arrival of his guest. The more he thought about it, the more this solution appealed to him.

If they walked through the crooked streets to the residency Prince Czartoryski was sure to be observed. The answer was to engage a cab—one of the few closed carriages in Istanbul, whose presence close to the port would be relatively unremarkable. It meant a longer drive—up the Bosphorus, and around to Pera by Taksim, at the top of the Grande Rue, but it could come down the road and pull into the gates of the residency without attracting too much attention. By then, the prince would be firmly housed—and Marta would guard them all.

Palewski almost smiled at the thought. A carriage was the thing: he would leave it at the Tophane gate, collect Czartoryski from his boat, arranging for his luggage to be sent on later, and whisk him to safety, incognito.

He recalled Yashim's advice to trust no one. Marta had to be told to expect a visitor, of course; but she did not need to know who was expected, and she could certainly be trusted not to talk. Old widow Baxi, in the former stable yard, need know nothing at all—but she could be relied on to engage a cab, if asked.

Widow Baxi returned triumphant several hours later, to say that she had engaged a good driver who would take the ambassador to the docks anytime he wished.

At two o'clock on Tuesday afternoon, the carriage rattled up to the steps of the Polish residency. It was not an especially well-fitted vehicle, and the horse in the shafts was a skinny nag; its driver was a sallow character with a domed felt hat and only one eye.

"The thing is," said Mrs. Baxi in a confidential whisper, "it's not the best on the street, but it is cheap."

Palewski cursed inwardly: he might have suggested that money was not an object, but Mrs. Baxi knew her customer. "As long as he can bring me to the port and back," he said doubtfully.

Mrs. Baxi did not know anything about back; that part, at least, she had forgotten; and of course the driver knew nothing about it, either. If he was to wait, he explained, he would expect to be paid half-fare up front, ambassador or no ambassador.

Palewski ground his teeth. Marta was dispatched for the money. By now a small crowd of little boys had formed around the residency gates: any hitch was worth watching. There were some men around, too, casual loafers and even a few students with nothing much better to do during their lunch break, standing at the back of the boys and gawking at the Polish ambassador's preparations to go out in a carriage.

Marta brought the money, the driver was paid, and at last Palewski claimed his fare by climbing into the cab.

Only now did it occur to him that he should have sent the cab to wait at the port, without approaching the residency at all. He shrank back against the tattered leather seats, gripping the sides as the cab lumbered forward at a gentle trot. He could see the crowd of boys parting as they passed through the gates, and some of them ran alongside, caroling and hooting. One of them jumped up onto the footplate and pushed his face against the glass like a gargoyle.

Palewski closed his eyes. There was sweat on his chin, and he leaned forward to open the window, detaching the leather strap that pegged the pane in place. Nothing happened; the window did not budge. He had not expected it to.

The boys fell away as the cab turned into the Grande Rue, lurching from side to side so that Palewski was thrown against the upholstery. The window dropped with a sudden crash, and hot air wafted in. The driver slowed. Palewski imagined him peering down to assess what damage had been done, and prayed he would not stop.

After a few anxious moments the horse picked up, and they carried on jouncing along the Grande Rue. Palewski laid his hat on the floor and took a grip of the window with one hand, bracing himself against the far side of the cab with the other.

At Taksim, the new building petered out. He glimpsed the tiled roof of the water tank, and then he stuck out his feet to brace himself as they half-slid, half-toppled downhill toward the Bosphorus.

"Should have walked," he muttered through clenched teeth. "Bloody conspicuous . . . ! Old man . . . shaken . . . to pieces."

His foot slipped from the wall of the cab and landed on his hat, denting the crown. "Damn!"

They slowed to a stop. Palewski retrieved his hat and stuck his head out the window.

They had arrived at the water's edge—with a flock of sheep!

"Push on!" Palewski shouted to the driver. "Quick, get ahead!"

There was still a gap—he whacked the hat in frustration against the window ledge. He'd have seized it—why did cabmen have to be such laggards? The sheep jostled against the wheels of the cab.

He flung himself back into the seat, and consulted his watch.

Seven minutes to two. At two o'clock, the prince would come ashore.

He closed his eyes in an agony of indecision. Ten minutes to walk to the quay. Without the sheep, five by carriage. The sheep would block the road for the next mile to Tophane, unless the driver maneuvered past them. But would he?

The inactivity was unbearable. He pictured Czartoryski stepping confusedly onto the quay, expecting—what? A friendly face, Palewski, a carriage . . . Loungers in the port, noting his arrival. Runners to the Russian embassy.

Palewski took out his handkerchief to mop his forehead and instead crumpled it up and bit into it.

With an oath he snatched at the handle of the door and leaped out, into the sheep.

"At the gates!" he shouted. The driver looked around in surprise. "At the gates, wait. You understand? Get there as fast as you can, and wait for me!"

He began to wade through the flock, then turned. The driver was looking straight ahead with his one good eye.

"Double fare, driver! When we get back—understood?"

A ewe butted him in the back of his knees and he lurched forward to avoid falling. He was wading through sheep, touching a hand to each head as he swam by. When he looked around, the driver was still staring fixedly ahead.

Palewski shoved and cursed his way to the edge of the flock, on the landward side. In a few moments he had overtaken them, pursued by the irritated shouts of the drovers. His dented hat was still in his hand.

A mile, he had guessed: it seemed like two. He walked like a man possessed, sweat streaming down his collar.

All that mattered was to reach the quayside before Prince Czartoryski came ashore. His legs scissored madly, he hunched forward, the afternoon sun beat down on his unprotected head—and he felt the most important moment of his whole diplomatic career turning away from him like a sunflower!

The boat would be late, he told himself, as the port inched itself toward him beneath his swirling feet.

He glanced back: he could see the flock like a pale rug spread across the road, and the cab still bringing up the rear. He'd secure his guest, get out of the port, and meet the cab under the trees. He was disheveled—why not? Czartoryski would understand—the drama. The haste. The excitement! Why, it was like Moscow, back in '12!

Palewski surged ahead, young again.

And found himself jostling on the crowded quay.

26

"I think it's disgraceful, to keep a horse like that."

Eliza pulled Compston back and pointed at the bony nag.

"They come like that. Special breed," Compston explained. It was not the time to discuss the welfare of Istanbul cab horses: it was miracle enough that they had spotted one when it was wanted. "Bred like greyhounds, all rib."

"Nonsense. In Ireland, horse like that, we'd shoot it. Doesn't the driver feed his animal?"

Compston chose to ignore the question.

"Hey, driver! Take us to Pera! *Pera götürür!*"

The driver didn't look around. Compston noticed that he had a funny eye. He led Eliza around the horse's nose, aiming to try from the other side.

"Hey, driver!"

The driver looked down.

"To Pera! We want to go to the British embassy."

The driver glanced over his shoulder, perplexed. If he had understood the arrangement properly, he was to wait here by the trees for the ambassador. But first it was a one-way fare, then they wanted fetching home, and finally the ambassador had leaped out of the cab with some unintelligible remark. What if his plans had changed again? These young Franks must be connected to the ambassador in some way.

"Twenty *kuruş*, blast it! I'll give you twenty to help this young lady get home."

The driver shifted uneasily in his seat. It was a lot of money. Twenty *kuruş* was twice what the ambassador had offered—and he might not be back for hours—if he came at all.

"Forty," he growled.

"Thirty."

"Thirty-five."

"Get in, Miss Day." Compston tugged open the door.

"Certainly not, Mr. Compston. Do you see how he treats his nag? Why, the nosebag's full of nothing but chaff!"

"Certainly not?"

"I've no intention—"

George Compston was solidly built. He scooped up Eliza by the waist and dumped her in the cab. Then he climbed in after her and slammed the door. "There."

Eliza was too astonished to protest. The cab moved off and she scrambled unsteadily into the seat.

"Mr. Compston!" she exclaimed, but her eyes were strangely bright.
To Compston's astonishment, she began to laugh.

"Oh, Mr. Compston! You're a rotten guide, but that doesn't really matter, does it? There's always a Murray's Handbook . . . I do like a fellow who can get a girl a cab!"

Compston flushed. Eliza was still laughing—she looked awfully well, he thought.

As he glanced through the back window of the cab, he thought he saw two men in the road, in top hats.

One of them was gesticulating.

Compston turned his head. There was a sudden bang from somewhere along the road, and Eliza clutched his arm.

"What was that?"

"Oh, firecracker," he said airily. He was on surer ground here. "Mahommedan festival stuff. Wedding, probably. It's typical Istanbul, Miss Day."

27

"OH Christ!" roared Palewski, as he watched his cab clatter away up the dusty shore road. "Come back!"

The prince laid a hand on his arm, and Palewski swiveled around. "Please, Palewski. Don't excite yourself. I am quite sure—"

Palewski was never to learn what Prince Czartoryski was so sure about. There was a bang, followed by a ripple of sounds like seeds popping open, and the breath shot from his chest.

28

FOR Giancarlo, Rafael, and Fabrizio it was also a rough morning.

La Piuma's instructions had been clear, down to the name of the ship and the date of its expected arrival. The mark, La Piuma wrote, was a European nobleman, seventy years old, tall, slender, and traveling alone. In all probability he would be met by the Polish ambassador, Count Palewski.

It was essential, La Piuma wrote, that the nobleman never leave the port. Once in Palewski's protective custody he would be hard to reach, and the intelligence he carried would have been passed on. It was vital, for the success of the cause, that the stranger be stopped—preferably on board ship, but if that was too difficult to arrange, certainly on the quayside.

Giancarlo had swept his fair hair from his forehead and gritted his teeth.

There was a final flourish: *Prepare yourselves*, and a small sketch drawing of a quill.

Rafael flushed when he read Palewski's name.

"Palewski! That complicates the business."

Fabrizio shrugged. "La Piuma doesn't say it is a problem."

"He's been good to us," Rafael said stubbornly. "I mean—he's a friend. And he favors the revolution."

"La Piuma may have information we can't guess at." Giancarlo gestured to the letter. "We have to be careful, Rafael."

"I don't like it, all the same," Rafael said.

"It's not what you like or don't like!" Fabrizio burst out. "We aren't here to talk and talk. We offered ourselves to the cause, and now it makes a demand. So, fulfill the demand, *e basta!*"

He chopped the air with his hand.

Rafael cocked his head: "What about Birgit?"

"She's asleep," Giancarlo said, as if that explained everything.

"Man's work," Fabrizio had said, smoothing his black hair. "I'll see you both later."

29

TWO figures shimmered at the foot of the bed: Palewski supposed they were angels. He was surprised that his side still hurt. He thought that a man on his way to heaven should be relieved of all pain and anxiety.

The anxiety returned: first he groped for it, then startled, and groaned aloud. He saw his own pale hand on the cobbles, and there was a cab, driving away, and a man—falling. A hand on his arm—the prince! Yes— then Czartoryski falling. Blood—had there been blood?

But it seemed that it was he, Palewski, who had fallen.

He was not surprised when one of the angels clarified by his bedside into the figure of Marta. He shot out a hand.

"The prince!"

Marta squeezed his fingers. "Kyrie," she murmured.

Palewski followed her sideways glance: "Yashim! The prince . . ."

Yashim moved up the bed and sat down gently at Palewski's side. "The prince? Tell us about him."

"I met him—at the port. There was—there was a cab. Mine. I took it there. It was gone."

He controlled a grimace; fresh sweat beaded his forehead. Marta took a flannel and dabbed it across his face. He closed his eyes.

"A cab. Sheep." His voice had sunk to a mumble.

Yashim leaned forward. "And the prince?"

His eyelids fluttered. "The cab . . ." His murmur was indistinct.

Yashim glanced up at Marta inquiringly. She pulled a face. "There was a cab, Yashim efendi. The widow Baxi found it for the kyrie, so that he could go to the port and bring his guest home."

"His guest—?"

"He did not give me his name."

"This prince, do you think?" Yashim frowned. Palewski's special guest, obviously, but prince of where?

"Who is the prince—and where is he?"

Palewski stirred, and his lips moved toward Yashim. "Cab . . . gone. Is Char . . . Ch—"

His teeth began to chatter. Marta mopped his forehead.

"Who brought him home, Marta?"

"Two men, efendi. They walked him back—he could walk, a little. They were Turks. Maybe fishermen. They would not stay."

When Marta had summoned Yashim earlier that afternoon, Palewski was already on his bed. Dr. Millingen was explaining to Marta how to pick out the pellets.

"Peppered with shot, on his left side," he explained. He held a pair of tweezers and dropped a lead pellet into a bowl by the bed. It pinged against the china. "Torn up. Must keep the wounds clean. He's out for the moment, which is no bad thing—this sort of probing hurts." He bent over Palewski's ribs, and stretched the skin with his fingers. With the other hand he inserted tweezers carefully into the little round hole. Palewski groaned and jerked.

Millingen paused. "Steady, old man." He began groping into the wound with the sharp metal jaws. "Bah, it's these tiny pellets."

Yashim peered into the bowl. The shot that Millingen and Marta had extracted was lying in a sticky heap at the bottom; a few had stuck to the sides.

"This shot—it's too small to kill a man," Yashim murmured. "Except at point-blank range."

The leeches arrived in a jar, sticking to the glass. Millingen rolled up his sleeve and plunged his hand into the jar. One by one, he began applying them to the wounds.

"A few steps closer," Millingen agreed, "and the ambassador would probably have died. Whoever let his gun off like this must be feeling pretty shoddy. Dangerous sport, hunting."

Another pellet clinked into the bowl.

"I'll say something for the ambassador, it's not his first wound by a long chalk. Saber scars." Dr. Millingen gestured vaguely with his tweezers. "Of course, he was a much younger man." He peered closer. "Bullet wound, too. Which war?"

"Borodino."

"Quite. Your friend's a survivor. We'll trust to that, and to these single-minded gentlemen," he added, draping another leech onto a wound. The leech curved slightly, and stuck; Yashim shuddered, seeing it begin to pulse.

It was only after Millingen had gone, cheerfully suggesting that he should send his bill to the fool who'd let his gun off like that, that Yashim was able to question Marta, and Palewski had briefly regained consciousness.

The widow Baxi was at home, sewing, oblivious to the drama of the afternoon. Yes, she knew the driver of the cab, she had engaged him herself, and got a good price. She promised to send him to Yashim as soon as she could find him.

He arrived two hours later, as dusk was falling, sinister in the half-light, with his single eye and ingratiating leer. He volunteered nothing: everything had to be prised out of him, bit by bit. Yes, he had collected the efendi at the residency. He had ordered him to the port. No, the efendi had jumped out of the cab before they got there but he had carried out his agreement, nonetheless. He had been paid as far as the port, but not farther. Even so, he had waited for the efendi. Ten minutes? Maybe more. A long time, anyway, in the blazing heat.

"And the efendi did not return?"

The driver shrugged. "I waited a long time. Then some unbeliever came. Not the same one, maybe, but an unbeliever, like him. They are many, efendi, and it's easy to get confused. He wanted the cab."

Yashim sat forward. "Where did he want to go?"

The driver sucked his lip. "To an embassy, also. I thought maybe he was the same one."

"He wanted to come here?"

"Some other one." The driver looked bored.

"A different embassy?" Yashim spoke sharply.

The driver looked up at the ceiling. "I have had a busy day, efendi. I cannot remember everything. Another one."

Yashim gritted his teeth and let a coin spin between his fingers.

"It was the Ingilstan house," the driver remembered, brightening.

Yashim frowned. "The Ingilstan house?" Why the British embassy? "So this man—he was a Frank? And he asked for the Ingilstan house?"

"Yes." The driver put out his palm. "With a woman."

Yashim let the coin drop, and sat back. The driver's answers surprised him. If Palewski was in danger from anyone, it had to be the Russians, or the Austrians, who would most wish to interrupt his diplomatic efforts. Someone might have taken the cab to the British embassy, and walked on from there. But with a woman, too?

"At the Ingilstan house, did you drive in through the gates?"

"Right to the door." The driver grinned. "The man paid. The woman walked inside."

"Other cabs at the port? Was anyone else waiting at the same place?"

The driver shook his head.

"And before you left—did you see anything strange? Hear anything?"

"No."

Eventually, Yashim let him go.

He walked to the window. A bee clung to the glass, moving up and down the single pane. He opened the window and took a sheet of paper from the escritoire and guided the bee out into the open air.

Palewski had met his secret visitor at the port, with a cab waiting. Then someone had fired on them.

A gust of wind blew in through the open window.

Palewski had called him a prince. A real prince? How many princes were there? Yashim remembered what he had said to Natasha about the Ottoman aristocracy: but in Europe there must be dozens, hundreds of them—French, Russian, Austrian. An idea struck him and he turned to the bookcase.

It took him a moment to find the volume he wanted. Palewski had shown it to him once, a huge calf-bound book stuffed with slips of paper and scraps of aristocratic intelligence: the Almanach de Gotha, a prodigious work of genealogy and snobbery which listed, Palewski promised, the oldest families in Europe. Yashim had laughed at him: every family, he countered, was old.

He brought the book to the escritoire and thumbed through the pages, trying to work out how the entries were arranged. Palewski had said something about arms, and quarterings, going back centuries—to the time of Charlemagne, and the Byzantine emperors, in some cases. Doherty's time, he thought inconsequentially: the time of real Latin.

There seemed to be hundreds, if not thousands of princes in the book: most of them long dead. Where was Palewski's prince—and was he, too, dead? Was his name to be one of those written on a slip of paper, and dropped between the pages of the Almanach de Gotha—*Prince So-and-so, b. Wittelsbach 1760; d. 1842—in Istanbul?*

Yashim glanced up at the window.

He had not stayed with Palewski after the shooting. Either he had vanished into the city of his own free will—or he had been made to disappear.

He frowned, and went to find Marta. The kyrie, she said, was still asleep.

"He has a fever, efendi. His body is hot and dry. I would like the doctor to come back."

"Send for him again. I'm going out, but I shall be back before dark."

30

YASHIM made his way downhill to the Tophane landing, his mind a blank.

Istanbul was not a city where people disappeared easily. It was not like London, or Paris: not yet. Every street was inhabited by people who had lived there for generations, or given over to specific trades. Any stranger would be noticed, almost anywhere—particularly a foreign prince.

Almost anywhere except, perhaps, around the Tophane landing. If there was anywhere in the city where you could shoot a man, or lose one, it was here, where the crowds threw up strangers of every description: foreign sailors from all the corners of the Mediterranean and beyond, Maltese ruffians, Genoese officers, French sea captains, even Indians and Chinamen; smooth bankers from the Phanar district, or their peons; urchins, touts, hotel runners, dockhands and storekeepers; burly negroes, emaciated opium addicts, foreign tourists. And diplomats, of course.

He supposed it had always been like that, even in the days when the Ottomans maintained a haughty disregard for the Frankish kingdoms and empires that had not, as yet, fallen under their sway. At the height of the Ottoman Empire's power the mix would have been different—more north Africans, no doubt, drawn from the corsair kingdoms of the southern Mediterranean, pirates in all but name and always consummate seamen, as the Turks never could hope to be; Egyptian crews who manned the great grain barques that fed the largest city in the world. He thought of the taverns clustered around the port, and of the people who frequented them.

The cab had waited by a clump of willow trees. Palewski had brought his man back toward the trees. Was that when he was shot? Or was it earlier, on the way from the Tophane gate?

Yashim found the trees without difficulty and he cast about while the light held, examining angles, retracing his steps on the town side of the street, peering up alleyways and into courtyards, searching for the place where a man might conceal himself with a gun. He imagined Palewski taking his friend's arm with his right, placing himself on the left; it was the natural thing. Palewski on the town side, the prince by the water, walking northeast—Palewski peering into the shade to make out the cab . . . Palewski half-turning . . . he'd have seen the cab was already gone. A shot.

A shot. Or maybe two. Yashim leaned back against the walls of a wharf, trying to piece things together from a few scattered phrases— and Millingen's observations. Once or twice he attracted the curiosity of passersby, shoremen or sailors or little boys, but traffic had slackened. Finally, still uncertain what he was really looking for, he returned to the clump of trees and squatted down, dangling his hands between his knees.

31

"I lost him, Yashim."

"It wasn't your fault."

Palewski picked fretfully at his sheet. "I took precautions to keep it secret. But somehow they were waiting for him." He sighed. "And don't say what you want to say, because it's true and I don't want to hear it."

"You should have brought me in?"

Palewski stared gloomily at his friend. "The whole Polish diaspora will call me an idiot. Or a traitor. At times like this, a wise man looks around for someone else to blame, but I can't see a soul. Just one self-styled ambassador playing with guns and secret messages like a twelve-year-old boy. Lemon juice!"

"Lemon juice?"

"Oh, you know, Yash. Invisible ink, secret codes."

"You could blame Midhat Pasha."

"I'm trying, Yash. We set this up together."

"Had you fixed a meeting with the sultan?"

"The sultan, his ministers, the whole works. For Friday. Midhat was briefing them. New policy slant in European affairs. Active and respectable. Something to entice the British and the French. What I mean is, *impressive*. And the prince had the authority to make it stick."

"Prince Czartoryski."

Palewski turned his head sharply, and winced. "Did—did I say so?"

Yashim pulled out a piece of paper. "'The members of this family,'" he read, "'bear the title Prince Czartoryski (Serene Highness). Voivode of Podolia. Grand Dukes of Lithuania. Chancellor of Lithuania.' Here. 'Adam Jerzy, Prince Czartoryski, Duke von Klewán and Zuków. Born in Warsaw on January fourteenth, 1770. Married, in Radzyń on September twenty-fifth, 1817, Anna, Princess Sapieha-Kodenska, born St. Germain-en-Laye, 1798.' That Prince Czartoryski."

"Yes." Palewski sank deeper into his pillows as if crushed. "That one."

"Not a very old family, if it's any consolation," Yashim remarked, folding up the notes he had taken from the Almanach de Gotha a few minutes earlier.

"They are as close as we come to a Polish royal dynasty," Palewski muttered.

"Very well. We have three days."

"To do what?"

"Find him."

Palewski put his fingers to his temples, and sighed. "I had him, Yash. I had him by the arm and we were going to the cab. Then I saw the cab roll away. I shouted. He told me not to excite myself and then—then there was an explosion. A gun." He stared at the lamp. "We won't find him. Not now. He was the target. They could pepper me with shrapnel any day of the week, Yashim, so obviously it wasn't me they were after. You think they'd fire on us unless they meant to kill him?"

"I don't know. Dr. Millingen—"

"That sawbones!"

"Dr. Millingen thought you'd had a hunting accident. He picked a dozen pellets out of your back this afternoon. Who'd use a gun like that for an assassination?"

"At point-blank range—"

"Possibly. Fire once, wing the pair of you. Reload, step forward. Coup de grâce, at point-blank range." Yashim paused. "It's not an empty street."

He thought fleetingly about the cab, rattling away. He got up and stood with his arms folded at the foot of the bed. "Where does he live, this Czartoryski? Where did he come from?"

"Paris. He's an exile, like the rest of them. *The* exile. I said his family was the closest we have to Polish royalty? Well, Adam Czartoryski is the leader-in-exile. His *Essay on Diplomacy* is our Bible, really. He's related to everyone, on almost every side of the equation—Russians, Germans, everyone. He has the Hôtel Lambert, on the Île Saint-Louis."

Prince Czartoryski was not just some aristocratic patriot, playing cloak and dagger with the European powers, and Yashim was beginning to understand the depth of Palewski's anguish. "If Poland was liberated, he'd become king?"

Palewski shook his head. "I don't know," he said petulantly. "If not king, he'd be the broker, at any rate. Oh God." He groaned.

"There's no body." Yashim did not want Palewski to yield to despair. "Would the Russians try this? The Austrians?"

"Either. Both. There's a committee that watches over European affairs like a hawk, pouncing on the slightest hint of change or rebellion. Russia's foremost. Austria behind. Prussia benefits, though this isn't really the Prussian style." He sighed. "All Metternich's old gang, from the Congress of Vienna. An agreement signed almost thirty years ago, Yashim, which froze the map of Europe into despotisms, and sold out Poland. The list of signatories is pretty long on the final treaty."

"And they still have an interest in maintaining the arrangements."

"Some more than others, no doubt. But yes, on the whole, the people whose voices were heard at Vienna govern Europe today. The Pope was there: he got his Italian states back," he added bitterly. "A lot of blood had been shed to liberate them in the first place. A drop or two of it was mine."

"Czartoryski's arrival here would have upset them?"

Palewski nodded. "He came to explain to Midhat Pasha and his people what an alternative Europe might be like, and how the Ottomans could benefit from championing it. That would have sent alarm bells ringing all over Saint Petersburg."

"He lives in Paris," Yashim said, feeling the agitation in his friend's voice. "Why not kill him there?"

"Paris? You don't assassinate a man in Paris."

Yashim ignored him. "There's one reason they might try to kill him here instead. But it doesn't apply in this case—so I begin to hope he isn't dead."

Palewski gave him a disgusted look, and said nothing.

"For an assassination, Paris would do as well as Istanbul. But for a public execution, Istanbul is better. Killers anonymous, and Czartoryski dead? It shows the Ottoman Porte conspiring with the architect of European revolution. That would throw the Porte onto the back foot. We would be forced back into our diplomatic shell—averse to taking any more risks, shy of tampering with the established order. Meanwhile, a warning is sent around Europe: don't underestimate the reach of the Powers—or the determination of that committee. Isn't that it?"

"Possibly." Palewski looked wary.

"Then where's the body? Why not leave him dead in the street— display it to the world? If Czartoryski were dead, we should have heard about it. If they didn't leave his corpse, then I hope they have him, alive. But I don't know why." He paused. "I hope he's still here."

"Why—why can't they just kill him, and be done?"

But Yashim shook his head. "I found him just now, in the Almanach de Gotha. I mean to find him here. In Istanbul."

32

"WHY can't we just kill him and be done?"

Rafael's question hung in the air. It was more a plea than a question: a question addressed to their consciences.

Why couldn't they just kill him?

They all knew why. On the docks, a few yards off, he had been—what? A pair of black trousers and a coat, with a hat on top, like something produced by an opera buffa costume department, with the label of *villain* pinned to his back.

For them, he had become the fine point of the machine of assassination they had constructed with cold attention to detail, the motive no warmer than a coiled spring in its housing, the emotion no louder than the ticking of cogs. The object of their labors was only a rivet that needed to be tapped neatly into place, firing pin to percussion cap.

But then the shot went wide and the revolutionaries were left with a machine they could not mend, as useless to them as a steam engine to a Bedouin. They hurried their intended victim away, only to discover that he was not made of rivets: he breathed, he wept, he spoke. He was thirsty, bewildered, frightened like them. And angry.

His anger confused them most.

"How dare you!"

Later: "I don't know what you hoped to achieve by this disgraceful charade, but it would be better for you to abandon it immediately. Do you have any idea who I am?"

They did not want to hear. They marched him to the cellar of the house, where Ghika had stored their trunks, and locked him in. But first they buttoned his coat on back to front, so that he could not move his arms, and tied his shoelaces together. That was Fabrizio's idea.

"If you make a sound, we will kill you," Fabrizio said. Forgetting for a moment, perhaps, that they meant to kill him anyway.

Upstairs the postmortem began; except that there had been no death.

Birgit had gone to visit Natasha at Topkapi, to goggle at palace life, so they could speak freely.

"There was something wrong with the gun," Fabrizio explained. "It misfired, I'm positive."

"Where is the gun now?"

"You brought it back." Fabrizio looked surprised.

"Me? I was helping to carry the man. The gun was your responsibility. Did you leave it downstairs?"

"*Cazzo!* I thought someone had it."

They were all breathing heavily. Giancarlo broke the silence.

"Rafael, you go and fetch it."

They squabbled about that. Giancarlo said he could not go, because he was tall and recognizable, and because he needed to think. Fabrizio had better stay, too, he had already messed up once—twice, if you counted the bad shot.

"It misfired!"

"Whatever you say."

Rafael went. In his heart he knew the gun would be gone already, so when he arrived at the port he did not find it. He did not look very carefully: he just walked by, with a sideways glance, and saw that it was not there. Then he went back.

"You searched for it? *Cazzo!* Fabrizio—did you carry it across the road? Did you look under the trees, Rafael?"

"Of course I did." Rafael was lying and the others suspected it. But they were all tired, and frightened and confused.

Giancarlo produced the note he had written for La Piuma while Rafael was out. "*Bird dispatched.* We must tell him something. Anything is better than silence."

"It's a lie."

"For the moment. He's as good as dead, anyway."

Each of them had a vision of the man in the cellar, raging, buttoned up in his frock coat. "How dare you!"

Had they killed the man, shot him dead on the pavement in the sun, they would have felt no remorse, only the satisfaction of a job well done, loosening another stone in the edifice of papal tyranny. Because they had *not* killed him, they were frightened and ashamed and full of guilt. As assassins they could have exonerated themselves, or so they each told themselves, quietly, privately. As men innocent of murder they felt all the weight of their guilt and their crime pressing down on them.

The crime, a murder, was yet to be performed.

"Why can't we just kill him and be done?"

33

"**AND** seven! I win."

"Fact is, Miss Day, I'm under instructions to let you, you know. It's what we fellows call diplomacy."

Eliza laughed. "Mr. Compston, I had no idea you sparkled as a wit." She let him gather up the cards.

"Another game, Miss Day?"

"I don't think so, not unless you know any new ones."

"Oh!" Compston's face brightened. "We had a fellow here last year, Rushford. Dreadful man, and a proven cheat, though up till then he had us playing a rather good game. At least, that is . . . I'm not sure I can remember the rules."

"Oh, come on. What was it called?

Compston blushed. "D'you know, I can't say. I—I can't remember what we called it."

Shithead, as he had just remembered.

"Well! It must have had a name, Mr. Compston. Rummy? Or racing demon? What was it?"

"Yes, George. What was it?" Fizerley unfolded from the billiard table, where he had been practicing his cueing. "You must remember. You and Fusspot played it all winter. Head-something, wasn't it? A funny name."

"Gentleman to see Mr. Compston." The footman spoke from the door. Compston leaped to his feet, overturning the flimsy card table.

"Absolutely!"

When he was gone, Eliza turned to her cousin. "Why won't he remember the name? Do you?"

"Yes, Eliza, but wild horses won't drag it from me. Keep trying George."

George had stepped into the vestibule.

"Yashim efendi! What a relief!"

Over the years, a friendship of sorts had sprung up between Yashim and the young Englishman. Yashim knew Compston as a good-natured ass; Compston, in turn, saw Yashim as a jack-in-the-box, popping up when least expected. Both, to some extent, had moderated their first impressions. Yashim had been surprised to discover that Compston spoke fluent Russian, while Compston had learned to rely not only on Yashim's cleverness, but on his kindness, too.

"Someone took a cab here from the port this afternoon. A gentleman with a lady, I understand."

Compston looked slightly wary. "Oh yes?"

Yashim had been wondering whether he should let word of the attack on Palewski spread. Now he decided to keep it quiet.

"Do you know who they might have been?"

Compston had a vivid recollection of the cab, and the way he had pinched it from under the nose of the man who'd hired it to wait. But surely Yashim efendi had more important things to do than track down cab snatchers? "That is—it was me. I was with Miss Day. Fizerley's cousin, um. She was awfully tired, and hot."

"You? But it was waiting for someone else, wasn't it?"

Compston remembered Miss Day stamping her pretty foot. "I felt it was, ah, an emergency. A sort of life-and-death matter, so to speak."

"I want to know if you saw, or heard, anything odd, while you were there. Anyone hanging about, for instance. Another cab, perhaps? Maybe someone you wouldn't have expected to see, down at the port."

Compston could think of nothing. "No other cab, that's for sure. We were darned lucky to persuade that one—take it, I mean."

"Is this Miss Day?" said Yashim, looking over Compston's shoulder.

"Yes, indeed. Miss Elizabeth Day. Yashim efendi, an old friend. Yashim is asking about the cab we took this afternoon."

Eliza returned Yashim's bow with a curtsy. "I had no idea our plain doings were of such interest, Mr. Yashim efendi. However, if it's the condition of the horse you're concerned with, I can assure you that I have seldom beheld worse. And I've seen the horses on Grafton Street. Quite shocking."

But Yashim was not interested in the state of the horse.

"I couldn't be expected to know what was or was not out of the ordinary, having only just arrived in the city," Eliza pointed out. "However, I admit I am unused to—*scrutiny*."

"Being looked at? I am sorry, I'm afraid that for many people in Istanbul a Frankish woman is still a rare sight."

"But not for a—what do you call 'em?—a Frank, I'll be bound."

Yashim frowned in puzzlement. "A Frank?"

"A young man, Mr. Yashim efendi. I caught sight of him as I was feeling the nose bag. Chaff, it was all chaff! But it was just as well that Mr. Compston said the right thing to the driver. As indeed you did, Mr. Compston. I was ready to dissolve."

Yashim found her words hard to follow. "My apologies, mademoiselle. You mentioned scrutiny."

A little crimson rose to Eliza's cheeks. "I noticed a young man peering out from the alley across the street, and he was *looking*."

"Looking? At you?"

"Not just. I'm afraid I'm making far too much of it, now. It wasn't important. I feel silly, mentioning it. He was just there, looking. And then, well, he wasn't."

"Oh no," Compston murmured. "Not silly, at all."

"What was he looking at, Miss Day?"

"Oh, just me and the carriage, and Mr. Compston, I suppose. He was young, about Mr. Compston's age." She tilted her chin. Her ringlets bounced. "A bit taller, possibly. I couldn't tell you if he was dark or fair. But does it matter, anyway?"

"Was it perhaps his cab you were taking?"

Eliza looked perplexed. "His cab?"

"I'm afraid the cabbie was waiting for someone, Miss Day," Compston murmured. "But dash it, Yashim, what's all this about? Tall Franks, popping their heads out of alleys to admire Miss Day, what? Could happen any day of the week!"

Clumsy as it was, Eliza's expression showed recognition of the compliment. "I didn't think of that," she replied, more seriously. "I don't think, now, he *was* waiting for the cab. He was just, there, you know. Looking out. Do you play cards?"

But Yashim did not play cards; not that evening, at any rate.

"How odd," Eliza said musingly, when he had gone. "I didn't know you'd stolen the cab. Did you do it for me?"

"Needs must when the devil drives," returned Compston, gruffly. "And the very devil *was* driving, don't you know. One eye. Horns, probably."

Eliza smiled. "And what was the name of the game you played last year?"

"The French might call it *tête de merde*," Compston said.

Miss Day tucked her arm through his. "Thank you, Mr. Compston. You do have the makings of a very fine diplomat. My own cousin wouldn't tell me, and I think it odious bad manners for a man not to tell. Don't you?"

34

COMPSTON, Fizerley, and his cousin Eliza were already in bed when Yashim arrived at the theater farther down the Grande Rue.

The lights, he saw, were doused. Earlier in the evening the torches would have blazed in their sockets, to attract the attention of passersby in a city that was generally unlit at night. The torches had been Yashim's idea. In most parts of Istanbul they would have been a hazard but Pera, the European quarter, had been rebuilt in stone and brick since the last great fire swept out the old wooden buildings.

Preen had been quick to see the benefit. "Incredible, Yashim. So simple—and so successful! A little fire attracts the men like dogs in camp."

He knocked, and Mina let him in. Like Preen, Mina had started her career as a *köçek*, one of the young boys whose feminine and suggestive dances had taken her to weddings, parties, and other, more intimate gatherings along the Bosphorus. The *köçek* belonged to a long tradition of ladyboy entertainers, whose origins were uncertain; perhaps Egyptian, and possibly familiar to the Byzantines, too.

Preen was no longer in her first youth, and it was Yashim who had encouraged her to establish the theater. It was not respectable, but it was secure.

"Hello, darling." Preen lay on a divan, drinking tea. "I'm afraid the pashas have all gone home."

"Pashas?"

"As if. Two snoring Russians, from a ship. What's your trouble?"

Yashim took a place on the divan.

"Tea? Mina."

Mina brought him a glass of mint tea, and Yashim sipped it gratefully. Preen watched him for a few moments.

"You can go, Mina. Leave the lamp on the stairs."

Mina closed her books, in which she had being doing the evening's accounts, and yawned.

"Big silence, and a big problem," Preen said when they had heard Mina close the front door. "Yours, I hope. I am not interested in the despise and fall of the Ottoman Empire."

Yashim smiled. When Palewski had suggested she perform Byzantine tableaux for philhellenistic tourists, Preen said the old stuff was too dull. Palewski had patted his ten-volume set of Edward Gibbon's *Decline and Fall* and challenged her to find a dull paragraph.

He'd been forced to give in. "I think you have to read it through," he'd protested. "What you need is Suetonius."

Preen took her tableaux from sources more calculated to interest sailors and porters: tragic murders, suggestive abductions, harem quarrels.

"Something of both," Yashim said, at last. "Palewski was shot in the street, at Tophane."

"You are saying it like that because he is all right?"

"He's hurt, but the wounds aren't serious, Alhamdulillah."

"You frightened me, Yashim." She gave his arm a push. "So tell me."

He left out nothing, not even the fact that Palewski had been meeting someone very important. "The prince has disappeared."

"The prince?"

"Very secret, Preen. No tableaux."

"Of course, darling. It's not all business. Where do we find him?"

"Remember the time you trawled the port taverns for me? The Janissary time?"

"Hmm. I was younger, Yashim."

"You don't look any older."

"You want to ask if anyone heard shots?"

"Heard a shot. Saw something." He thought of Miss Eliza Day, and her mysterious Frankish admirer. Tall, like Palewski, but young. He remembered her blush. A handsome man? Perhaps. Not that she could remember . . . perhaps she had been constrained by Compston's presence. A tall, handsome young man.

"Yashim? You aren't listening. You want to start now?"

"We'll go together. Like old times."

"What, I look older now? You said—"

"I'm older, Preen. You're just the same."

"Sweet," she said. "I'm older, heavier, and I've got short hair. But you know? I cut more ice. Let's go."

35

MARTA remembered the times she thought the kyrie would die.

Once he had been almost drowned, and once someone had wanted to kill them both, the kyrie and Marta. Marta remembered that warmly. She had saved them, so the kyrie had said, with her toe. Of course, it could not have been quite that way, but she liked to think of it sometimes.

He had even proposed to her. Not meaning it, of course, but thinking just of her toe. The kyrie! Earlier he had gone to Frangistan, to Venice. She had been lucky to have him back—and afterward she had thought that the danger had been not only death, but also maybe a woman.

The idea made her shudder.

When she first came to run his house, before she understood his ways, she often used to think he was dead. She'd come upstairs to find him sprawled in the armchair, with the lamp burning and the fire gone out, and his face pale as string cheese. He wasn't breathing, and the room would be strewn with bottles and books—she thought the reading had killed him.

Twice she'd found him dead on the stairs. And he'd called her in the middle of the night—Marta, Marta!—convinced he was dying himself, after catching a fish bone in his throat. Cough cough, and a little blood.

Once, coming upstairs, she'd heard his fiddle playing break off, and the unmistakable sound of the kyrie dropping to the floor. She tossed the tea onto the steps and rushed in, only to find him scrambling across the furniture after a wasp, with the score in his hand!

Marta smiled. The kyrie was not for dying, she thought. He cheated it. He laughed at it. He was peppered with lots of little holes but the doctor said they weren't too deep, and he had scars from long ago—saber cuts and bullet wounds.

She smiled, and let the tears squeeze from her eyelids. If he asked her to marry him she'd say yes, yes if—

Palewski's eyelids fluttered. Marta lifted the sponge from his forehead and, without moving her eyes from his face, dipped the sponge into the bowl.

Palewski looked up. He saw Marta, and the nightmare about his guns dissolved, leaving a faint trace of cordite.

36

"Let's go to the tavern with musicians," Preen suggested, as they came down onto the Tophane road. "It gives us something to look at."

They stepped over a dog on the threshold and went down a few steps into a vault where the air was close and smelled of wine and sawdust. Half the tables were occupied, and in the corner a solitary musician was sliding his fingers up the frets of his baglama, rocking back and forth as he stared into his audience.

"A good musician," Preen said, professionally. "He's from the Cyclades. Syros, or Tinos."

They crossed to the divan. Preen ordered wine, but when the waiter returned it was Yashim who paid.

"A shooting on the quay, this afternoon. Did you hear about it?"

The man clacked his tongue. "The tavern was closed."

He went back to a wooden cubbyhole near the entrance, where he dropped the money into a box. He said something to a boy, and the boy picked up a crate and went out.

Preen took a sip of wine. "You were going to let me do the talking."

"That wasn't talking. More of a polite cough." From his seat he could see the baglama player and the door. He saw the musician nod, and his tempo gradually picked up. The notes came faster and louder, and the conversation in the tavern rose in volume.

"I said he was good." Preen had to lean in to be heard.

"Yes. And dutiful."

Yashim nodded toward the door, its frame filled by a man almost as broad as he was tall; he had to turn his shoulders to scan the room. Without changing his expression he started forward and settled with surprising lightness onto the divan at Yashim's side. His huge hands dangled between his thighs.

"You're asking questions." His voice was rough, with a lisp, like a file on board. Yashim took in the broken nose, the curiously absent eyes and blue-gray stubble from the top of his head to his chin.

"A friend of mine was shot. Maybe somebody died."

"This is not a good place." The prizefighter stood up and started for the door.

Yashim got up to follow. "You don't have to come."

Preen gave him an indignant look. "I was meant to ask the questions."

The prizefighter plunged into the dark streets and Preen's sandals flapped on the cobbles. After a few minutes the man stopped at a gate in the wall. He muttered something and the gate swung open onto a courtyard. Some men were squatting around a brazier but stood up as they came in.

Preen drew her scarf to her lips.

The gate fell shut behind them and Yashim heard a wooden bar being slid home.

The prizefighter turned. "Any knives? Weapons?"

Yashim raised his hands in a gesture of peace.

"Follow me." He hesitated. "Not the lady. It's a man's place."

Yashim and Preen exchanged doubtful glances.

"I am a man," Preen explained, sweetly. "You can check if you don't believe me."

The big man's eyes widened fractionally, and he shrugged. "Come."

The door was swept back onto a damp corridor. Beyond the corridor they found themselves enveloped in fog.

"A steam room!" Preen exclaimed in surprise.

The steam cleared slightly, showing them a tiled and domed hammam. In the middle was a raised stone slab, and on the slab lay the hairiest man Yashim had ever seen.

He was black from head to foot, his body hair smooth and glistening like the fur of a giant otter. His head was cradled on a pair of massive forearms. Even lying down he looked huge.

He turned his head and looked at the new arrivals through the steam. "You ask questions. What for?"

Yashim rubbed the steam from his forehead, and loosened his cloak.

"A friend of ours was shot at today, on the port road," he said. "He was badly hurt. He was with a companion who seems to have vanished."

The big man let his lids droop. "And you are?"

"I am Yashim. I work for the sultan and his household."

The hairy man stretched out a hand and the attendant handed him a towel. He raised his head and rubbed it across his face and then, with a sucking sound, peeled his massive frame from the slab and swung his legs over the edge, where he sat working his huge head from side to side. Yashim felt the steam and sweat sliding down his back; his shirt stuck to his skin. The man rubbed his chest thoughtfully, making all the hairs start up.

"In the port, you say? I am a friend to the *kadi* who supervises the port of Istanbul—in an official sense. My name is Balamian."

He got to his feet, bowed his head, curled his fingers loosely at his side, and the attendant swung a bucket of water and sloshed it over him. Yashim guessed the water was cold, but Balamian did not flinch as the water splashed onto his furry pelt, and only brushed the hair from his eyes with a pass of his hand.

"The *kadi* has many responsibilities, Yashim efendi. I help to regulate his affairs." Balamian reached for a towel and tied it around his waist. "His affairs, and the affairs of the port. We settle the loading and the unloading of ships. Victualing crews, finding replacement sailors. I give work to the men. Help them if they are sick, look after their families. I know them all. I know the ships." He paused. "And if anything happens in the port, I know that, too."

"Anything?"

Balamian smoothed his hands over his head, like a bear washing itself.

"Eventually, everything."

Yashim didn't doubt him for a moment. Balamian was like a sultan, and power dripped from him like the steam on his beard.

"The port's a busy place, Yashim efendi. Ships, men, coming and going. It takes an effort to control—and we don't like violence."

Balamian's position, Yashim guessed, was founded on violence: those huge hands could crush a man as easily as they squeezed a sponge. He meant, of course, that he reserved the violence, or the threat of it, to himself.

He patted his face with the towel. "We will be in touch."

The man with the face of a boxer led them back through the corridor and across the courtyard. The gate swung shut behind them and for several minutes they walked uphill without saying a word, the sweat slowly cooling on their backs. The streets were dark and empty, but now and then their way was lit by a crack of lamplight between closed shutters. Cats slipped across the cobbles. Overhead the stars were bright and cold.

Preen shivered. "What a gangster, darling! Did you see his eyes? His hair? Did you see his hair?"

37

GIANCARLO was beginning to feel like a gangster.

"Shoot me, damn you, or let me go. You can't keep a man like this!"

Their prisoner seemed ready to believe in Fabrizio's gun, pointing through the fabric of his jacket pocket, as the caïques went slowly up the Golden Horn.

"Nobody would understand a word you said," Fabrizio told him, truthfully. They counted on that. "But if you make a move, I'll shoot you."

The trip seemed to interest their captive, who looked out at the dark silhouettes of the great mosques as they unfolded, one by one, in stately progression along the seven hills. Lights twinkled on the shore: old wharfs, a caïque stage, fishermen selling mackerel off the boats. Now and then Fabrizio caught a whiff of frying fish, and remembered that none of them had eaten all day.

At Eyüp they walked in a huddle through the sleeping village. Dogs yanked at their chains, goats bleated nervously in their stalls, and the moon rose to show them the entrance to the woods.

"I don't understand you," Czartoryski said. "Who are you? Pah! You're well fed and flashily dressed. Kidnappers—with their own tailors!"

That night they kept watch in turns, fastening the rope that encircled their captive's waist to the wrist of the man awake. In the morning he had slept better than them, on a pile of straw. They moved his rope to a ring in the wall and gave him the stool, which was the only piece of furniture they could find.

All through the day they took turns to watch him, while the other two went outside and argued. Once, Fabrizio went to Eyüp to buy some food, because of the three he looked most Turkish.

The stool creaked. "It's something—what, political? Nothing to say to that? Let me guess. Catholic hard-liners—knights of some fusty medieval order or another. The Golden Fleece. Malta? No, too young, and not grand enough. Knights of the Sacred Rose? No, I made that one up. Like you did, probably. I need to pee."

"Again?"

"It's my age. It comes with certain infirmities."

Rafael sighed in exasperation. He went forward and undid the cord that held Czartoryski's leg to the ring in the wall, and led him outside.

"Lovely bit of country, this," Czartoryski said, as he unhitched himself. "Reminds me of Dante." He began to recite:

> *Già m'avean trasportato i lenti passi*
> *dentro a la selva antica tanto, ch'io*
> *non potea rivedere ond' io mi 'ntrassi;*
> *ed ecco più andar mi tolse un rio,*
> *che 'nver' sinistra con sue picciole onde*
> *piegava l'erba che 'n sua ripa uscìo.**

He chuckled. "*Purgatorio*. Canto twenty-six, if I'm not mistaken."

"Twenty-eight," Rafael said, in a surly tone.

"Twenty-eight, is it? Well, you may be right." He took a deep breath. "There. Shall we go in?"

Rafael fastened him to the ring, and Czartoryski resumed his musings. "I don't think of Dante and zealotry—or bigotry—in the same

---

* "So far into that ancient wood had my steps,
Though slow, transported me,
That I could no longer tell the place
   Where I had enter'd; when, behold! my path
Was bounded by a rill, which, to the left,
With little rippling waters bent the grass
That issued from its brink."

bracket, to be honest. Dante—the patrimony of all Italians, I should have said."

"Of course!" Rafael chimed in hotly. "He's our national poet."

"And it's people like you who prevent Italy from becoming a nation," Czartoryski pointed out. "Just as you would smother Poland under a blanket of foreign occupation and repressive laws. In the name of what? Catholic stability? Some lost medieval dream of Christendom? Tchah! Your fantasies create half the suffering in this world. You make me sick."

He folded his arms and let his chin sink to his chest, eyes closed.

"It's not me who would smother anyone," Rafael retorted; yet he felt confused. "It's you. I am for freedom! It's you and your people who keep Italy divided and oppressed."

But Czartoryski would not reply. He took several deep breaths through his nose, and settled his weight again, so that the stool creaked.

Rafael folded his own arms and sat back moodily against the wall, chewing his lip.

The man who should be dead wanted to sleep and he, Rafael, could not close an eye for a second! Why was Fabrizio such a fool—to throw away a single shot?

38

YASHIM kindled a small flame in the stove, and heaped it with charcoal. He wrote a note to the Italians to tell them Palewski had had an accident and was confined to his bed.

When he had folded the note he leaned out the window and gave a piercing whistle that brought a boy running out of the shadows.

"Elvan," Yashim called down, when he saw the boy's face like a moon looking up at him. "Can you run an errand? Take this."

He gave an address, and let the folded note flutter down into the street below. Elvan caught at it, missed, picked it up from the ground, and sped off.

Yashim turned back to the kitchen. He added charcoal to the fire, put on a pan, and rolled in a couple of lamb shanks, with a short drip of olive oil, to brown. Now and then he gave the pan a violent shake.

He took the pencil and on a second sheet of paper wrote down everything he had learned about the attack.

He glanced at the shanks, gave them another shake, and peeled an onion, chopping it fine. Holding the lamb back with a wooden spoon, he poured the fat into a bowl, then dropped a knob of butter between the shanks. It sizzled and he added the onions.

He reached out for various small pots and took a couple of cinnamon sticks, a few cloves, and a big pinch of salt. He pounded peppercorns and allspice berries into his mortar, and scraped them up and stirred them into the pan. They began to catch. A ladleful of water calmed the pot. He added a scattering of sugar.

From a flat basket on the side he selected four plump pomegranates, halved them on a board, and scraped the jeweled seeds into the mortar using a metal spoon. It was a fiddly job. He added a little more water to the pan, crushed the seeds under the pestle, poured the dark, tangy juice into the pan, gave it all a stir, and clapped on the lid. He moved the pan slightly off the coals, and went back to his paper, wiping his hands.

Who knew? he wrote. *Paris? Midhat/Porte? P.*

He put a ring around the last two names, then drew another line and wrote: *Where is the prince?*

He sat back, tapping his teeth with the pencil. There was something else he wanted to add to the list, but it would not quite take shape.

Yashim sighed.

In the end he simply wrote: *Visitors.*

39

YASHIM found the valide in a bad mood.

"*Tiens,* Yashim. I told you I wanted the girl entertained, and now you tell me you have to go chasing all over Istanbul for some imbecile who has taken a shot at your friend. It's not as if he was dead, is it? And what I want counts for nothing."

She rubbed her fingertips together irritably.

"Natasha enjoyed your *déjeuner sur l'herbe.* It sounds rather cosmopolitan to me." She snapped her fingers at her shawl. "What are all these Franks doing in Istanbul, Yashim? It didn't use to be like this."

The valide was right, of course. Yashim could think of a number of reasons why more foreigners were in Istanbul, starting with the opening of the Ottoman market to British goods. The sultan's decree placing all his subjects, Muslim or otherwise, on the same legal footing had emboldened the merchants and the bankers and stimulated trade, and foreigners washed in with the tide.

"Many people in Europe," he said, "want change. Their own governments resist it. People look to the sultan to help them."

"Like our Natasha."

"Natasha. Palewski. Even those Italians feel more free here than at home."

"Hmm. I hope, for their sake, they don't overestimate our patience. Istanbul is not London. But talk to Natasha," she added. "I must think what I shall write to the tsar."

Yashim found Natasha asleep on the divan in her apartment, a book in her hand. He watched her for a while: her features were beautiful.

He sat gently on the divan.

"Natasha."

Not quite awake when her eyelids flickered open, she saw Yashim and smiled and let them close again.

He put his hand on her arm. "Natasha."

She was awake in an instant. "Don't!" She snatched back her arm. "Oh, it's you, Yashim. I'm sorry—I was dreaming."

She sat up, and hugged her knees. Her hair was mussed up, and the side of her face was red where she had been lying on it.

"A bad dream?"

"I was at home," she said slowly. "Only you were there, too. You were throttling Petovski. At least—then I woke up." She smiled. "Saved you from the gallows, I expect."

"By waking up? Thank you. Who's Petovski?"

She was slow to reply.

"Our jailer. My parents despised him."

"Then I'm glad I throttled him."

She gave a little shiver. "He was a fat old man who came around to check that we didn't have too much comfort, or that we had enough bread. To find out what we were reading, and dig around in our correspondence. He sent reports to the tsar. My father said he was just a minor functionary and the tsar never read anything he wrote. It just went to an office in Moscow and after a while they threw it all away. But of course, he decided everything about us."

"I see. It's a shame to let him into your dreams, too."

She looked at him long and hard. "He's not the only one, Yashim. I can't—I can't always keep them out." She swallowed. "So. He used to bring me sweets, and try to sit me on his knee. I thought he was trying to find out things about my parents, hoping I'd tell him something he could use in his report. He'd pin me to his fat knees and pinch my cheeks.

"I didn't tell him anything, ever." She bit her lip. "I used to wriggle to get away, until I found—that is, I thought—well, he liked that."

"Did your parents know?"

She shook her head. "It began around the time my mother died. But once, Petovski and my father had a scene, a real row. It was about the sweets—and he'd asked me for things in return. My father told him to get out and never come back. But he did. We couldn't stop him."

There were tears in her eyes.

"Petovski said that I was grown up, and that from now on he had to interview me properly. I had to go alone."

She shook her head and stood up abruptly, and walked over to the window.

"He'd given me so many sweets and I should give him something back." She put her hand on the lattice, and spread her fingers. "What could I do? He said if I didn't do what he wanted, he'd have Father sent back to the mines. And he could. Maybe he was nothing to the tsar, but in Irkutsk? It made me sick. There was nothing I could do except try not to let my father know. I was afraid he'd get angry again, and endanger himself. Maybe he'd have killed Petovski. I don't know."

She was wiping her fingers, pulling them through her other hand.

"Yashim, I'm sorry. It must have been the dream."

"Go on."

"Petovski had a yellow house outside the village, and an old woman who cooked and cleaned for him. But when I knocked it was Petovski himself who opened the door. He had put something in his hair, to make it shiny, and a sprig of heather in his buttonhole. The woman wasn't there—he said it was her afternoon off.

"It was just a log house, really, with a room on either side of the hall and a kitchen and scullery out at the back. He had a fire going in the bedroom, and a table with some tea things. Some cake. He said it was cozy, and he took away my muff, and my coat, and my hat. He told me he'd buy a little house and make me the mistress of it, and he would come and see me just as if we were married. He said it would be good for my father, and he would see to it that he was more comfortable and had the books he wanted, and French wines, and everything.

"I said I couldn't live on my own, and that we couldn't be married.

Something like that. So he said—" She swallowed. "He said it didn't matter. Because we"—she began to dissolve into tears—"we could always have an interview there, at his house, when the cleaning woman was out."

"Interviews." Yashim put a hand to her shoulder. She drew back and took a breath.

"Interviews—without any talk. And then, afterward, he talked. He talked to say I mustn't tell. I didn't mean to, because it was so disgusting. Every week I had to go. After a while he stopped bothering to give me cake." She clasped her hands together in front of her, and straightened her arms. "It's not over."

"You mean—he still . . . ?"

"I mean, the story. I don't know why, but I want to tell you. I have never been able to tell anyone else, before you." She paused, and gazed at her hands in her lap. "The shame, Yashim. You try to block it out, but it's not like that. The lie—the horror—they say it gets under your skin but it *is* your skin. You can't block it out without hiding yourself. It's like being locked out of the world."

"I know," Yashim said, gently. "I know exactly."

"My whole body crawled with what Petovski did, and I kept it a secret. My father never guessed that anything was wrong, even though Petovski did do some of the things he promised—more fuel, sugar, that sort of thing. No French wines." She gave an unhappy smile. "Every week . . . Sometimes he drank. Sometimes he was so drunk I would just leave him and come home. He wasn't very important, he was just a little man."

In the cave, Yashim thought: in the cave, where cruelty met innocence and innocence was lost, there had been shame, and self-disgust at so much damage inflicted by little men.

"I found that out. One day I came for my interview and when he opened the door he looked quite frightened. Instead of taking me into his bedroom, we went into the parlor, and there was a fire in there and he introduced me to two other men who were standing by it. They weren't as old as he was, and they were better dressed.

" 'Some vodka, Lev Ivanovich,' the tall one said. He snapped his fingers and Petovski's hands were shaking so much he spilled the drink on the tray.

"One of the men drank the vodka, and then he said: 'So this is your little secret, Petovski. Eh?'

"Petovski was cringing in front of these men, and all I could think was that he'd been discovered, and would be punished."

Natasha had slipped into a monotone, staring straight ahead of her.

"That was not their idea." She shrugged. "The men were by the fire, and Petovski was trembling and groveling. In Siberia, everything is down to rank. Where you live, your pay, your chances of promotion, everything lies in the hands of your superiors. I don't know how they found out about me—maybe they saw me visiting, or maybe he talked, Petovski. He was so often drunk."

She took a deep breath.

"The man who had drunk the vodka, not the tall one, ordered me to undress. I didn't understand. I wanted them to rescue me. I stood stock still until Petovski slapped my face and began to unfasten my buttons. 'You do anything the gentlemen ask,' he said. And then the tall one kicked him, and told him to go out to the scullery and wait."

Natasha looked at Yashim. "They never went to the bedroom, never took me there. And Petovski never touched me again. But every week I went to the—the interview. Sometimes one, sometimes both of them. Every week. I had to hide it, as if there were two Natashas, the one who looked after her father and taught at school, and another one, who went to those men . . ." She trailed off, biting her lip.

"But after a few months I started to look ill. Even my father couldn't help noticing. He got me goat's milk, and eggs and meat. He did portraits, little sketches, for people in return. And after a while I started to look better. My skin grew clear, my hair was shiny again. I even put on some weight—I had become very thin, you see.

"My father was pleased. He said the eggs did me good, and I believed it, too."

Natasha stared for a long time at the wall, without speaking. At last she said: "Am I frightening you, Yashim?"

"Yes. Go on, if you want."

"You are the only person I have ever told."

"Your uncle Sergei?"

"He had gone. They'd all gone. There was only my father, and it was easy to deceive him. I had been deceiving him for a year, or more. But of course, in the end, I found out what to do."

"You were pregnant."

She nodded, slowly. "One of them said he liked it like that. He liked me to be pregnant. But the tall one was angry. They argued about it. In front of me, as if I were a piece of furniture."

She twisted her fingers together. "There were old women in the villages—my father used to speak with them, about the flowers and the plants. They knew everything about them. For the spirit. And for the body."

She glanced up at Yashim. Her eyes were hard and her jaw clenched.

"Even that—it was something else to hide. I don't mean just the pain, because that was nothing. It passes. I mean—the ground was too hard. For three months I kept the bundle of cloth hidden in the outhouse. In the spring I dug a hole and buried it in the yard."

Yashim put out his hands. "Natasha."

She looked uncertainly at his hands and then, very deliberately, slowly, she lifted her own, and placed them on his. He felt them shaking. His thumbs slid across her fingers.

They stood there, silently, holding hands.

"Have you—escaped now?" Yashim asked at last.

She shrugged. "The valide asked me to Istanbul."

"You must have—" he hesitated. "You must have many dreams."

She closed her eyes, and moved imperceptibly closer to him. "My dream, Yashim, is not to dream anymore," she said.

40

YASHIM waited by a pillar, looking out over the cobbled yard of the Sublime Porte. Two officers in uniform stood to attention by the gates in the full glare of the sun. Several windows were open overhead; from one of them a man with long mustaches was scattering crumbs for the pigeons on the windowsill.

There was no harm in feeding birds. On the contrary, it was a meritorious act, a kindness. Yashim heard a clapping of wings, and took a deep breath.

Perhaps the man with the mustaches had limed the window sill?

"Do you expect a reply, Yashim efendi?"

A door opened on the court and a *chaush* in yellow livery jogged by, carrying a message. At the gate he saluted; the officers acknowledged him.

Yashim had encountered cruelty before; had been its victim, when his mother was murdered and he had been pinned down, trapped struggling and screaming in the cave.

He remembered the soft hiss of his mentor, years later: mentor, tormentor. "*The eunuch.*" He'd blotted out the cruelty, moved on; rebelled, finally.

He swayed, as if he stood at the edge of a dark abyss.

"Efendi? Are you all right?"

Yashim blinked. Natasha's story had dimmed his vision. He saw design in simple gestures, cruelty in gentle faces.

"I'm sorry. What did you say?" There was the courtyard, in the sun, and here was a secretary.

"I wondered if you expected any reply, Yashim efendi."

He saw a young man wearing the fez and the stambouline, with a gentian in his buttonhole. He was one of those modern young men, undoubtedly fluent in a foreign language, who had joined the service since Yashim's day, without moving through the traditional palace schools. The gentian signaled ambition, Yashim suspected, rather than romance.

"Possibly. I'll wait."

When the secretary had gone, an old man in slippers and a fez emerged from a basement staircase onto the courtyard, dangling a tray of coffee cups from his finger. He crossed the courtyard and pushed open a door and disappeared.

Yashim thought of Natasha's bundle, of the grave she'd dug in the thawing ground.

A thin gray lizard zigzagged down the pillar and sped off across the stones.

"Yashim efendi? The pasha would like to speak to you."

He followed the young secretary upstairs, to the creak of his leather shoes.

The secretary knocked at a door.

"Come!"

"Yashim efendi."

"Very good. You may leave us, Orhan."

The door closed. Midhat Pasha was standing by the window, erect in his black tailored coat, with tightly curled gray hair cut short and pince-nez on his nose. He looked at Yashim over them.

Eventually, Midhat Pasha removed his glasses and tapped them on a paper he held in his hand.

"Bad business, young man."

"Yes, my pasha." Yashim was not sure how much he should reveal he knew. It was supposed to have been a perfect secret, but now . . .

"Ambassador Palewski has been shot."

"Hmm?"

"He had Prince—"

But Midhat Pasha raised his hand, dangling the wire spectacles. "Tsk, tsk. If you know, so be it."

Yashim bowed. He had known Midhat Pasha for many years. Almost twenty years, when as an unhappy youth he had been taken into the palace school. Older than the others, wounded in body and in mind, he had found a friend in the pasha's only son, a boy almost as reckless as himself. Yashim was the older boy, still working through the agony of his castration and his mother's murder, but Bayezit at seventeen simply chafed against the demands of school life.

He was not clever like his father, Midhat, who was carving out a career for himself in the palace administration. Nor was Bayezit by any stretch of the imagination beautiful, as his mother was said to be. He was strong as an ox, bored to tears by his lessons. Anxious, too, to live up to the example set by his illustrious father, who was already by then considered an expert on foreign affairs, and had pulled strings to enroll his son in the schools.

"Can't you help Bayezit at all?" Midhat had asked Yashim once, in exasperation. "He's a lump of granite. Languages! Recital! Logic! They wash off him."

Yashim had repeated what Bayezit himself always told him, that he should like to be a soldier. Bayezit, Yashim had found, had all the military virtues. He had courage and immense physical strength, a well-developed sense of loyalty, and an openness that inspired confidence in the people around him. He had only to speak, and the other boys listened. They laughed at his efforts in class, but they respected his big hands, his honest judgments.

Midhat had set his heart on having his son in the same service, tripping along the corridors of power, following in his own footsteps— maybe giving him the support that only a son could provide. But Bayezit's grades were shocking; even with Yashim's help, sitting up at night going through his French vocabulary, slipping him answers in class, patiently taking him through the suras of the Koran until the words had mashed into a meaningless babble of sound: even with this encouragement, Bayezit had seemed likely to fail his graduation. Midhat had finally given way, and agreed to let the boy try soldiering.

He joined a mounted artillery unit. In an army infested with appointees and placemen he had risen quickly on his own merits. He had the makings of a first-rate soldier when he was killed, three years later, struck by a ricochet when the Russians besieged the Shumla Pass in 1828.

Hence the "young man": in Midhat's eyes, Yashim was the friend of a man who had never grown old. The boy who survived, too: he read it always in Midhat's eyes.

"Ambassador Palewski will pull through, inshallah," he said. "No sign of the—other."

"What does that mean, no sign? You've been working on it?" Midhat Pasha sounded surprised. "Who instructed you?"

"Palewski is a friend," Yashim explained. "I didn't need to be instructed."

"So this—ah, guest, whom we have been expecting," Midhat murmured doubtfully, twirling his spectacles. "He never came?"

Yashim read a flicker of hope in Midhat's eyes. He shook his head. "He came, pasha. They were together, at the port. And then—then, Palewski took a shot. The guest disappeared."

"Disaster." Midhat passed a hand over his eyes. "Disappeared, you say? Disaster. It's very sensitive. For your friend, for us, for—the other one you mentioned." He rubbed his fingers on the bridge of his nose, and began to mutter his thoughts: "Discretion, yes. Obviously. But speed. A quick solution, hmm?" He fussed with his thoughts aloud, it seemed to Yashim. "By Friday? You'll need men."

Yashim shook his head. "If I need them I'll ask for them. Right now, if there's any chance of a solution, we must work in secret. The more noise we make, the worse the outcome might be. Don't you agree?"

"By Allah," said Midhat, laying his spectacles on the desk, "this is a mess. Our own resources are limited. Carry on with your investigation, but report to me. I will consult with the sultan." He sighed and shook his head. "Altogether, a mess."

Yashim bowed. It wasn't a wholehearted endorsement, but it would do. Midhat Pasha said their resources were limited.

Informers? Watchmen? Army officers? To search Istanbul for a vanished prince, who else did they really have, except Yashim?

41

Aᴀ F T E R they had wandered through the bazaar, out through the court of the Bayezit mosque and to the Süleymaniye, which rivaled Ayasofya, Yashim meant to give Natasha coffee. But when he smelled the meat sizzling on the spit he realized they were hungry, too.

"Please sit down, effendi, hanum. *Ayran?* Umit—fetch *ayran* for our guests! Skewers—one, two, or three?"

The cook picked up three skewers, threaded with tiny cubes of meat, and presented them across his arm, like swords.

"How hungry are you, Natasha?"

Natasha raised her eyebrows. "Is it lamb?"

"Only the liver. Two?"

The cook laid four skewers on the grill, jostled some others into better position, and whipped out three plates, which he began to pile with bunches of coriander and parsley.

"Fresh salad! Fresh for you," he declared cheerfully, putting an onion on his block. With a dozen swift strokes he reduced the onion to dice, and swept them onto a plate. He split a lemon, drizzled it over the onion, and then scattered the plate with a handful of *kirmizi biber*, toasted pepper flakes.

Yashim and Natasha watched quietly as their meal was assembled— the salad, the herbs, the tender pieces of lamb liver, the huge blanket of bread, thin and supple as fine leather, the *ayran*, a soothing yogurt drink. The liver was the speciality of the house—that is, there was no other: just liver, cut small and cooked with a hint of smoke.

The man's working rhythm soothed Yashim: it was part efficiency and part show, to reassure them and other passersby that the cookery was swift and well rehearsed. The plates came swooping to their table: the lamb, still sizzling on its spit, across a plate. Yashim began tearing at the thin bread, choosing morsels of meat and herbs, adding a pinch of onion, dabbing the little parcel into a dish of spicy red pepper flakes.

Natasha watched him.

"You eat too fast."

Yashim considered this. "I'm sorry. It's force of habit," he admitted. "On the street, at least, I take my rhythm from the cook."

"He's fast."

"And methodical."

Natasha wrapped a morsel of lamb the size of a hazelnut in a sheet of bread and put it in her mouth.

"You forgot the salad."

She nodded with her mouth full, and almost laughed.

"Try it like this."

He made her a parcel of lamb and onion and coriander. "Is chili too hot?"

"I can try," she said.

He sprinkled a little chili over the meat, and passed her the wrap.

"I suppose Saint Petersburg, or Paris, is like this, too," she said, gesturing along the street. "Ordered, and methodical."

"I don't know Paris, but rhythm and order governs Istanbul, at any rate. From the kebab vendors to the water carriers."

"And those caïquejees bringing their boats to the landing stages without a bump."

"And imams watching the sky for stars, to time the call to prayer."

Natasha nodded, and bit into her food. "It's better like this. Delicious."

After a moment, she said: "I don't know why it doesn't all go haywire, though. So many people, all having to do the right thing, at the right time."

Yashim smiled. "From time to time, it does, almost." He told her about the eerie days that followed the elevation of a sultan, when time seemed to stop in its tracks. "Everything gets confirmed by the new sultan, bit by bit. The army and the guilds and the old taxes. And after a while, it resumes its normal rhythm. City life goes on."

He thought of Palewski, falling to the ground in a hail of shot. "It closes up again, like the tide," he said.

"A dog barks, the caravan moves on. It's a Russian proverb."

"An Ottoman one, too! *It ürür, kervan yürür.*"

"*Sobáka lájet, a karaván idjót,*" Natasha murmured. "But where does it go, Yashim? The caravan?"

Her eyes met his.

"I don't know," he said slowly, gazing at her. "Down the old road, I suppose. The well-worn track, year in, year out, that leads to—to the same place."

After a moment she lowered her eyes, and smiled.

"The city of domes and spires, whose very streets are paved with gold."

Yashim had felt, for a moment, the tug of the caravan on the road itself.

"Natasha—"

But as he glanced toward her, a movement between the tables caught his eye.

It was the hands he saw first: those huge, loose fingers curled around a length of burlap which the prizefighter was carrying at his waist. Yashim recognized his heavy shaven head, his rounded ears, and the lumbering delicacy of his tread. He seemed to swell into view, like a balloon: like a djinn, uncorked from his bottle.

Yashim raised his head.

The prizefighter stood like an ox, surveying the scene with bland disinterest. What he thought of Yashim's entertainment, or of his Russian guest, could not be said: he might have been looking at a crate of fish, or a wrestling opponent. For Yashim was sure the man was a wrestler: he had the wrestler's dainty way of standing, small feet, legs slightly bowed, deep chest.

"They told me I would find you here," he said.

Natasha looked up in astonishment. Yashim nodded.

"So you found me. There's a message?"

The man raised his hands. "I brought the gun."

It took Yashim a moment to grasp what he meant. "You brought a gun here?"

The man gave that sound which Yashim had interpreted as a signal of amusement. "You weren't at home, efendi."

"I'm sorry, Natasha. Where did you get this—gun?"

"Some joker thought he could make trouble. He won't no more." The man's features tightened very slightly in what Yashim suspected might be an effort at a smile. "He was had, efendi. The gun don't work. Lovely to look at. It fires wide. He should have checked afore he started."

"Started what?"

"Boh! Little guy, being tough. Nothing to do with you, efendi. We says, where d'you get it? Asked him a number of times, efendi." He paused.

"Very patient of you."

The big man gave an amused huff. "He remembered better in the end, he'd bought it off a man in the tavern. He's promised us an introduction but it looks like the fellow's gone off somewhere. How it came to be doing the rounds we'll find out. The boss thought you'd want to see the gun."

"I am indebted to him," Yashim replied. "What makes your boss think this is the piece?"

The big man scratched a protuberant ear. "It's logical, he says. There's guns and there's guns, efendi. This is one of 'em. Never seen its like."

He hefted the burlap tube. To Yashim it now looked conspicuously like a gun. He glanced at the cook, who was busy at his chopping board.

"It's light, some Frankish make," the man said. "Maybe not so old, not like some of them old Janiss—" he stopped short, automatically swallowing the forbidden idea "—them old army guns you find in the bazaar. Lovely pieces, good range, even though they are old—but some people find them hard to fire, I'm told."

"Give it to me." Yashim glanced anxiously around.

The big man propped the sacking against the low table. Just like a gun, Yashim thought.

"Thank you. Thank you, very much." He gestured to the food on the table. "Can I offer you—?"

The big man shook his head. "Not that it doesn't all look very nice, efendi." And he gave one of those tight faces that Yashim read as a smile, and which seemed to include the idea of his lovely companion, as well as the bread and lamb, cooling on its spit. Perhaps Natasha thought so: she turned a radiant smile on the visitor.

"A dog barks, Yashim," she said, when the man had clumped off down the street. "A man bearing a package? Highly mysterious."

Yashim seemed not to have heard her. She reached out and touched his sleeve.

"And where does the caravan go now?"

He looked up. "It goes, Natasha—" He paused. "There's a friend I'd like you to meet. Or are you tired?"

"Not at all. We Russians chirp like crickets all summer, didn't you know that? And I'd like to meet your friend. Just first explain the mystery."

"As we go along, I will." He stood up and put some money on the table. He would tell her everything that had happened to Palewski, omitting only the story of Czartoryski.

"Woof!" She laughed. "Let's go."

42

"The ambassador is in the drawing room, Yashim efendi. We made up a divan. He wanted to be moved."

"We'll go up and surprise him," Yashim said. "But in a few minutes I may need you, Marta."

"I am here, efendi," she said simply.

Yashim led Natasha upstairs. At the top he knocked.

"It's me, Yashim. I've brought Natasha Borisova. Natasha, Count Palewski."

"Come in, do. It's an honor, Mademoiselle Borisova. The famous Russian guest! Forgive me for not getting up. Yashim has told me quite a lot about you."

He was lying against the sofa cushions, wrapped in a dressing gown that Yashim recognized as the silk-embroidered coat he'd once persuaded the ambassador to wear to a palace reception—as he recognized the slight lisp that Palewski acquired when he drank spirits.* A quilt lay over his legs. He held out his hand over the back of the sofa.

"Count Palewski," Natasha murmured, touching her hand to his. She removed her bonnet and laid it on a chair. It seemed to Yashim that she was extravagantly pretty.

"Do come and sit down. There's not much room, Mademoiselle Borisova, but you may sit on my legs if you don't mind. I can only offer you brandy or warm beer, and I recommend the brandy. It's not as good as the stuff that wretched Doherty siphoned up this afternoon, but it is cognac. Do fetch glasses from the cupboard, Yashim, there's a good fellow."

He winced as he moved his legs to let Natasha sit down. "Thank God, a pretty face—and conversation. No, don't worry. Not my legs that hurt." He let Yashim refill the glass that he held on his chest. *"Nasdrovie!"*

"So Doherty was here again?"

"Came to drink my brandy, I suspect. Gave me a lecture on Orthodoxy to cover up his obvious alcoholic designs. Marta aside, I haven't seen a truly Christian face all day. Doherty and Dr. Millingen bleating about scars."

"I sent the boys a note," Yashim said.

"Yashim told me what happened," Natasha said. "It must have been very frightening."

"'S nothing, my dear," he said airily. "Line of duty and such. But what's that?"

* See *The Janissary Tree.*

He strained forward from his pillows, looking at an object Yashim had stood on the fireside rug.

"Recognize this?"

"It's the Boutet. Finest fowling piece that ever came out of France," he explained to Natasha. He ignored her look of surprise, as she glanced at Yashim. "Why did you fetch it up here, Yash?"

"I didn't. This gun was delivered to me about an hour ago. Natasha and I were having lunch. You're sure it's yours?"

"Unless it's Napoleon's," Palewski retorted. "Let me look."

He handed his brandy to Natasha and turned the gun over in his hands. "Mine, of course. I don't understand. Midhat sent it?"

"Midhat?"

Palewski frowned. "No, I give up. I thought perhaps I'd somehow mixed up guns, or left this behind and forgot. Memory might be a bit shaky, mightn't it, after all the recent excitement? But this isn't the one I took shooting. This one's the dud. I never took it out."

"Someone did." Yashim told Palewski about the giant who had returned it, and Balamian's hunch that it had been used in the port attack. "He hasn't caught up with the man who sold it yet. But I think he will."

"Gets what he wants, does he, this Balamian?"

Yashim pulled a face. "I would hate to be the one keeping secrets from him. You say this is the gun with the faulty mechanism. I take it you don't remember when you saw it last?"

"Of course I do. Well, roughly, anyway. About a week ago."

"Was it locked away?"

"Locked away? How would I know? I suppose so, yes."

Yashim frowned. "I'd better call Marta."

"Yashim, you're babbling. Is he babbling, mademoiselle, or am I going mad?" Palewski laid the gun aside and took the brandy. "Nothing to do with Marta, bless her. Your idea, Yashim—I took it to the bazaar as you suggested, to a professional gunsmith. You do remember saying that?"

"Yes, but I thought—"

"Whatever I said, Yashim, I took it to the bazaar. To be quite honest, I was interested in what they might say. I saw old what's-his-name? Man with the patch, Milosevic, knows a thing or two about guns. I just meant to get an opinion, but you know what those people are like. Whatever he knows about guns, he knows a lot more about selling stuff—including his impeccable repair service. Fact is, he'd hardly taken it into his grubby paws before it was all stripped down and lying in pieces on his bench. Quite impressive, for a man who had never seen a Boutet in his life. I swallowed it. Not the gun, I mean. His line. Told me he'd have it right in no time, without a scratch."

Yashim slumped back in his chair. "You kept a receipt?"

"I took one, for what it's worth. Not much, judging by the way it turned up in your friend Balamian's big mitts. It's in the escritoire, second drawer down." He patted Natasha's hand. "I'm afraid this must be all very dull, Mademoiselle Borisova. Not quite *The Arabian Nights.*"

She glanced at Yashim, and smiled. "Oh, *The Arabian Nights* . . . But everything's new to me."

Palewski closed his eyes, and when he opened them he was looking curiously at Yashim. "You're right, mademoiselle. It's all very exciting. I only wish I could share your dispassionate enthusiasm for new experiences. I haven't been shot for twenty-five years."

"I'm sorry, I—"

"No, no. Let me feel your hands. Why, they're cold! Brrr. Would you like a fire?"

Natasha shook her head. "The brandy is lovely. They're warming up already."

Palewski turned his head. "Any sign, Yash? Maybe the drawer underneath."

Yashim was by the escritoire with a packet of papers in his hand and a frown on his face. "These letters—about some visitor of yours. Have they been lying here all the time?"

"Hidden in plain view, Yashim. Old trick. I had dispatches once, for Moscow—this might interest you, mademoiselle—"

"It's all in here, is it?" Yashim broke in. "The seal's broken."

"Never sealed it, Yash. It's just an old envelope I used, put all the letters in it together. I'm sorry, Mademoiselle Borisova—"

"They're not—" Yashim checked himself. It was useless talking to Palewski now.

His friend was wrong if he thought he had secured all the letters in the envelope. When Yashim returned to the drawer he found one lying loose at the bottom. Beneath it lay the receipt he'd been looking for, from Milosevic the gunsmith for a Frankish gun.

He pulled out the chair and sat down, staring at the letters. He half-heard Palewski telling Natasha a story about riding on Moscow, years before: ordinarily, Yashim would have wished to listen, for Palewski was wary of telling old tales. "Shoot me if you ever catch me reminiscing," he'd once told Yashim. "Dull as listening to somebody else's dreams. Which is what reminiscence is, I suppose. Old men's dreams."

Palewski appeared to be laying out the disposition of troops in 1812, as the Corsican marched on Russia. Yashim frowned.

"Forgive me," he said. "There's something I need to do—could you entertain Mademoiselle Borisova here for an hour?"

"Don't hurry back," Palewski said.

43

AT the arms bazaar Yashim found men putting up the iron shutters, under the supervision of a stony-faced sheik leaning on a brass-tipped staff. Across the street, half a dozen brokers, or criers, drank their coffee. All day they had wandered the arcades of the bazaar, calling out prices on articles that had been pawned. By the entrance the hamals entitled to work at the bazaar were standing in a knot; farther off, leaning against the wall, or squatting in the dust, were a number of ill-fed Jews who picked up work as interpreters and runners.

Yashim hurried inside. Like all bazaars it was a warren of alleyways and covered ways, bristling with antiquated muzzle-loaders, atavistic cannon, worn sabers, and curving knives—an armory that extended a near-mystical protection to the valuable treasure stored in basement safes. Istanbul's fabled arms bazaar was more than a gallery of old weapons, blades, and guns: it was the city's strongbox, too.

Old people still called it the Jewel Bazaar, for it had been a jewel market long ago, built like a fortress to protect emeralds and rubies, turquoise and sapphires, from all the eastern mines. But the Ottomans treasured the jewels of war, too: encrusted daggers, octagonal-barreled carbines inlaid with ivory and ebony, scabbards of silver and velvet, etched powder horns. There were still emeralds and diamonds, but now they were part of an arms trade that valued beauty and utility together.

In a city without locks, for the most part, people had started bringing their precious goods to the arms bazaar for safekeeping, or to put in pawn: at the bazaar you could always raise some cash.

Yashim found Milosevic at his cubbyhole, closing the shutters.

"Milosevic efendi?"

"That's me," the gunsmith replied without turning around.

"I have a receipt."

The gunsmith began taking in some fine old guns stacked against the wall, wiping them with a cloth. All along the passage men were closing their shops, and the air rang with the sounds of rifle stocks hitting the ground, and the clash of sabers as they were taken from the walls.

"It would be better if you took a look at this receipt."

Milosevic sighed, and reached for the paper. "The ambassador's gun?" He squinted at the paper. "Very fine piece, really priceless. A Frankish gun."

He nodded, almost to himself. "To be honest, no gunsmith in Istanbul could appreciate the craftsmanship better than me. They buy and sell guns like vegetables here. 'Milosevic efendi, fix me this old gun, I beg of you.' 'Milosevic efendi, is this a good one?' Pah! I do everybody's work."

He looked down at the receipt and began to smooth its edges with his thumbs.

"This, my friend, is no Montegrin jezail from your grandfather's time, with an action made by the village blacksmith. Bam! Bam!" He mimicked a hammer thwacking onto the paper. "It's a fine piece, delicate, many, many hours of work, and by an experienced artisan. Ah, well. The Franks, they win all the battles these days."

"Where's the gun now?"

"It's in my workshop, efendi." He gestured to a dark hole at the back of his shop. "You can't expect a gun like that to be fixed overnight. Tell the ambassador that I am working on it, and I will call on him when it's ready."

Yashim put a foot up on the step, and leaned forward. "I think it's gone."

Milosevic looked baffled. "Gone? What do you mean?"

"Three days ago it was used in an attempt to murder someone here, in Istanbul."

"It's not possible."

The gunsmith turned and disappeared feet first through the hatch in the floor. After a few minutes his face reappeared, glistening with sweat.

"I must talk to my son."

He clambered out of the hatch and brushed past Yashim.

Yashim settled cross-legged on the mat in front of Milosevic's shop. The gun had gone, and that was that. He was more concerned about the letters lying open in Palewski's escritoire, for anyone to find. But anyone reading the letters could have seen the receipt for the gun, too.

Milosevic's son remembered the gun. He had been minding his father's shop at the time. Someone came from the Polish embassy to ask about the gun that had lately been brought in. Young Milosevic could see that it was an expensive piece, and had made two assumptions, both of them, as it turned out, wrong.

"I thought the gun was in for cleaning," he said. He was stubborn on this point. He could not explain why he was so sure, except to say that the gun had lain alongside two others, modern types, which he himself had accepted for an overhaul the day before.

Besides, the man who called was a Frank. As he kept repeating, the gun was a Frankish piece that belonged to a Frank. "With an ambassador, do you need a receipt?" he asked, with aggressive naïveté. He had parted easily with the gun.

156 • JASON GOODWIN

Yashim's efforts to get a description of the man were largely in vain. Milosevic junior could not remember much about him, not at this distance in time, though he'd certainly never seen him before. Five days? You say only, but that's a long time in this business. It's a busy place. Young? He was not old, he was sure of that. As to the color of his hair, or his height, or the shape of his face, it was—with a shrug—normal. About medium height. He might have been fair or dark. Perhaps more dark than fair. A Frank.

Didn't Yashim know what a Frank looked like?

"He's young," Milosevic said. He pinched the young man's flabby biceps. "At his age, it's all here—and not there," he added, giving the young man a playful, but apparently rather painful, cuff on his ear. Young Milosevic shook his head and wondered if that would be all.

"I'm busy, all the time. Like I say."

Yashim dismissed him and declined an offer to drink coffee, to Milosevic's evident relief. "Nothing like this has ever happened before. I am trying to pass on my methods, and my skills, but it takes time. He's not a bad boy, efendi. I have to say, in the end, I take some reassurance from your words."

"What words?"

"You say someone tried to use the gun. It would not work, so that is good, no? Maybe Allah himself has chosen us to be the instrument of the criminal's frustration. Allah be praised."

"Praise to him," Yashim replied.

Milosevic took this as an encouraging remark. "And better still, you have recovered the weapon. So in the end, no harm and a little good has been done, you see. It is kismet, is it not? We are merely made to submit."

Yashim had an impulse to poke the man in the eye. "I wish you joy of your son," he said, thinking up half a dozen better retorts before he had reached the gates of the bazaar.

44

GHIKA sprawled fully dressed on the pallet bed, one side of his face pressed into the gray sheet. Two empty bottles lay on the floor, a broken glass and an empty jug, but the room no longer smelled of aniseed. It smelled of sour alcohol, like Ghika's ragged breath: alcohol, and decay. A thin wire of drool spun from his lips to the sheet. Each time he snored, the wire shivered.

It had been a night of drink, and fuddled memories of a girl with white-gold hair and breasts that curved like apples above a slender waist. The drink had brought her closer, at first, until he could almost touch her skin; but after that, it was only the drink.

He opened his eyes. The pale daylight jabbed at them with knives; they seemed to bleed, red rimmed, filigreed with broken veins.

Ghika groaned and wiped the side of his face with his hand. After that he lay still for several minutes, sliding back into a dreamless sleep to resurface again and again on waves of nausea.

At long last he began to move. Very slowly he levered himself into a sitting position, one foot striking the bottle, which rolled under the bed. He groaned again, then belched. He swallowed some vomit, and clutched his chest as the bile burned. His ulcers whined.

When he finally stood up he gave a grunt and flung himself back down on the divan, his leg in the air. A piece of glass was sticking out of the sole of his foot. He took a swipe at it, grimacing with self-pity, and managed to dislodge the fragment but cut his finger. He put it in his mouth.

Ghika stumbled, trembled, groaned, and cursed as he floundered around the room, searching for water and sucking his wounded finger.

At the sight of the raki bottle he pulled a face. The bottle winked back. Ghika stiffened and pursed his lips in disapproval. There was no call for such familiarity, not with Leandros Ghika. Respectable family, the Ghikas. Owned the whole house. Lost the furniture. Father dead.

He dropped the pile of glass onto a table and picked up the bottle and set it on the table next to the glass. The other one, he remembered, had rolled under the bed.

Going down there made his head hurt. He groped for the bottle, and pulled it out.

It was not a bottle of raki. It was another shape. He stared at it stupidly for a few moments, then sniffed it. It smelled of starched coiffures and silk drapes and applewood *chibouks*. There was a little amber liquid at the bottom, too, and he drank that. It tasted of brandy. He mastered an urge to vomit, and felt slightly better.

Brandy was too expensive for Ghika. He must have stolen it, he reasoned. From the men who kept the whore upstairs, the woman who shamelessly bared herself . . .

He enjoyed that thought for a while. He'd stolen the brandy, found her alone in the room, alone . . . asleep . . . she'd been asleep, down on the divan the way he'd woken up just now, but naked . . . her rump . . . that's it . . . buttocks . . . he parted her thighs and she stirred. Quick! Pressing her nape down onto the bed, he fumbled with his trousers . . . she was writhing now, yes . . . Not like those stolid lumps at the whorehouse but white and lithe and bucking—presenting her perfect rear, a little higher, that's it . . . In! She was tight, and alive . . . He gave her little screams to scream, and then he stifled them with his hand on her neck as he pressed her down into the pillows.

He wiped his hand across his face. It was a dream. It hadn't been like that. One of the men—someone had given him the bottle. He could vaguely remember being outside in the corridor. A noise. The men, and someone—someone else.

"Wha—wha's going on?"

After that he couldn't remember. But it didn't matter. He'd liked the dream.

45

IN time, everything and everyone drifts through a port. The merchandise, silver, bills of trade and exchange that justify its existence. Men, of course: stevedores, dockers, lightermen, merchants, inspectors, tax collectors, and sailors of every creed and color. There are port rats and prostitutes. Altogether they bring news—gossip from the hinterland, prices from abroad, new jokes, the latest disasters.

So although the body was not discovered in the port, Balamian got to hear about it almost as soon as the *kadi*, in whose jurisdiction the man had died. It did not concern him directly, but he remembered Yashim, who had been brought to see him in the baths, and sent his man.

Yashim had left his stew to simmer and gone down to Kara Davut to find the quince man coming up the road with a basket on his back loaded with big yellow quinces, set off against sprays of bright green leaves. The man solemnly unhitched his basket and helped Yashim choose four hard quinces, each with its spray of leaf.

Back home, Yashim sliced each quince in half and cut out the cores. He pared them into slices, dropping them into the pan before they had time to brown. He ladled a little more water into the pan and set the lid on.

He put the bright leafy sprigs in a small vase, and put it on the windowsill.

He barely had time to settle on the divan and pick up the sheet of observations before there came a knock on the door. He opened it and recognized the huge man from the tavern, unsmiling.

"The boss gave me a message," he said, jerking his thumb over his shoulder. "They found a man dead, below the Frankish cemetery. Looks like he fell." He shrugged, expansively. "The boss thought he might be yours."

Yashim knew exactly where the man meant: the old Catholic cemetery beyond Taksim, beyond the pest hospital and the old walls of Pera, where the ground shelved steeply down to the shores of the Bosphorus.

"Thank you—and please, thank Balamian efendi for his solicitude. Is anything known about the man who fell?"

"That's the message." He stuck a finger in his ear and worked it there, glancing around the flat. His enormous feet shuffled on the rug. Yashim raised his eyebrows.

"It's where the Franks go, don't they, when they die? The old Genoese place. I went up myself once, as a kid."

With that unexpected confidence, the big man gave a short bow and clumped off down the stairs.

Yashim glanced around his apartment. He checked his stew: the water was barely simmering, so he decided to leave the fire in, and let it die down of its own accord. He slipped his cloak off a peg, folded it over his arm, put on his shoes, and followed the messenger down into the street.

At the Balat stage he engaged a caïque as far as Karaköy at the mouth of the Golden Horn; experience had taught him that rowers preferred their own stretch of water. From Karaköy he took another, gliding up the Bosphorus past the Tophane arsenal, and the port, which Balamian seemed to control, until they reached a small stage west of the sultan's palace at Beşiktaş.

It was well after noon, and the sun was hot on his back as he began to climb toward the Frankish cemetery. The land here was broken into a series of ridges, sometimes reinforced by masonry, and the buildings that had grown up on each broad shelf. The lane wound between them without direction. To his right the sloping ground above Dolmabache was dotted with the cypresses that always marked an Ottoman graveyard, fluting skyward like natural minarets. Many of its headstones were centuries old, veering crazily through neglect, smoothed to illegibility by years of wind and rain, some deliberately smashed in the rage that followed the destruction of the Janissaries almost sixteen years before. But the Frankish cemetery above was older still, consecrated when Pera was a Genoese colony battening on the Byzantine trade.

Yashim was sweating when he overtook a carter urging his ponderous horse up the broken road. He gestured politely, to offer Yashim a lift; but the empty cart jounced and thundered across the cobbles and Yashim found that he preferred to continue on foot.

"You're wise!" The carter leered jovially at Yashim. "My next load's a dead 'un."

Yashim doubled his pace. He had hoped that Czartoryski was still alive. He had counted on the widening gap of silence after the assault to mean that the prince was, in some way, protected: more useful to his abductors alive than dead. Balamian's news was what he had dreaded most. It was scarcely twenty-four hours since Palewski had been shot: if the intention was to cause an éclat, then to hurl the body down from the Frankish cemetery into the Ottoman one could still be counted a success.

If the aim was to frustrate liberal hopes and to embarrass the Porte, the choice of the Frankish cemetery as the place to murder the prince was, he supposed, impeccable. A dead man in a graveyard caused no comment if he reached it by tumbrel, attended by mourners, and was lowered into a hole in the ground. If he was murdered there—pushed from a cliff, or bludgeoned and left for dead—then the infraction stank to high heaven: it became a story the whole city would soon hear.

"It's where the Franks go when they die."

He glanced up. In the distance he could already see the little mortuary chapel of the cemetery, tactfully surmounted by a modest wooden cross, but what engaged his attention was a knot of people standing by a low wall, looking down into the Ottoman cemetery.

He hurried up to them, conscious that he cut a poor figure in his damp shirt, his turban slightly askew, his shoes dusty from the road. He looked about for the *kadi*, but perhaps he had already gone.

"Where's the body?"

The men at the wall turned to look at him, suspiciously.

"Over there," one man said, with a jerk of his head. But it was hard at this distance to see much at all: only a couple of men standing by a dark shape on the ground. Yashim assumed they were gravediggers.

"The *kadi* said to let no one through," the man said. He put out an arm.

Yashim shook his head. "I've brought the cart," he said, and at that moment the cart itself crested the rise. The man stood back.

"The cart's coming," Yashim explained, as he approached the gravediggers. Above them, the cemetery's retaining wall rose fifteen feet, ending in a broken line of loose stones and scrub that marked the boundary of the old Frankish graveyard. Yashim looked up at it, and frowned.

The corpse lay facedown on the stones and grass in a small declivity at the foot of the wall. That he had fallen from above seemed obvious at first sight: one arm outflung, the other awkwardly pinioned beneath the trunk; a knee was bent at an unnatural angle. But what mattered most to Yashim at that moment was the fact that the dead man was dressed in European costume: leather shoes, black trousers and frock coat.

Yashim squatted down beside the corpse.

"Does anyone know who he is?"

The sexton shrugged. "Maybe a Frank."

Maybe, Yashim thought. But also, possibly, a Turk.

Whoever he was, Yashim was certain that he was not looking at the body of Prince Adam Czartoryski.

It was also plain to Yashim that the man was already dead when he fell.

46

DOHERTY, the Irish priest, brought Palewski a vial of holy water.

"What am I supposed to do with it? Drink it?" Palewski asked testily. He was in a bad mood, and quite enjoying it. Birgit's failure to rush over, full of concern and warmth, was a legitimate cause of annoyance, of course; but he took a bad mood to be a sign of convalescence, too, and that cheered him. His wounds were still sore, but the leeches had done their work; Dr. Millingen had declared that the danger was, for the most part, over.

"We'll have you up and about in a few days," he'd said cheerfully, in the bedside manner he reserved for foreign diplomats; Palewski resented him for it. "With a few honorable scars."

"All my scars are honorable."

"Of course, I meant . . ."

"You won't find any on my back."

"No, no. Don't excite yourself—the dressings . . ."

Doherty chuckled, and suggested the holy water might be sprinkled over his wounds, a proposition that Palewski treated with marked aversion.

"Blessed it may be, Father, but I'd rather not douse my wounds in water you've lifted from some dank font. Why, the stuff's alive! Meanwhile," he added, pointing a finger at a dark bottle on the bedside table, "this is suitable for external and internal use."

Doherty uncorked the bottle and sniffed. "Brandy-like, it is. Still, as a friend, perhaps I ought to taste it, to be on the safe side."

He had the brandy in a glass before Palewski could think of a reply.

"Ah. A grand marque, if I'm not mistaken. One of the French houses, am I right?"

"Doherty, you may be a priest but I think you're an ass." Palewski put his hands on the mattress and shifted his position, grimacing. "Here. It's for my pain."

"Of course it is. I came to tell you, now, that my work in this city of infidels is almost done. I leave for Rome at the end of the week, and not, in my opinion, a moment too soon. This is no place for Christians, Palewski."

"So you'll be taking more than half the population of Istanbul with you?"

"Schismatics, my old friend. Half Turk, the lot of 'em. I'd gladly lead them to Rome if they'd admit their errors and put themselves under the protection of the Vicar of Christ. But they are all frogs in pots, Palewski—and I fear you are, too."

"Frogs? What are you talking about?"

"Come, come. You know the story of the frog that was boiled alive? They heated the water slowly and he could just about bear it, a little hotter, a little hotter, until it was too hot for him, after all. And by then, he was dead. You've been here a long time, and I daresay you don't notice the signs. Why, you're lying there shot and you call it a decent place for a Christian?" He shook his head. "They'd have me by the heels if they got half a chance, I know it."

"Who? The Orthodox?"

"The Mahommetans," Doherty said darkly. "It starts with looks, and then it goes onto jostling, and jeering, and it'll be stoning and burning before there's an end on it, you mark my words."

"Have you been jostled and jeered at, then?"

"I have. I've walked these very streets and been spat on, insulted and reviled. There's an evil spirit in 'em, Palewski, and it's gathering strength, when a man of the cloth can't walk down a public street and escape the dark looks of that pagan race of idolators and blasphemers."

"I don't suppose many Mahommetans would know a Catholic priest from a tattooed Chinaman. You're simply an object of surprise."

"It's the fires of eternal damnation that'll be the surprise for them, Palewski. They don't know it. Can't see it. You'd best keep your eyes open, too, my friend, after I'm gone."

Palewski allowed a pause to develop. "Well, we shall be sorry to lose you," he said finally, without obvious conviction. He had thought the priest engaging company; he had not expected this fanatic. Anyway, he wanted Birgit. "I expect you'll be seeing the Italians before you go?"

Father Doherty jostled his empty glass onto the bedside table, among the books and bottles. "No doubt. And I'll be telling them the same as I've told you. They can't go on playing games with their souls forever in this life."

"Well, somewhere in between the fire and the brimstone, Father, would you mind telling them I'd appreciate a visit, too?"

"Aye, I can do that much, I suppose." A puzzled frown appeared on the priest's face, and he leaned in a little closer to the bed. "Tell me, Palewski, what exactly did happen to you, when you were shot? Your friend said you were at the port."

Palewski felt suddenly very weary; he wished the priest would go. "Look, Yashim has all the details. Ask him. I'm afraid I'm not up to it. Need to rest."

"You were alone, I take it?"

Palewski grunted. His eyes had closed. Father Doherty glanced covetously at the brandy.

"I'll be off, then. So long. I'll drop by again, never fear."

Palewski made no reply. His chin dropped onto his chest, and he was snoring gently when Father Doherty tiptoed from the room.

Father Doherty did not immediately go downstairs. In a room on the floor above, he surprised Marta, who was folding sheets.

Marta gave a little cry.

"Peace, dear lady!" He gestured to the window. "I wanted to see the view from here. The view?"

Marta pursed her lips. Doherty went to the window, from where he could see the roof of the Galata Tower and, in the distance, the woods and turrets of Topkapi Palace across the Horn.

"Very nice," he said. He tipped his hat and went off downstairs, leaving Marta puzzled and indignant.

47

THE *kadi* had been summoned when the body was discovered, and Yashim was still at the cemetery when he came slowly up the hill, leaning on a stick, sometimes pausing to catch his breath.

He looked at the body for a few moments, and shook his head. "Well now, cover him up. Cover him up. It would be just as well to get him down to the mosque, at least. A lot of flies at this time of the year."

"I have sent for a sheet," Yashim said. "The carter here will take him away."

The old *kadi* looked at him with interest. "Are you a relative of the deceased?"

Yashim stepped forward and bent to speak in a low voice. "Yashim, from the palace. I heard what had happened and came to see."

The *kadi* cocked his head. "The man is dead. It's a long way to come, Yashim efendi."

"Not if a man has been killed, *kadi*."

The *kadi* planted his stick in the ground and leaned on it, looking up at the cliff.

"The fall was enough to break his neck," he murmured.

Yashim followed his glance. "It's possible," he agreed. "But from the position of the body I think he was already dead when he fell. A man's instinct when he loses his footing is to put out his arms to protect himself. He didn't. There's bruising to the neck, too."

The *kadi*'s chin sank. "What to do, Yashim efendi?" He glanced at Yashim out of the corner of his eye. "There's never been anything like this in all my time. A murder, you think? We don't even know the poor man's name, unless it is written in his jacket, perhaps."

"I've looked," Yashim said. The dead man was either a Turk or a Jew, youngish, in his late twenties at most, clean shaven, reasonably well dressed at moderate expense in the fashion popularized by the late sultan, which consisted of the frock coat, trousers, and black shoes. The shoes were good, but worn: Yashim had particularly noticed the soles, which suggested that the young man had spent a good time walking in them.

His pockets contained nothing above a few coins, some shreds of tobacco, and, folded very small and almost lost in the seam of his trouser pocket, a scrap of yellow paper with the words *coffee: 2 kebab 4* written in pencil. There was also a pencil, much sharpened, in the inside pocket of his coat; Yashim satisfied himself that it was the same sort of pencil that had been used to scribble the note. Otherwise there were no clues of any kind to the wearer's identity.

The *kadi* sighed. "What took him to a cemetery where he had no right to be?"

Yashim nodded: it was just what he had been about to say. "Why would a believer be in a Frankish graveyard?" He paused. "We may suppose that he went there for a purpose—to meet his killer, or someone else. Or to avoid him."

"Or to examine a grave."

"Yes, that's a possibility." Yashim looked keenly at the *kadi*. He might be old and quiet, but he wasn't missing much. "The chapel. Is it attended?"

"Only when a funeral is in progress, I believe. But we can ask, can we not?"

"I wish I could be of more service, *kadi*, but I am afraid my coming here today was chance. I thought something else might have happened, and I needed to eliminate the possibility that your man was connected in some way."

The *kadi* smiled. "Very little is left to chance, my friend. Come, let us walk down the hill together. You are in a hurry to be off, but the walk will do you good and carry you where you want to go."

Yashim blinked. "Very well." He had a strange sensation in his ears, as if listening to the *kadi* could be the most delightful thing he had ever done. "His clothing cost him three hundred *kuruş*, and his shoes half as much."

"He pushes a pen, perhaps."

"But punishes his feet." Yashim told the *kadi* about the excessive wear on the man's shoes. "The shoes are polished very bright, all the same."

The *kadi* jabbed at the ground with his stick. "Most illuminating."

"In what way?"

"He walks a lot, and jots down his expenses for coffee and a kebab. This tells us that he is literate, of course, and suggests that he is employed while he is walking. After all, to manage his own money a small note-book would be sufficient."

Yashim shook his head. "I don't follow you, *kadi* efendi."

The *kadi* laid his hand lightly on Yashim's arm. "So. I was a teacher, long ago. Some of my students carried just such a notebook to help them calculate their expenditure through the week. It helped them work out how much allowance they had left. It was a private book, because some of their expenses were made on—shameful things."

Yashim nodded. "So he wrote on paper, and kept a list of expenses to show his employer, rather than for himself. Who could the employer be? What sort of firm employs Turkish clerks?"

The commercial revolution that had swept Europe, creating armies of clerks to keep the ledgers, had barely touched the Ottoman Empire. Trade, like industry, was still conducted on a personal level, where deals were sealed over coffee; and Ottoman gentlemen did not, for the most part, engage in trade. That they left to Greeks, Armenians, and Jews.

"Indeed," the *kadi* murmured. "A firm? Perhaps the biggest of them all?"

"The biggest?"

"I wonder if our friend worked for the government? Well, well, it is a possibility."

He picked his way carefully over the rough ground, and at the road he stopped and gestured with his stick.

"So beautiful, the Bosphorus at this time of year."

They walked slowly downhill. At the bottom the *kadi* nodded. "It requires some thought."

"I will let you know, *kadi*, if anything occurs to me."

The *kadi* turned to him and bowed. "That," he said, "would be very gracious."

Yashim bowed in return, to hide his blush. He was aware that the old *kadi* was laughing at him.

48

IN summer, Istanbul was very hot. In winter, it froze. Ice heaved paving stones from the earth, and the spring rains washed the earth away, to rise as dust all through the long, hot summer. Agreeable as the city was, and perfectly sited to be the navel of the world, it was unquestionably dusty, muddy, and flyblown.

Yet its inhabitants were among the cleanest people in Europe, for the filth of the city had produced a remedy. At the public baths men and women could be washed, steamed, scrubbed, rinsed, lathered, soaked, bathed, and exfoliated; their hair could be cut, their body hair removed with wax and unguents, their nails pared, their nostrils and ears washed, their skin softened with creams and oils, their muscles manipulated, their hands and feet rubbed, their temples massaged; they could be roasted on hot platforms, and chilled in cold baths; then pummeled and stroked, kneaded and splashed down, before they emerged shining for a glass of tea and a sweet cake.

The process could be performed express, or it could be—and usually was, by the women of the city—drawn out into a day of rigors and relaxations, accompanied by conversation, laughter, and sometimes dancing, performed by troupes of *köçek*.

"Ouf!" Birgit raised her head from the hot slab, and winked at Natasha, who was lying on a hammam towel beside her. "Like a sauna, but rather grander." She rolled over onto her back and adjusted the rolled-up towel under her head. "It's like being in a church," she added, gazing up at the dome.

Natasha did not reply. Eventually she murmured: "In Siberia, the native people have places like this, to sweat and become clean. It is seen as a spiritual purification, led by a shaman."

Later, it seemed less like a church; Natasha was not sure that the languorous and intense massage she received led automatically to spiritual purification, and the tea and sweets they were offered, as they reclined in the tepidarium, were anything but shamanic.

"I could spend days here," Birgit mumbled sleepily, as she brushed the cake crumbs from her lips. She raised her leg and ran her finger up a shin that had been depilated and buffed by expert hands.

"Yashim is meeting us at four," Natasha reminded her.

"Hmm? It's six. He said six."

Natasha closed her eyes. She reached behind to pull her damp hair to one side, and settled her head on the firm little pillow. "Four o'clock, Birgit. You must have forgotten."

"What's the time now?" Birgit asked, after a long pause.

Natasha was even longer replying. "It's Wednesday," she said finally, and they giggled.

49

"The two Frankish ladies? But they are gone, efendi, this hour or more."
The fat old lady glanced involuntarily at the till: they had been lavish with
their tips, the Frankish girls.

"Gone? How did they go into the street?" Yashim asked, surprised.

The old lady raised her eyes to the ceiling. "Murad! Murad! There you
are," she added, as a man stepped into the little domed office by the hammam entrance. "The Frankish women. You saw them home?"

Yashim's lips tightened. "Where to?"

Murad scratched his head. "Not far. Ghika's place."

"But they were supposed to meet me here."

The old lady said: "Perhaps they got tired of waiting?"

"So—Ghika's place. Where's that?"

It took Yashim less than ten minutes to reach the house, but his anxiety dissolved in an instant when he saw Natasha on the stairs. She was
descending slowly, one gloved hand trailing against the wall, the other
clutching her skirt to keep her from tripping: the last rays of a dying sun
suffused her hair with an almost unearthly light.

She raised a finger to her lips.

"Shhh! Birgit's asleep—with Giancarlo!"

Yashim tried to give her a disapproving look, but failed. "The valide
would have had my head if anything had happened to you," he said.

"Are you scolding me? I'm sorry." She lowered her eyes. Then she
glanced up again, and laughed.

"Are we going back to the palace?"

Yashim smiled. "I see you've grown accustomed to Ottoman life. Is it such a chore?"

Natasha blew out her cheeks. She looked radiant, Yashim noticed: as though the baths had sloughed away a layer of Siberian frost. Her skin shone.

"No, not a chore, exactly," she said slowly, her eyes dancing with amusement. "But it is how the valide warned me it might be, a little. Talking to the ladies, well. They only want to discuss the latest fashion—and I'm not a very fashionable person. I think they're disappointed in me."

An idea seemed to strike her. "It's rather like being at the baths, isn't it? All those women, trying to be beautiful? At least there everyone goes naked—there's nothing to pretend, and everyone is the better for it." She told Yashim about an enormously fat woman who wasn't obviously beautiful. "But she was magnificent, Yashim, jowls and all. I thought, when I'm old and fat, I want to be like her."

"It doesn't seem very likely," Yashim murmured.

"I wouldn't mind," Natasha continued gaily, sliding her hand under his arm. "Fat or thin, or gray, or bent—I'd be myself, wouldn't I? But at the palace it's worse somehow. Sad. Not the valide—she does exactly as she pleases, and she's magnificent, too. But the others live to please, I suppose—and there's no one to please, except her."

"And she's not easily pleased," Yashim pointed out.

They stepped out into the street.

"No. She doesn't much care. But everyone else wants me to tell them how the ladies dress in Saint Petersburg these days." She shrugged. "How many petticoats? Does a skirt spring from the waist—and is it true that sleeves are being worn long this year? They are always fingering my hair here"—she pulled at the dark strands that framed her cheeks, and grimaced—"and questioning my bonnets. The only thing they really approve of is my shawl—and not because they think it's pretty. They have much lovelier ones. Just because they think it's more *à la mode* these days."

She gave an exasperated sigh. "So that's what I think when you ask if I want to go back to the palace. Not a chore, of course not. But not the

Arabian nights." She gave him a sly look from under her lashes. "You know, I feel astonishingly clean. My skin feels clean and bright after all that scrubbing and pounding. It gives me—energy."

She said it with a fierce little twist, and Yashim had to laugh—partly to still the little hollow that had just flickered in his chest. Natasha looked beautiful—and he had thought her plain!—with those lively, intelligent dark eyes framed by the two perfect arcs of her eyebrows, her lips dark and full, and her high Russian cheekbones scattered merrily with the lightest of freckles. And she had spoken of her skin . . .

He had shown her the sights, in daylight—Ayasofya, the Blue Mosque, the Egyptian bazaar—and she had accepted them like a list of indisputable facts set out in a child's copybook. *The sky is blue. The church is old. Air is composed of oxygen, nitrogen, and carbon dioxide.* But daylight was a ruthless pedagogue.

At dusk, the muezzin's call sounded the half-plaintive, half-triumphant note of man crying in the void, while all around his handiwork was blurring into insubstantial shadows. Then the Bosphorus, almost still, became a silver gleam; the bats swooped out from the archways and the domes; the minarets grew long enough to touch the stars. The hills of Asia, across the water, beetled closer for protection. The markets emptied out, the coins lay stacked, the merchandise slumbered in piles, and—

Somewhere out there, Yashim reflected, Prince Czartoryski lay hidden, or dead.

"We could go anywhere," he ventured. "Are you hungry?"

"I thought you liked to cook," she said, squeezing his arm.

"I do."

She pushed and pulled his arm, like a child. "Then ask me home. Take me there slowly—but don't make me walk. All that dust!" She crinkled her nose. "It would be too much like Siberia."

"I thought Siberia was a land of endless snow?"

"Ah, white and very clean—like me? You are absolutely right, Yashim. But it has another face—a dirty one, in summer. Then nothing is hidden anymore."

They were walking slowly down toward the Bosphorus, arm in arm. Below them lay the village of Galata. "Karaköy," Yashim said. "That's its Turkish name. *Kara* means 'black,' so people think it's the Black Village, but it's really Karaköy after the Karaites."

"Who?"

"A Jewish sect. They build synagogues underground, I don't know why. There have been Karaites here for centuries, but more came from the Crimea after you Russians took it from us."

"I suppose many people feel like exiles," Natasha said. "Not just us—my father and me, I mean. The Jews make a religion of it," she added, as they passed a synagogue. "The Greeks are exiles in their own country. The Turks—do they yearn for a return to the steppe? The valide—born in Martinique. Your Polish friend, without a country to return to. Even those boys, Birgit's Italians. Is Istanbul a city of exiles?"

"Mind the steps," Yashim warned her. "We'll take a caïque from here."

Minutes later, they were rocking gently up the Golden Horn.

"A city of exiles?" Yashim came back to her theme. "Perhaps it was always like that, from the moment it was founded as the second Rome. A city of people who came from somewhere else."

"Like the Turks?"

"Turks, Latins, even Greeks, many of them. Armenians, and Jews, and Laz from Georgia. The Genoese, who founded Pera and built the Galata Tower. After the conquest, Mehmet brought a whole new population into the city—Serbs and Greeks, and Muslims from Anatolia, and so on."

A thin wind whipped at the water, and Natasha slid her arm beneath his.

"What's making you smile?"

"I've been complaining," Yashim said, "how Istanbul is overrun with foreigners these days. As if it was ever any different."

At the Balat stage he helped her ashore. A lantern swung at the landing stage, but the streets were dark and he held her hand as he led her up the hill toward his home.

They climbed the stairs in darkness. Inside the flat, he lit lamps, settled her on the cushions, offered tea.

"What I said about exiles. Are you one, too?"

"An exile?" He looked around. "This is my home, Natasha."

"Not like that. I mean—perhaps you are, in one way. In a kind of internal exile."

She spoke haltingly, feeling for the right words like someone searching for a hidden spring.

Yashim gazed up at her. He had never considered it this way. It was something he tried not to consider at all, working each day to its end so as not to have to think.

"From the world? Not really. It's not—exile."

"Not exiled from the whole world, but from a part of it. Perhaps you impose it on yourself? Inner exile, where you control the borders." She bent forward and touched his arm, on the inside, where his sleeve lay open; he shivered. "Exile from—women," she faltered. She looked earnestly into his warm gray eyes.

Yashim felt suddenly very tired. "It's not—it's just—" He shook his head.

Her arm went up and she took his head in her hand and pulled him closer. At the last moment she turned her head aside, and gave a little gasp. "Please. Please don't kiss me."

She glanced back sideways at him through lowered lids. "I—want"— she began, inching her words out in breath, not quite using her voice—"I want you—to do it. To do it—want it." Her hand closed on the back of his head, her body twisted; it was as if she were speaking from some other place, deep inside her. Her mouth tensed, as though in pain.

"Natasha," Yashim murmured.

She let go of him, sat back, and picked up the hem of her long skirts, allowing them to ruffle upward, over her knees. "Like this. Please, Yashim." She flung one hand back across her eyes, while the other bunched her skirt up between her thighs. "Do it. I want you to."

She raised a knee; the skirt fell back along her thigh, its hem drifting among the petticoats and frills. "Come." She lifted her hand from her skirts to reach out to him, looking at him from beneath her wrist. "Come here."

He heard the catch in her voice, a little sob, a gasp almost, as her raised knee dropped to one side, making the frills bounce and stretch against her naked thigh. "Quickly, please. Yashim, I want you to do it. Ah!"

It was a tiny cry, like a bird, and Yashim was there, while her hand slid down the muscles of his back, dragging at his shirt, snatching at it, catching the hem. She opened her thighs, and as he pressed forward she squeezed her thighs together for a fraction—a fraction of resistance that seemed to be also a wince of pleasure, and then both of them thrust, she from the bed, he from his knees between her knees. Natasha groaned, bit her lip, and her chin was rising, the smooth skin of her neck tightening into hollows and cords, taut, abandoned, oblivious.

She spoke only to cajole him, to ask him to go harder, to go faster, to go slower: to hold her there, to touch her thighs and buttocks, while she dug her fingers into his back.

Yashim let go: he who was always measured, always in control, was allowed this once to let his mind go free. "Do it," she gasped: and she freed him from the pain; "Now! More!" and his memory was dissolved into a sweet now, a ravenous more, so that his whole body seemed to echo with her commands, her rising gasps, seemed to ache with the ache of her arms, now taut against his back, now flung akimbo over her head, driven by a need and a longing that was her longing, and her need, too.

She came with the same startled cry with which she had called him to her; with a flush that rose in her cheeks, the color coming and going over her neck like the shudders and the stillnesses of her hips. Sleepily she turned her head and gave him the flicker of a smile.

He smiled back, and felt her fingers running through his damp hair.

50

THE blood gathered in dark clots, coagulating gradually against the severed skin, hardening the dull surface of the drop that would never fall now that the blood was growing cool and had stopped flowing. Beneath it, on the floorboards, the flies had clustered already in the pool.

It was red in the bowl, too, where La Piuma had so carefully rinsed one hand with the other, paring the little moons of cloying blood from every fingernail, one by one. Not so much blood, there: yet it was enough to stain the water, so red and dark it had seemed that the basin was sloppy with pure blood.

Blood and water. Water and blood. It was a kind of transubstantiation.

51

"Is this how exiles make love, Yashim? Fiercely? Forgetfully?"

She touched his eyelids, twice. Yashim blinked and smiled. "Am I such an exile?"

"No," she admitted gravely. "No, you're not." She leaned back, propping her cheek on her palm, looking at him.

She shifted her leg and scratched his bare calf with the heel of her buttoned boot.

"Ouch."

A mischief came into her eyes, and she laughed softly.

"Very *Arabian Nights*, after all. I'm glad you didn't take me to the palace."

"Me, too." He meant it. He felt giddy and full of joy, daring to hope that in an instant of forgetting he had forever escaped something he had always been unable to forget. And yet he did not want to think. "Are you hungry?"

"As a horse."

Yashim got up, dancing into his pantaloons. Natasha's slim bare legs scissored on the divan: she had never even removed her bodice. The thought of her utterly and gloriously naked made him hop as he dragged the pantaloons to his waist. Natasha saw, and laughed.

"I see I was wrong about exile."

Yashim drew the strings tight, and padded over to the kitchen. He struck a light and lit two lamps.

He made her a simple omelet. There was fresh bread from the Libyan baker, and cheese and pickles from the picnic.

"I should go," she said finally, when they had eaten. "They get cross at the palace if I'm late."

He began to dress. "Do you need another shawl? It can be cold on the water."

"Perhaps you'll sit close beside me, Yashim, and keep me from it."

Yashim blew out the lamps, blinking as his eyes adjusted to the moonlight. She stood beside him, and he heard her soft breath.

He had only to turn his head, and he could kiss her. But she stopped him first, with her fingers on his lips.

"No kisses," she whispered. "All the rest."

He took her hand and led her down the dark stairs.

52

AND what of the boys, those ardent revolutionaries, all this while? Still dreaming of a new dawn, as the real one broke over the ruined farmhouse where they had spent yet another uncomfortable, frightened night? The autumn dew lay heavy on the grass, bent and dark where animals had slipped past in the night: the tiny, broken track of a stoat, the stripe of a low-slung fox, the dark, dewy pools where a deer had jumped across the clearing.

As the sun rose, it revealed a world festooned with gossamer threads that shivered and sparkled in the light. They laced the grasses, spun from the grass to the trees, ran almost invisible from the window ledges and lintel of the old, half-broken door. They enclosed the revolutionaries, and their prisoner, in a fine-meshed net, all but invisible to those who were caught up in it. And another net was drawing closer around them every moment.

It was Czartoryski who drew it to their attention. He had woken up at that moment when the sky, from being true black night, begins to lean toward the dawn. Far off, too far away for his old ears to perfectly hear, a muezzin was calling the morning prayer; or perhaps it was a cock on a distant farm. He had, until that moment, slept well. The fact surprised him, for in Paris he was a notoriously light and difficult sleeper, prone to bouts of indigestion—and irritation, if anyone in his household made the slightest noise. He went to bed each night, safe and sound, and fell into uneasy sleep; but here, on a blanket pulled across the straw, in imminent danger of execution . . .

He reached out and slapped the nearest man. "I sleep here," he roared out cheerfully, "like a Lithuanian corn merchant!"

He chuckled to see Giancarlo's red face emerge snarling from the blanket, his fair hair stuck with wisps of straw.

His appetite! That was what had woken him, no doubt: a litany of deep, satisfactory grumblings in his belly. They had turned in as soon as it grew dark: the bandits were too afraid to have a light, or even keep a fire, at night. He had slept a whole ten hours, and had the hunger of— who? Gargantua?

He rolled to one side and poked a shrouded figure in the straw.

"My hunger is Rabelaisian," he growled. Fabrizio responded by snuggling deeper into his cocoon, pulling the blanket up around his ears. "Hear me? Breakfast?"

He laughed and wondered if he was going mad. Not he. The truth was, for years Czartoryski had led a life of intrigue, diplomacy, incessant work, incessant worry. He suspected everyone he came into contact with. He had pots of money, as the English would say: a staff of fourteen at the Hôtel Lambert, another twenty-five in the country. *"Bonjour, mon prince. Bonsoir, mon prince. Voulez-vous prendre une tisane? Une bière? Château Lafite '02?"* The valet brought his correspondence to him on a silver tray, each morning sharp, at nine o'clock. Voluminous letters, begging letters, letters of support, letters from Poland, from Germany, from socialists, from liberals, from log cabins on the Ohio, from an Englishwoman who sought advice on her Pomeranians, coded letters from his agents, terse communications from his bankers—*"O Prince, mon prince, vous souvenez-vous de moi? Répondez-moi. Un seul mot . . ."*

Answers, decisions, ulcers.

And now all he had to fear was death, which comes to everyone. All he had to do was wait. No calls, no salvers, no letters. Not a care in the world.

He lay back and rubbed his stomach. For the next hour he amused and tortured himself by making an inventory of the finest breakfasts he had ever eaten. He set to thinking about the food he had left untouched. White butter subsiding into the heart of a warm roll, condemned by a crumpled napkin. A dish of eggs *en cocotte* that he had once petulantly mashed and sent back, cold, to the kitchen. Silver dishes of deviled kidneys, of crepes so buttery they glistened over the tiny spirit lamp that chafed the dish; mounds of fresh croissants, baskets overflowing with brioches, baguettes whiter inside than the snow in Warsaw, or the inside of a redhead's thigh!

Ah! He began to compile a list of all the beauties he had kissed, had flirted with, had actually come to grips with—lots. Polish, Russian, German, French, parlormaids and duchesses. He thought of them all, and began to pile them up, like brioches, in his mind—mounds of sugary girls, their breasts as white as confectioner's paste, all limbs and dimples and . . .

He stretched and the straw crackled underneath him.

The terms of his confinement had unquestionably improved. The more these buffoons thought about killing him, the easier those terms became. From the stool where they had bound him at first, he had graduated to a rough wall, and a beaten earth floor, and a heavy rope around his waist. It would not do: they saw that. They had thought long and hard about the problem: how to tie him in such a way that he could move about but not untie the knots himself.

It was he, Czartoryski, prince, diplomat, flower and hope of his unhappy nation, who had proposed the obvious solution.

"Why don't you simply let me loose?"

Where could he run to—supposing that at his great age he still could run? The house was hardly well barricaded, but the windows were quite high, and he would make a fearful noise trying to climb out. Well, would he give them his word?

"I am prepared to give you my word, as a prince of Poland, that I will make no effort to escape."

Face to face, hands in the open. No crossed fingers, no tricks. Czartoryski scorned the vulgarity. For a nobleman of his rank and lineage, only his oaths to God could be considered binding.

53

PALEWSKI was wrong if he thought he had seen the last of Father Doherty. The cleric had even taken up position in his dreams. He was standing by the window and urging Palewski to stir himself because the streets were full of Orthodox bishops, baying for blood.

"Get up, man! It's death! Death, I tell you! It starts with blood and ends with jostling in the street, so it does."

Palewski woke up with a start, and it was the dream again, with Father Doherty wild-eyed at the end of the sofa, shaking Palewski's feet and talking urgently of death and blood. Palewski closed his eyes, and then opened them with a start.

"Wha—what are you talking about? Where's Marta?"

And Marta was there, close beside him, wringing her hands.

"It's the priest, kyrie. He seems to be out of his mind."

"Get me coffee, there's a good girl. Don't mind him. Just coffee, Marta. Quick as you can."

"You must wake up, Palewski! Holy Mary and Joseph!"

Palewski inched himself upright against the arm of the sofa, and winced. "All right, Father. Sit down. Sit. Take a deep breath."

Father Doherty sank his head almost between his knees: Palewski could see the nape of his neck, and his grimy collar. He hoped Marta would be quick with the coffee.

Doherty finally raised his head, with his fingers pressed against his eyebrows, and groaned.

"I went this morning to see the Italians, Palewski. Meaning to say goodbye, you know." The idea seemed to dislodge him: he slid a hand to his mouth and heaved. "I—I—went in, up the stairs," he continued, slowly, parsing his words like a patient child, "and . . ."

"What?" Palewski said sharply. For the first time he felt uneasy. "What, man?"

"I knocked." Doherty's eyes were wide as he made the gesture. "No answer. I pushed the door—it wasn't locked—" He gulped. "There was blood all over the floor."

"How could you tell?"

"I—I called out. 'Who's here?' The blood was sticking on my shoes. And when I looked, it was everywhere. On the floor, on the walls. Everywhere. Like a shambles, man. An abattoir."

Palewski looked horrified. "Go on."

"I wanted to go in—but then I heard a noise. Clicks, like an insect or a door, or I don't know what. God forgive me, I was afraid then. I can't quite remember how I came out. I thought of you, Palewski. We have to do something."

Palewski's face was drawn. "I can't move. We must get Yashim."

Marta came in with the coffee for Palewski and his visitor.

"Unless you'd prefer something stronger?" Palewski said. But Doherty cradled the little cup in his hands.

"I followed the coffee," Yashim announced from the doorway.

"Yashim—thank God. Get him a cup, Marta." When the door had closed he said: "Father Doherty's been to the Italians' apartment. Blood, Yashim. On the walls, on the floor."

"So much blood. I—I came away."

"He heard some sort of clicking noise. He thought there was somebody in there."

"Very well. Can you show me what you saw?"

Doherty took a deep breath. "I can show you the place. But—"

"I know the way. You don't have to come in."

At the front door they met Marta, who presented Yashim with a cup. Yashim took a gulp of the coffee, and steered the priest out into the street.

"What prompted you to go to the flat, Father?"

"I'm leaving Istanbul in a day or so. I hadn't seen them in a while, and I wished to make my farewells. They are so foolish, Yashim. Foolish but still young."

They struck off downhill, into the warren of ill-made streets that led to the port.

"It's not far. Not far at all. But this morning, coming up—with that behind me—it seemed to take hours. Oh, Jesus."

When they arrived at the gateway to the courtyard, Yashim told Doherty to wait. Stillness reigned in the darkened hallway. Ahead, the stairs rose to a gallery that encircled the little backyard. Yashim went up slowly, keeping to the wall. He paused and glanced back over his shoulder.

Was it his imagination, or had the shadow widened a fraction beneath the hallway door?

At the top of the stairs he found the door shut. Yashim turned the handle: the catch clicked and the door swung open.

A cloud of flies rose from the floor, buzzed, and settled back.

A couple of low inlaid tables stood by a divan covered in a printed quilt. The cushions against the wall were arranged neatly, point upward, in a tidy row. A book lay facedown on the divan. It was unbound, but its title page was written in a language Yashim did not recognize. The author's name was Kierkegaard, and Yashim remembered that Birgit had talked about him, in the woods.

Birgit and Giancarlo. Fabrizio and Rafael. He stood motionless in the silent room. He remembered them all from the picnic in the woods, Giancarlo stripped for swimming, pale and muscular as he stooped over Birgit on the grass and dashed the wet hair from his eyes; Fabrizio, wiry and dark, slipping into the water secretly, like an otter, shy of the girls watching; and Rafael beside them, smiling awkwardly because he had refused to swim, twirling his cap between his fingers. It was like an exquisite old miniature painting in his memory, flattened, foreshortened, each character in the picture taking up his or her particular space. Natasha's dark head bent over Birgit's fair one. Both girls laughing at a private joke, glancing at Rafael.

He crossed the room, hesitating between two doors. The one on the left opened into a small room with a single latticed window overlooking the street. Some clothes were folded neatly on top of a chest of drawers, men's clothes, and on the divan opposite the window were two cushions less carefully positioned than the cushions in the main room. Rafael and Fabrizio? The window was shut but the room smelled fresh and clean.

The other room must have belonged to Birgit and Giancarlo. The boy used it for sleeping, and making love, presumably, but it was much more hers than his, a boudoir scattered with pots and bottles and all the girlish tools and devices Yashim recognized from the harem— tweezers, a small razor with its blade carefully tucked into the handle, a single pearl earring lurking behind a pot of cream. A mosquito net dropped to the divan from a wooden ring suspended from the ceiling, and the door of an old armoire bulged with pale striped skirts and white petticoats.

Birgit was there, but not the boy. Her neck was open in a wide smile of welcome, her bloody head flung back over the edge of the divan, her hair stiff and matted where it had cascaded to the floor beneath a water-fall of blood.

Yashim walked slowly around the divan. His lips were drawn into a downward curve that hollowed his cheeks; only with effort could he maintain his reluctant gaze. It was only ten feet from one side of the divan to the other, but to Yashim it was like ten miles, ten years, each step harder than the last.

He went next door and slumped to the floor, his back to the window, and for many minutes he sat wrapped in his own arms, wondering what he should do.

He would inform the *kadi*. A priest would be needed for the burial, which must happen within hours; but the *kadi* was the point of justice.

A *kadi*, a priest—and a consul, for the Italian boys. Where were they?

The blood on the walls was dry. He took a deep breath and went back into the bedroom and knelt by the divan, assessing the condition of the blood and the degree of movement in her limbs.

Father Doherty said he had heard a noise, as if someone was moving about. But Yashim was certain that Birgit was long dead when Doherty arrived. The nights were cooler now, and that affected the onset and the passing of rigor mortis. Maybe she had been killed last night.

Natasha had left her with Giancarlo around six o'clock, when she met Yashim and they went back to his flat. Rafael and Fabrizio were not at home.

He examined the front door. There was no sign of a forced entry: no broken wood, no splinters around the lock. Perhaps Birgit herself had opened the door to her killer. Suspecting nothing. Opening her door to someone she already knew.

She didn't know many people in Istanbul.

Once again he had an image of the the picnic. A tableau: Giancarlo and Birgit, and the two boys, the dark Sicilian and the solemn intellectual, and Natasha, all laughing under the trees, unaware that within days one of them would be dead. He blinked. It was not, he sensed, quite the right picture. Natasha and Birgit, the dark and the fair; and the three boys. He saw himself standing at the edge of the pool, looking back. Paintings dissolved when you stepped up close; the picnic scene was touched by dark strokes he had not noticed on the day: shadows under the trees, the dark empty windows of the ruined house. Doherty's hat on the grass.

There was a knock on the door and Yashim jumped.

"Yashim?"

"I'm coming, Father. We must go back to Palewski's."

"Palewski's, yes. That's a good idea. I'll—I'll go now, then. You can catch me up."

Yashim let him go. There would be a priest, but perhaps it would not have to be Doherty.

He opened the door quickly, and called after him.

"Yes?" Doherty was on the stairs.

"When you came in up here, earlier—how far did you come?"

He could see the white moon of Doherty's face in the gloom of the hall.

"Well, I—I just stepped in. One step, ah, maybe two? Enough to—you know. Is there someone, well, is anybody there?"

"I'll join you at the residency."

He moved to the wall and watched the priest go out. He stood, watching, for several minutes.

At last he closed the door behind him and went downstairs and pushed at the door in the hallway. It opened easily and he went inside.

The room was dirty. The walls were a muddy yellowish gray, and a gray muslin, thick with dust, hung across the window. The air smelled stale.

Someone stirred on the divan.

"Who are you? You can't come in here." A tuft of black hair and then a face appeared above the blanket.

"My name is Yashim. Are you the caretaker?"

"I'm the landlord. It's my house."

"What's your name?"

"Ghika. It's my house. You've come to see the Franks?"

"Are they here?"

Ghika rubbed his face. "I don't know. Take a look, if you're so interested."

Yashim heard the hesitation. "I've been up already." He took a step farther into the room.

Ghika propped himself up on one elbow.

"Earlier," Yashim said, "you saw the priest?"

"What if I did? You don't scare me."

"Upstairs scared me."

The man's slippers were just inside the door, where he kicked them off. Yashim bent down and picked one up. "But it didn't scare you."

"Scare me, scare you, I don't know what you mean. You can put my slipper down."

But Yashim did not put it down. Ghika, who saw everything, barely saw him move; but he felt the blow between his ribs, and the wrench as Yashim took him by the hair.

His head snapped back and he gasped.

Yashim wiped his mouth for him, on the sole of the slipper.

"Taste it, Ghika?" he hissed. "Blood."

He flung him back onto the divan.

"That's the blood from the floor upstairs. You knew she was alone?" Yashim knew he was starting the wrong way, but he didn't care. Fury possessed him: the good girl dead, the flies buzzing, and this creeping lizard who pattered through pools of blood in his slippered feet.

His fury almost made him miss the knife.

Ghika put up his hand to rub his neck. His hand dropped and something just caught the light as the blade whirled through the air. Yashim swiveled automatically, mechanically, too late to stop the point from sinking into his arm. A moment earlier, the target had been his heart.

Quick as a lizard, Ghika was off the divan and swept past Yashim on his way to the door. Yashim gripped the hilt of the knife with a curse and pulled it out, delicately, trying not to rip the skin.

He heard Ghika's feet pounding across the hall. Shame swept over him, rooting him to the spot. He heard the crash of the door. He looked at the knife in his hand.

And felt the hot sting of the stab wound in his arm, and saw the blood welling up between his fingers as he clutched his sleeve.

54

YASHIM advanced grimly into Palewski's drawing room. All the way back he had been working out how he should break the news, but now he had no clever ways, no gentleness.

"Birgit is dead."

"Oh, Christ."

"Somebody cut her throat."

Palewski turned pale. "Birgit? Why"—and then he noticed Yashim's arm. "You're bleeding."

Yashim shrugged his waistcoat off and let it slide to the floor. "Marta's coming. I'll be all right." He didn't want to look at Palewski. His arm felt numb.

Doherty rose from a window seat. "You're hurt?"

"Get the brandy, Doherty," Palewski said. "Come here, Yash. Let's get that shirt off."

Yashim sat wearily on the divan. Palewski helped him tug off the shirt and looked closely at the wound. He pinched it between his fingers. "The brandy, man." As the skin opened he sloshed the liquid into the wound and Yashim winced.

"Hold still. It's the best thing for this stuff. I had some better, but it's gone."

Marta came in with bandages and a salve, but when she saw what Palewski had done she nodded. "It's good, even if you stink."

The men were silent while Marta applied the bandages to Yashim's arm. "I can fetch you tea," she said simply.

When the door had closed, Yashim told his story. Doherty interrupted, with comments and exclamations—"Holy Jesus!" "I was right"—until Palewski told him to shut up.

"Forgive me, Father. Would you mind?" Palewski shook his head. "Who would kill Birgit, Yashim?"

Yashim trickled a little brandy into a glass. "I'm sorry."

"Ach, Yashim. I had her destined for happy things," he said simply. "Lovers, husband, children. I thought she'd eat cake and grow fat."

Yashim knew what Palewski meant. Birgit had inspired them all with feelings of contentment: her gentle irony, her beautiful blue eyes, her delicious curves. None of them had seen anything but a generous loveliness. Not a man with a knife. It was as if they bore responsibility for being blind.

"No sign of the boys. I found the man who claims to own the place. I lost my temper—he'd been up there, treading in the blood. Then I threatened him. He stabbed me with a throwing knife, and bolted."

"Was it him, then?"

"I'm not sure. He would have known who was at home, and who'd gone out, that's true. He had a knife." Yes: guilty or not, Ghika belonged to the dark fog that had crept upstairs.

"That landlord's a shifty one," Doherty remarked.

"He knew what had happened," Yashim went on. "He didn't tell anyone, but on the other hand, he didn't try to hide. I found his footprints in the blood by the door, and I showed him the blood on the soles of his slippers. Whether he's a killer, I don't know." He thought of the dingy room, and Ghika lying on the divan. "I think he went upstairs to look around, found her dead, and probably stole whatever he could lay his hands on." Yashim worked his arm. "I'd better go and find the *kadi*."

The priest uncorked the brandy and tilted it to his lips. "Needed that," he muttered, wiping his mouth on the back of his hand. "I'd better get on."

He paused at the door, but Yashim lay back looking faint and Palewski just jerked his head. The door slammed.

Palewski nodded at the door. "Yesterday Doherty was here ranting about blood and hellfire and all the rest, and I dismissed him because— well, because it isn't how things are. Blood doesn't just well up on the street, by some divine or diabolical command. And yet—it has done. At least, it's a better explanation than anything I can think of. Czartoryski vanishes into thin air. A good and harmless girl . . ." He shook his head. "It's like some biblical plague, hitting without rhyme or reason. The city devouring itself."

"I know," Yashim said. "I know exactly."

55

A young district magistrate accompanied Yashim to the Italians' apartment. He brought two orderlies along with a stretcher and a canvas cover.

There was no sign of the Italians. No sign of Ghika, either.

The young *kadi* went very white when he saw the corpse.

"This is a crime of Nazarenes," he said, as the orderlies maneuvered the body onto the stretcher. "It is not in our imagination, such a violation of a woman. There is no way a Muslim could have done this."

Yashim, who had been looking for jewelry or money, stopped his search for a moment.

"Say that again."

"A Muslim could not have done this. Many other crimes, yes. I have seen many bad things. But this kind of killing? I will not believe it." He shrugged. "She was a Nazarene, and she died at the hand of one of her own. Come, we will leave this to the orderlies."

In the main room the *kadi* opened a window and stood looking out into the court.

Yashim prowled the room, opening the drawers of the chest, running his fingers along the shelves. He could hear the men arguing in low voices through the door.

"What are you doing, Yashim efendi?"

"Looking for her jewels."

"She doesn't need them anymore," the *kadi* said. He gave Yashim a thin-lipped smile. "You saw her wear them?"

"Once, yes."

"Probably the killer took them," the *kadi* said. "Perhaps that was why she was killed."

"Ghika could have taken them."

"Ghika, the Italian men. All these sorts of people love money." He stood at the window patting his hands together. "I have been wondering, Yashim efendi, if this is strictly any affair of mine. My concerns are with the faithful, not with Franks."

"But this is your district," Yashim reminded him. "Your jurisdiction."

"These people, these unbelievers, come and go," the *kadi* said. "I don't mind telling you, this sort of inquiry doesn't look good. It takes me away from my people, and gives them a—a—" He bunched his fingers together and shook them in the air. "A wrong association."

Yashim looked around from a stack of bottles. "You mean—you won't investigate?"

"It will be long, it will be in many languages I do not understand, among people for whom I feel—nothing. Do you see? On the one hand, I am a young *kadi*, at the beginning of my career. Who knows?" He looked up into the sky. "But on the other hand, the old ones watch me all the time. They think me inexperienced. They would think I am like the others of my age, who are Muslims on the outside but Franks inside. Those men who read Frankish books, and study how to dress and talk like giaours."

He leaned against the windowsill, silhouetted against the daylight where Yashim could not read the expression on his face.

"In this business, this shocking business, the old men and my superiors would see only this. The giaour *kadi*! The young man who runs around for giaours! Sling the mud, that's the proverb. Even if it doesn't stick, the stain will remain."

Yashim stepped up to him. He had found nothing in the flat. "I understand that a *kadi* follows justice, above all else."

"Of course, of course, I was not forgetting justice. That's what we all seek, isn't it? But, Yashim efendi, among the giaours I am like a dog, who can bark but not talk."

He laid his hand on Yashim's shoulder. Yashim sucked in his breath. "It's sore. The inflammation."

"Yes, I forgot." He dropped his hand but his voice remained soft and low. "I don't say you are a Frank on the inside, Yashim efendi, because you're not. You are a Muslim, and a Turk. I see that about you. But you know the ways of these sorts of people, hmm? Their talk, how they live, that sort of thing. Yes?"

He put a hand to his breast and bowed, smiling. "So we will have the Franks arrested, and also this Ghika, as soon as any of them appear. This is my job, and no one will think me a giaour if I am swift, and act without favor. Let them go to prison. You, my friend, must gather the necessary evidence—keep it simple, I need hardly add, we don't want the judgment to involve many hours, and foreign speeches. Simple evidence. If it's the Greek, if it's the Italian—pshht!" He shrugged. "One of them did it. Maybe all of them, together. You know how these people are, working together, plotting and such. So that way we are swift, and not afraid to show all men are equal. I'm glad we can do this."

"We work together," Yashim echoed.

"Exactly." Either the *kadi* missed the irony in Yashim's tone, or he preferred to ignore it. "I will provide men, to set a trap. If those giaours—those Franks, or the Greek, turn up here, my men will pounce."

"And if they don't turn up?"

The *kadi* waved a hand. "I'm sure they will. By all means look for them if you can. Meanwhile, I'll put two men in downstairs."

The orderlies emerged from Birgit's room with the stretcher.

"Take it down," the *kadi* said. He turned to Yashim. "I'll have her sent to the Catholic cemetery beyond Taksim."

Yashim wondered if Birgit was a Catholic. He had a vague idea that the Danes were mostly Protestant, like other northerners. Doherty might know, if indeed it mattered where you were buried, or how the rites were observed, once you were dead.

It would matter to her people, he supposed. Her mother and father, the brothers and sisters she might have left behind, a family which no one in Istanbul knew anything about; friends and neighbors in a faraway country.

They followed the stretcher bearers downstairs. Birgit's corpse was covered by a sheet.

"I'll start by looking through Ghika's room," Yashim said.

The *kadi* nodded, and hurried out.

It took Yashim less than a minute to find the jewelry: it had been carelessly thrust under the mattress of the divan. There were several silver bangles, a string of pearls, and an earring that matched the one he had found upstairs, which Ghika must have missed. If Ghika had killed her he would have had time to hide the jewelry somewhere safer.

When he had pocketed the jewels he scanned the room again. He had found a bottle under the divan, and he set it upright on the small table. Otherwise there was little furniture, nowhere to hide anything. He squatted down and patted the floorboards one by one. In the far corner, beyond the grimy window, he felt movement.

The board lifted easily. The nails had been cut off on the underside, and in the cavity below, Yashim found several hundred silver *kuruş*, wrapped in a dirty cloth. He put it back where he had found it, let the dingy curtain fall back into place, and went out, closing the door.

56

"CZARTORYSKI was lifted off the street," Yashim explained as he sat with Palewski in the drawing room. "Birgit, who is romantically attached to the boy who wants to overthrow the Pope, has been murdered. The boys have disappeared.

"Is there any connection? That's what I can't make out. On the face of it, yes, obviously: Czartoryski and the Italians are liberals, whose common target is the settlement made at Vienna almost thirty years ago. A settlement that locks both their countries in an iron grip.

"But then, as you said yourself, the Italians aren't really serious, are they? What did you call them? The Baklava Club?"

Palewski acknowledged the remark with a mirthless snort. "And Birgit didn't care about politics."

"Birgit, no." Yashim ran his fingers through his hair. "I was such an idiot to provoke Ghika. He's the only one who could possibly say what happened last night. I—I was enraged, sickened. Stupid."

"It's done, Yashim. And Ghika will come back. For the money."

"I hope you're right. He'll need to drink." He told his friend about the bottle beneath the divan.

"Revolting," Palewski said. "I hate drunks. It's what puts me off Doherty."

"You were the one who befriended him."

"Mea culpa. And I introduced him to the Italians."

"Yes. He liked them."

"Liked them? Doherty's one of those who'll go anywhere for a swig. They had the champagne."

"And why is he in Istanbul?"

"As far as I can make out he's come to ransack the Patriarchal Archives. Hunting for old documents. I have a hunch, based on speculation, prejudice, and various hints he's dropped, that he's looking for anything that might bolster the Pope's claim to territorial dominion in Italy. Something like the Donation of Constantine, only more plausible."

Yashim looked blank.

"You never came across the Donation of Constantine? Big thing in its day. The emperor Constantine divided the Roman Empire into an eastern and a western empire, when he founded his own capital here, at Constantinople. The city of Constantine."

"I know all that."

"So, several centuries later the popes found themselves struggling against the German emperor to be top dog in Europe, arguing over which of them had the right to appoint the bishops and collect the tithes. The Vatican produced a musty old parchment showing that Constantine had handed Europe—the western Roman empire—over to the popes. That was the Donation of Constantine. It shut the Germans up, for a few moments. It wasn't until the fifteenth century, when it was all old hat anyway, that Lorenzo Valla proved it was a forgery. He analyzed its Latin, and it wasn't current in the fourth century. Good bit of detective work, in fact. Egg on the pontifical tiara, and all goes quiet."

"So it was just a piece of wishful thinking?"

"Yes. Unless, of course, Constantine did make the donation, and the Vatican just couldn't prove it."

"Because they couldn't put their hands on it?"

"Exactly. And there have always been rumors that other forms of the donation do exist, confirming the Pope's control of western Europe. They can't be in the Vatican Library, obviously, or we'd have heard about them. After 1054, of course, the schism between the Catholic and Orthodox churches was irrevocable. The Orthodox church would have kept anything to the popes' advantage to themselves. The Greeks hate a schismatic more than an infidel. 'Better the sultan's turban than the bishop's miter,' as they always said."

"It's very ancient history, though," Yashim said dubiously. "This donation."

"Don't underestimate its importance. A foolproof donation would come in rather handy, when the Pope's being assailed by all those liberals—like Giancarlo and his friends—who think he should concentrate more on God and less on Tuscany and Rome. That, I suspect, is why Doherty is in Istanbul. He's ferreting among the Latin documents in the second library of Christendom, after the Vatican. The Patriarchal Archives."

"He's found what he wanted, then. Isn't he going back to Rome?"

Palewski nodded.

"When did he arrive?"

"Three weeks ago. Shortly before the fourteenth. He reminded me of the date at the time, celebrating the Christian victory at Lepanto—it's actually in the mass," Palewski said thoughtfully.

"A lot has happened in those three weeks," Yashim said. His glance fell on Palewski's writing desk. "He sat there, you know, writing you a note. The Italians were all here—and all your Czartoryski letters were in the desk. The whole plan."

"Bah! He's just an old drunk. And he's an Irishman, Yashim. He sympathizes with the Poles."

Yashim stood up. "I need to think," he said. "I'm going to walk."

Palewski called him just as he was going out the door. "Yashim! You can't walk around like that. You're covered in blood, and your shirt's torn."

Yashim looked down at his shirt, as if seeing it for the first time. "All right. I'll go home and change."

57

YASHIM'S landlady put her head out the door as Yashim went by.

"There's a gentleman waiting for you, efendi. A *kadi*. I said he could go in, I hope you don't mind."

"It's all right," Yashim said. "Would you bring me some hot water, hanum efendi? I need to wash."

He went upstairs, expecting to find the young *kadi* with new information. Perhaps he had changed his mind, and wanted the case? It was more likely he'd decided to drop it altogether.

But when he reached his flat, it was not the young, ambitious man who sat on the divan fingering his prayer beads, but the old *kadi* from Taksim.

Yashim greeted him politely, and offered him coffee.

"No, thank you, efendi," the old man said peaceably. "I just came by to hear your thoughts. If you will forgive me. I'm not used to this sort of work."

He noticed the blood on Yashim's sleeve and raised his eyebrows. "You, on the other hand, seem very experienced."

"You're right," Yashim said, with a slight bitterness. "Murder, again. Someone tried to get me, too."

"I am sorry."

Yashim gave him a wan smile. "Would you mind, *kadi*, if I washed my arm? I need to change."

"Not at all. Perhaps we can talk in the meantime."

There was a knock on the door and the landlady came in with a brass jug. "Water for you, Yashim efendi. *Kadi*." She put the jug by the washstand. "What is that? Blood? Your shirt is ruined. Tsk, tsk. Come, give it to me. I'll see what we can do with it."

She helped him off with the shirt: Yashim found he could not lift his arm above his head.

The old *kadi* peered at his wound. "It's a nasty cut. You should have a stitch."

Widow Matalya nodded. "He's right, Yashim efendi. I'll come back with some things. Like the old days," she added cheerfully, thinking of her husband, the sipahi cavalryman.

Yashim poured the water into the washstand and began to sluice his arms.

"I'm afraid I haven't given the case much thought," he confessed. "His shoes were good, but there are too many cobblers in the city. I did wonder if the paper might throw up some sort of lead."

The *kadi* nodded. "I'm glad you say so. It took me much longer to think of that." He took a notebook from his pocket and shook a scrap of paper from its leaves. He smoothed it on his knee. "You wouldn't believe how much paper there is in Istanbul. I took it to the stationers' bazaar, as a matter of fact. Rag, they call it. Yellow rag."

"It's common?"

The *kadi* wagged his head slowly. "Yes and no. For people who so respect the written word, we don't make very much paper. We have beautiful paper for imperial firmans, Korans, and works of calligraphy, it's true, but the ordinary types of paper mostly come from abroad."

"Like this yellow rag?" Yashim dried himself on a towel, dabbing it gently around the wound.

"Strangely enough, no. This is made in the Meander Valley, by a Greek. To make a lot of paper you need to build a big mill by a river, and put a great deal of money into it. This Greek, Anton Staviopolis, came over from Chios after the troubles there. Now he makes many kinds of paper, including this yellow rag."

The widow Matalya pushed the door open. "Now, Yashim efendi, I will sew you up."

Yashim sat on the edge of the divan, where the light was best. "It's interesting, *kadi*. But I don't see that it gets us too far, knowing only the maker."

The *kadi* tilted his head. "As a matter of fact, it gets us farther than you might imagine. They don't sell this paper in the bazaar. Do you know why, Yashim efendi? It's contracted."

"Contracted?"

"This will sting, efendi. Hold tight."

"Yes, contracted. I will talk to him, hanum, and keep his mind off the stitching. Staviopolis found a market for his paper before he built his mill. He talked to people here in Istanbul, and they gave him a good idea. A special paper, a single buyer, and all contracted. That's what it means. Someone signs a contract, and pays him money before he even starts making paper. Maybe even before he has built his mill! That must be how these businessmen operate, I suppose."

Widow Matalya pursed her lips, and drove the needle through Yashim's skin.

"Very likely," Yashim said. "So who buys his paper? Ow."

"Two more," said the widow.

"Can you guess? Who uses a lot of paper these days?"

Yashim squeezed his eyes shut: the stitching hurt. But the old *kadi* was right—the questions kept his mind off the pain. "I'd have said the newspapers. Or the Porte?"

The *kadi* nodded. "But there are many newspapers, and only one government. Staviopolis persuaded the Porte to buy his paper instead of some foreign make. But it wasn't cheaper. Do you know how he managed it?"

"I daresay he sent the officials some boxes of mastic, and a lifetime's supply of *lokum.*" Mastic, the raw ingredient of Turkish delight, was the bedrock of Chios's prosperity.

The *kadi* chuckled. "Maybe. But he also promised the Porte that in return for money and some tax advantages, which would allow him to set up his mill, he would ensure that the paper was specially made for them. How would they know he was telling the truth? He'd make it yellow. Nobody but the government could use that color."

"There," said the widow Matalya. "It's done. I had to make the stitches quite big, but you should have come to me sooner. Now we must keep the wound clean."

"Yellow rag," Yashim murmured, as his landlady began to loop his arm in bandage. "Which suggests your clerk worked for the government. That makes sense. Of course, there's a lot of government these days. All those new departments."

The *kadi* wagged a finger. "When those new departments were created, Staviopolis thought they would use his paper, too. Some of them did. Some of them didn't. Perhaps he couldn't get them enough mastic?" The *kadi* chuckled. "Some of them insisted on having their own supply. The so-called Department for Religious Affairs, for instance, uses green paper. Quite a respectful touch. Staviopolis himself provides it."

Yashim smiled: the Department for Religious Affairs was heartily despised by traditionalists. "You could write an essay on the subject."

"Perhaps I will. An essay on the absurdity of human vanity. Yes, that might amuse someone. In the meantime, the yellow paper is still used exclusively by the older offices of state. The office of the grand vizier. The office of the foreign ministry."

Yashim felt a surge of admiration for the old *kadi*, who had done such patient footslogging.

"The next thing would be to see if they have anyone missing." He opened a chest and found a clean shirt.

The old *kadi* nodded. "Yes, I did that. The grand vizier's roster is complete. No one missing there." He gave Yashim an amused look. "At the Ministry of Foreign Affairs, on the other hand, I spoke to a very busy young man, who said they always had people coming and going. He didn't think anyone had been reported off work, but he had so much to do he couldn't check further. He was tidying up his desk, and cleaning his nibs."

Yashim struggled into his clean shirt. The *kadi*'s discovery might mean nothing, but it was suggestive, nonetheless. He knew from experience that it was always difficult to discard a new theory: it tended to roll around the mind, gathering corroborating detail like fluff. All the way home he had wrestled with the thought of Doherty discovering the details of Czartoryski's visit as he rifled Palewski's escritoire. But perhaps that was not how it happened. The Ministry of Foreign Affairs was Midhat Pasha's office, another potential source of a leak. The busy young man had denied the possibility that anyone had gone missing—but the *kadi* didn't necessarily believe him, and Yashim had growing respect for the *kadi*'s judgment.

The coincidence was troubling, if a clerk at the ministry was murdered a day after the attack on Palewski and the prince.

It didn't take much imagination to suppose that the clerk gave Czartoryski's anonymous assassin the necessary information—and signed his own death warrant into the bargain. The dead tell no tales—and someone had been careful to ensure that the body was not easily identified.

It was a lot of weight to hang from a flimsy scrap of colored paper.

58

OUT at the farm, only the condemned prisoner seemed cheerful and carefree.

"It's this place I can't stand," Rafael confessed. "The silence. The dark nights. Every time a twig snaps I want to scream."

Giancarlo threw a stone into the pond. Rafael scowled as it splashed in the water.

They could hear Czartoryski whistling inside the house.

"That's what I can't stand," Fabrizio said. "It's like we're his prisoners."

"That's obvious," Giancarlo muttered.

"Obvious, is it? Big apologies."

"He quoted Dante to me yesterday," Rafael said peaceably, to change the subject. Lately Fabrizio and Giancarlo had taken to incessant sniping at each other.

Giancarlo sneered. "It's more Shakespeare than Dante. Fabrizio as Hamlet."

"Me?"

"Why not? You had a job and you flunked it—"

"The gun was broken—"

"—and now you've waited so long none of us can do anything."

"The—gun—was—*broken*," Fabrizio spat out between clenched teeth.

"So you toss it into the street. Palewski's gun." Giancarlo shook his handsome head in disbelief.

"No one's going to find us here," Rafael assured him.

"Nor can we ever leave. We'll be thirty years old, and still here."

"Someone has to leave," Fabrizio pointed out. "We need more food."

Giancarlo flung another stone into the pool. "I should see Birgit," he said. "Let her know what's going on, at least."

"What *is* going on?"

"See Birgit? That's a pleasure trip," Fabrizio said. "You go to your mistress while we sit about here waiting."

"Is that all you can think about?"

"What do you mean by that?"

"Complaining you don't have a woman."

"Complaining?" Two red spots appeared on Fabrizio's cheeks. "I could have anyone," he said, snapping his fingers. "And I don't have to pay for it, either."

"Pay?" Giancarlo echoed incredulously, and spat. "Birgit follows me because she's a woman. A woman who likes a real man."

"Of course. Not because you keep her. Not because you buy her jewels and clothes and food. She comes because she 'loves you.'"

"Fabrizio, Fabrizio." Rafael knew he had gone too far.

Giancarlo snatched up a stone and skimmed it; there was a crack and Fabrizio grabbed his forehead.

"Ow! *Cazzo!* I can't see!"

Rafael dashed forward. "Let me look," he said urgently, taking Fabrizio by the shoulders. "It's all right."

"It's bleeding," Fabrizio insisted, looking at his fingers. "I'm fucking bleeding."

He began to struggle against Rafael. "Just let me go! I'll kill him for this."

Giancarlo stood up. "I'm going to get food," he announced.

"Another beautiful day!" the prince declared, close by. "I intend to swim."

They all turned. Their prisoner stood naked in the sunshine, holding a blanket between his fingers. His skin was very white, and he looked magnificent with his broad chest and his gray curls, the handsome patrician face, the slender bridge to his nose, the level, appraising eyes. He seemed a fine specimen of natural authority, enhanced rather than diminished by his being stark naked.

He advanced majestically to the edge of the pool. He let the blanket drop to the ground and waded into the water. When Rafael caught sight of the stockings of mud on his white legs, he groaned. They could never kill him now.

The prince waded in as far as his hips, then sank into the water. He swam for ten minutes, ignoring them. They stood foolishly on the bank, watching. Dragonflies hovered and darted through the warm air. The prince sank under the surface of the water and reappeared, blowing, a few yards farther on. Then he turned on his back and began to lazily circumnavigate the pool.

When he emerged, he stood dripping on the bank and stretched his arms. Then he bent down, retrieved his blanket, and walked back to the house.

At the door he seemed to remember something, and turned. "Lunch would be good. In about an hour."

Nobody spoke. Fabrizio rubbed his head thoughtfully. Rafael glanced at Giancarlo, who cocked his chin.

"Someone should go. We haven't anything to eat."

The situation was absurd; they all felt it. Czartoryski was supposed to be dead, and no one had planned on staying at the farm. No one had brought any extra food, beyond the cold chicken and a loaf of bread.

"We need some wine," Fabrizio suggested. It was a climbdown, but he did not mean it to be complete. "Take Rafael."

Rafael shook his head. "It's all right," he said.

"No, I'd like you to go." Fabrizio nodded significantly at Rafael, raising his eyebrows.

Giancarlo caught his glance. "Very well, he can come," he said. "Will you—you know?"

"I'll be all right. And he won't get away, if that's what you mean." Fabrizio smiled. "It's maybe like having a pee. You can't do it when someone else is watching."

Giancarlo nodded, and went to fetch his wallet.

When he had gone, Rafael said: "I should stay."

"Look, we need food, whatever happens. If—if I do *the thing*"—

Fabrizio added, and pulled a face—"we still need to eat. And Giancarlo will take hours if he's let out on his own. Seeing Birgit—she'll take care of that, won't she? He might not come back until tomorrow." A thought struck him. "He might never come back."

"How can you say that!" Rafael was shocked. "It's his cause, too."

Fabrizio looked at him with bright dark eyes. "Is it? Is it your cause, even? Or mine? You know, Rafael, it isn't some fiend of the Vatican we've got prisoner, is it? He's Polish, like Palewski, or so he says. He calls himself a prince but he told me he's in exile."

Rafael spoke in a low voice: "He lives in Paris."

"So whose side is he on? Palewski's? I am, too."

"What does it mean?"

"Maybe La Piuma's cocked up."

"I don't think so. It was La Piuma's warning that got us out of Rome before the police caught up."

Fabrizio laid his hand on Rafael's arm. "La Piuma. It was just a note. Who is La Piuma?"

"We've been through this, Fabrizio. La Piuma—it's just a code name. Without the code, we'd all be vulnerable, you know that."

"We've got the code. And I feel vulnerable." He raised his chin. "That's it, Rafael. While you're in town, go and see Palewski yourself, and ask him about the prince. Who he is. Not directly, obviously. Just fish—see what you can find out."

Rafael looked doubtful. "He'd smell a rat, Fabrizio. We aren't supposed to know anything about the prince. Not that he came to Istanbul, nothing. I can't just start a conversation about someone I'm never supposed to have heard of."

"All right then, Doherty. The priest. He'll know something about this fellow. See what his politics are. Anything. Check his story, if you can—Paris, all that."

Rafael nodded. "I will." He squeezed Fabrizio's hand. "Good luck. We'll be back as soon as we can."

Giancarlo came out of the farmhouse. "Have you decided?"

"He'll come."

"Fine." He hesitated then stuck out his hand, and they shook hands. *"Courage, mon colonel."*

Fabrizio opened his mouth to speak, but then changed his mind. He stood for a long time at the farmhouse door, shading his eyes as he watched them go.

59

"THE pasha is not here, Yashim efendi," said the secretary; the same secretary who had ushered him into Midhat Pasha's office the day before. "He left a few minutes ago," the young man volunteered. "To go to Topkapi."

"I'll find him there, then. I was on my way . . ." But at the door Yashim turned back. "Actually, we could save Midhat Pasha some trouble. There's a young clerk from the ministry who hasn't been in to work these past two days. The pasha had asked me to keep an eye out for him. I'm afraid I've just forgotten his name. Ahmet . . . Selim . . . Tchah!" He gave a rueful chuckle and tapped his forehead.

"Perhaps you mean Abdullah Ozgem? He's been away for days. Do you have some news?"

"Ozgem, that's it, and, well, yes. Some news, of a kind."

The young official looked around anxiously. "Not here." He beckoned Yashim into a side room and closed the door. "That's not good. Tell me what happened."

Yashim bit his lip. "I don't know that I shouldn't report this directly to the pasha himself," he said hesitantly. "It's just that—well, do you think Ozgem has much experience at this kind of thing?"

The secretary gave a noncommittal shrug. "He's tailed people before," he said.

"I know, but don't you think this one's different? Harder, maybe."

"Because they're foreign? I suppose that makes them less predictable. I don't know. The woman, of course. But why, is there something wrong?"

"I think he may have come under suspicion."

The young man pulled a dubious face. "The Italians are a fairly low priority—low risk. They haven't done anything, as far as I know. Between you and me, we sent Ozgem to cover ourselves, in case anyone thought we were careless about the 'great revolutionary threat' they worry about over there." He smiled. "Pretty routine. I suppose if he's blown his cover, we should pull him off."

So Ozgem had been tailing the Italians, for Midhat Pasha. Now he was dead. Birgit was dead. The Italians had disappeared. Midhat was speaking to the valide.

"Where does Ozgem live?"

"Is it important?" The young man sighed. "Very well."

He was gone for two minutes, returning with a handwritten card.

Yashim walked from the Porte to the palace like a blind man, seeing nothing. His mind was spinning, crammed with thoughts and speculations that rose and fell like caïques in a storm. Pumping the secretary had been child's play, but now he was left with causes and consequences that he struggled to pull into any kind of shape.

If the Italians had discovered they were being watched, the cemetery was a clever place to choose: it would have forced the unlucky Ozgem into the open. That suggested the Baklava Club had something to hide. Something to fear. Something that turned Ozgem's task from routine to dangerous.

The attempt on Palewski's life? He tried to imagine how the Italians would have reacted to the news that Palewski had been shot. They were almost allies, weren't they, his friend without a country and these young men seeking to unite their own? Was an attack on Palewski an attack on them? Or the prelude to an attack? In Istanbul, they said, they felt free: but perhaps the freedom was qualified, after all. Perhaps for all their bravado they lived in fear of papal agents coming after them. Tense, alarmed, they discover that they are being followed. Panicked—and Yashim could well imagine the effect the discovery might have on the three of them—they kill their tail to gain time, and go underground.

So Birgit was at the baths with Natasha. Giancarlo waited for her, at the flat. He got rid of Natasha easily by setting up a tryst. And then what? Birgit refused to go into hiding? Maybe Giancarlo and Birgit agreed it wasn't necessary: after all, she's a Dane and a woman. She's wasn't involved. Maybe they needed her as a link to the outside world.

But they underestimated the ruthlessness of their opponent. Someone who had already fired on Palewski and arranged for Czartoryski to disappear. Someone who that night came to the flat and found Birgit.

Or even Birgit and Giancarlo, together? He killed Birgit. Made Giancarlo, perhaps, give up his friends.

In which case, Yashim thought grimly, the *kadi*'s men were wasting their time. The Italians wouldn't be coming back.

Their bodies—following that of Czartoryski himself, no doubt—would have been dumped this morning. Into the Bosphorus. Into a shallow grave. Lost somewhere in the woods and waters that surrounded the city.

Yashim put out a hand and leaned for a moment against the wall, breathing heavily. It was a steep climb. Two smart young officers in kepis divided at his approach, and slipped past him on either side, still chatting.

Doherty wasn't young and beautiful: he wasn't charged with that sensuality, no, that search for sensual meaning, shared by the young.

Yashim worked his way through the narrow streets at the foot of Ayasofya. Doherty was there because he liked the liquor, and perhaps the attention. He'd come into Palewski's circle quite by chance, always ingratiating, looking to make friends.

Until yesterday, when he'd outraged Palewski with some bigoted remarks. Now he was about to leave, and perhaps he didn't care anymore. Perhaps, as Palewski said, his job was done.

Yashim went past the Fountain of Ahmet III without looking up, as he usually did, at its broad sheltering canopy and the delicate scrollwork on the marble panels.

Could the priest have killed a woman with whom he had joked and laughed that afternoon, beneath the trees?

60

"Ah, Yashim." Midhat Pasha blinked owlishly in the crepuscular shade of the eunuchs' gallery. "I've just come from the valide. I wouldn't go in, if I were you."

Yashim hesitated. "You brought her bad news, my pasha?"

"Pfui. She is no fool. She understands. But yes, for the moment it's a little rain . . ."

"They told me at the ministry that I would find you here, my pasha. I've news for you. Bad news, too, I'm afraid. Abdullah Ozgem, one of your people, was found yesterday at Taksim, dead. He'd been strangled."

Midhat's eyes shrank to the size of currants. "Ozgem? What—how do you know?"

"There was bruising on his neck. He was strangled and thrown over a wall."

But perhaps that was not what Midhat Pasha's question meant: not how the man was killed, but how he knew it was Ozgem.

"We traced him to your department. That is, the *kadi* worked it out from a scrap of paper. It's a long story, my pasha. I'm sorry."

Midhat took a staggered breath. "The *kadi*," he hissed. He had his forefinger pressed into Yashim's chest, and his face was tight. "So be it. So be it. Maybe there is no harm done."

He dropped his hand. "I want to have a report from you. I want to know everything you are doing."

Yashim bowed, and held it, humbly, listening to Midhat Pasha's footsteps retreating down the passage. The gate at the end creaked, and he was gone.

Yashim raised his head, and straightened up. He did not move for some time, but gazed at the gate with unseeing eyes.

He found the valide just as the pasha had warned him: spitting with fury, and looking rather well on it. She was angry enough to have got off the divan and to be standing, majestic in spite of the stick, in the middle of the room. Anger, not artifice, had rouged her cheeks, and her eyes flashed.

"You, Yashim! Have you come to teach me diplomacy, too? No—don't speak. If another man dares to lecture me . . . ! That old fright! That *snake!*"

Yashim folded his hands, saying nothing.

"He advises, does he! Our better interests—tchah! Meddling old fool. What are those interests? The *better* ones? *La!* Midhat, whose only interest has been to escape the curse of his birth in some provincial dung heap, decides them now, does he?" She banged her stick on the floor. "*Sacre bleu!* The valide writes letters at the dictate of every horse-tailed pen pusher! And you, Yashim. Stop simpering and fetch me some coffee!"

Outside, Yashim found two of the valide's handmaidens huddled together on a bench. He asked for coffee.

"You will take it to her, efendi?"

While Yashim was gone, the valide resumed her seat on the divan.

"Take this!" She thrust her writing box into Yashim's hands. "The valide will not be needing it again."

She put her nose in the air, but then she fiddled with her spectacles and Yashim saw that she had tears in her eyes.

"*Tiens.*" She squeezed the bridge of her nose. "I sit here, Yashim, and think that I have Europe at my feet. The tsar. The emperor."

She lowered her hand and gave Yashim a sad smile.

"I think of all the people I have corresponded with. All the great rulers.

And you know who will remember me best, when I am gone? The children of La Bouboulina. You seem astonished."

"Well, La Bouboulina was no friend of the Porte, hanum."

It was an understatement. La Bouboulina was a wealthy Greek widow who had fitted out—and almost single-handedly managed—a Greek fighting fleet in the war of Greek independence, twenty years before. The Ottomans called her La Capitanessa, the lady captain: and feared her.

"Pouf! That was politics, Yashim. La Bouboulina was a woman of my own sort. She was a friend."

"A friend? I had no idea."

"No, because I never told you. You know she was born here, in Istanbul? In prison, as it happens. Her family were great revolutionaries, Yashim, seamen. They were always fighting. The father had colluded with the Russians so we put him in prison, where he died. A ridiculous waste.

"She was raised on Spetses, in the Aegean, and before she was twenty-five she had been widowed twice. Her second husband also fought us when the Russians came, and he was killed fighting Algerian pirates. If more men had shown his courage, I might not be here," she added, thinking of her own capture by pirates many years before. "La Bouboulina showed courage equal to if not greater than his. She took over the business, and had new ships built—including a warship. Imagine!

"To punish her dead husband, the Porte decided to confiscate all La Bouboulina's property. Some type of Midhat Pasha of the day, no doubt, intended to seize her ships, her goods, her house—everything. So there she was, a widow with many children, facing ruin. But La Bouboulina did not give up—you know what she did?

"She came to see me. She sailed one of her ships to Istanbul, and came to visit me, to beg me to help her. Oh, she was *charmante*—and funny! She had so many children, and so many ships, and she told me it was only the children who gave her any trouble. She could have been a queen—we understood each other very well. As valide, I told her not to be naughty anymore, but as a woman I understood her. And I told my son, the sultan, that he should not let one piece of her property be taken from her. And it was not."

Yashim smiled. "I can believe that."

"Later she was naughty. Of course. She did what she liked, and she became a great rebel. She raised a navy with her own money, and sailed about in her warship, and made a lot of trouble for the Ottomans. But she did not forget what I had done for her. When her fleet took Tripoli, and the Greeks wanted to take revenge on the garrison, there were some women of our household there, and she stepped in to rescue them. She looked after them with proper decorum and sent them back here, to Istanbul, safely.

"She spent her entire fortune fighting for independence. It ruined her—and do you know? The Greeks put her in prison. They killed her daughter's husband. She had a son, George, who was very good-looking—I'm sure they all were, as she was—and he eloped with a beautiful girl from another big family on Spetses." The valide frowned, and waggled her fingers. "*La famille Koutsis, c'est ça.* When the girl's family came to complain, La Bouboulina faced them from the balcony of her house—and some coward shot her, out of the dark. Seventeen years ago. I still think about her. *Elle était très méchante*—naughty, very—but she had a big heart."

Yashim nodded. The valide looked at him and smiled.

"*Voilà.* That wretched pasha pricked my vanity, Yashim, and I needed something to restore it. I did La Bouboulina a kindness, and her children will pray for me. Not the kings."

There was a scratch at the door. Yashim opened it, and found one of the girls standing with the tray.

He took it to the valide, and set it on a low ivory inlaid table.

"I don't want it anymore," the valide said. "It was when I was feeling angry. But there it is." She shrugged. "I cannot write."

"For Natasha's father?"

"Since you tell me nothing, Yashim, I have to find out in other ways what is going on. Your friend, Palewski—he was shot? And someone taken away? Midhat tells me—*qu'est-ce qu'il a dit?*—that this has changed the *atmosphere*. It is no longer appropriate for us to ask for favors from the tsar."

"Why not?"

"Why not, why not?" The valide placed her fingertips to her temples and closed her eyes. "Because it would suggest that we do not take seriously the outrage committed on our streets. It may be supposed that the affair has Russia's hand behind it. If I write to the tsar, it might be construed as a form of exoneration. *C'est tout.*"

"I see his point," Yashim admitted.

"I see his point, and I blame you, Yashim. Had you kept me informed of events, it might have prevented an unpleasant scene. Coffee."

He passed her the tiny fragile cup.

"And Natasha? What will you tell her?"

"I will tell her the truth, Yashim." She rang a bell, and asked that Natasha be sent in. "She's an intelligent girl and she doesn't deserve to be kept in the dark."

It was the first time Yashim had seen Natasha since they made love. She stood for a moment on the threshold, hand on the door frame, the light gilding her hair.

"Valide?" She curtsied. "Yashim."

Was there something in the way she looked at him—the slow smile, a tiny widening of her eyes? Something the valide would not miss.

"Valide hanum," he said. "You've mentioned the need to be informed. It might be as well to tell you—both of you—what has happened in the past few hours."

He told them about the discovery of the clerk's body at the cemetery. "As a man unknown, there was nothing to link him to the other events, including the abduction and the attempted assassination of Palewski, that have, as you say, Valide hanum, so changed the atmosphere."

He was making it easier for Natasha to understand, when the time came, why the most important thing for her was no longer possible: why the valide was going to dash her hopes.

"Things have changed," he went on. He explained how the murder of the clerk might be linked to the Italians—who themselves had disappeared.

"But—" Natasha began.

"The worst," he said, "is to come. Last night, Birgit was murdered." The valide's face went taut. Natasha put a hand to her mouth. "No!"

"Doherty, the priest, found her this morning. Things are still not clear in my mind, and I have only really begun to pull the pieces together. It does seem, at the moment, that there's some sort of plot to destroy a certain type here, in Istanbul. Liberal, revolutionary, call it what you will. Istanbul is an open city—and the Ottomans are generous. Even you, Natasha, are here because of that. Maybe some people in Europe resent it."

"It seems to me quite clear," the valide declared. "We are dealing with a religious maniac, with political views. And one who holds very distorted views on women, too," she added, vehemently. *"Quelle tristesse. Quelle horreur."*

There were questions he needed to ask Natasha, and he supposed it was better to ask now. Later, when the valide had said her piece, Natasha would be upset.

"About last night. After the baths. You returned to the house?"

"We found a—a *chaush*? Is that what he's called? He escorted us. We went upstairs and then, like I told you, I came down to find you."

"And you left her with Giancarlo?"

She twisted her fingers. "I didn't actually see him, Yashim. I've just been thinking—I felt I'd seen him, but it's not true. We went inside, Birgit and me. She said something like 'Giancarlo's back.' The bedroom door must have been slightly open. We'd talked a lot about these things, at the baths," she added, with a glance at the valide. "So I came downstairs and found you."

"It might not have been Giancarlo, then?"

Natasha looked anxious. "Oh God, Yashim. You know how sensual she was. She stretched like a cat, and I felt out of place. I knew what she was thinking—all fresh and warm from the baths, like that." She hesitated, blushing.

The valide's eyebrows rose a fraction, but she said nothing.

"It's not your fault, Natasha," Yashim said, gently. "How could you have known—if Birgit didn't?"

"It makes me feel so—ashamed."

Yashim nodded. They both knew what she meant: not just her assumption that Giancarlo and Birgit were about to fall into bed together, but them, too. She and Yashim had wandered the moonlit streets and made love while Birgit—suffered.

The valide's eyes moved from Natasha to Yashim and back.

"Go, Yashim." She waved a bangled arm. "There has been quite enough blood and mayhem for one day, and I trust you to prevent any more. Natasha and I have a great deal to talk about."

61

ABDULLAH Ozgem, the clerk, lived not far from his work at the Sublime Porte.

It was a street of timber houses, narrowly packed together, whose jutting upper stories almost touched and kept the street below in perpetual shade. The broken ground was damp and muddy in parts, and Yashim had to pick his way carefully.

He knocked, but there was no reply. The ground-floor windows were high and barred, but they were not shuttered and one was open, releasing a scent of onions frying. Yashim knocked again, harder, and eventually an old woman put her head out the window and looked down at him through the iron bars.

"Yes?"

Yashim took a step back. "Good afternoon, hanum. Is this Abdullah Ozgem's address?"

She munched her lips and inspected him. "That's right," she said at last. "Are you from the mosque?"

"No, not exactly. May I come in?"

She continued to move her lips, considering. "You look like a gentleman from the mosque."

"I'm with the *kadi*, if you like."

"There you are," she said triumphantly. "Ozgem?"

"That's right. I'm sorry, hanum. It's hard to talk out here in the street."

"Push the door, then. It's not locked."

Yashim met the woman in the hallway. She wiped her hands on her apron. "He isn't home. Abdullah. I see all my students home at night."

"Students?"

She shrugged. "It's what I call them, efendi. Most of my gentlemen are at the technical college. But Abdullah has a job, obviously. I suppose that's why he got so rich," she mused. "New clothes, new shoes, wants meat every night. Splash it about, he does. Not that anyone dislikes him for it. He works for it, see? Coming in at all hours. Not coming in at all."

"You haven't seen him lately, then?"

"Gone since the day before yesterday, and not a word."

"I'd like to see his room."

She cocked her head. "What? He's not moving on, is he? I give him meat and I look after him like a mother. That's what they need, isn't it?"

Yashim agreed that that was exactly what they needed.

"It's a lovely room, efendi. I'll show you."

She led the way upstairs. The stairs were clean, the walls newly whitewashed. On the landing several doors led to what Yashim assumed were the tenants' rooms.

"This is the one, at the back," she said, pushing the door. "Oh!"

Yashim peered over her shoulder. It was a lovely room—wood-paneled, with a large window at the far end overlooking a yard, simply furnished with a divan, a table, and a glass lamp.

The window was open, and the sudden breeze picked up a ball of fluff and sent it surfing across the boards. The old woman peered into the room with her mouth open.

"I never!"

Yashim stepped past her. The divan had been dragged sideways, and stuffing from its mattress was spread across the floor. The lid of Ozgem's chest was raised and the mattress slashed, his clothes scattered across the floor along with feathers from the quilt and the pillows.

"I never heard anything," the old woman said, staring aghast at the damage. "He must have come in mad, or something."

Yashim leaned out the window. The yard was bounded by a low wall, giving onto an alley. Anyone could have come into the yard and climbed the back wall.

"I don't think he did this himself. It's a burglary."

"Burglars!"

Everything had been ransacked. Yashim picked up the lamp on the little table. It was a brass oil lamp, cheap but workmanlike; it was surprisingly heavy. He removed the mantle, laid it on the ruined mattress, and unscrewed the wick and the turning mechanism.

He took the lamp to the window and tilted it away from him. The oil slid to one side.

"Burglars," Yashim agreed. "Who didn't look in the right place."

The oil chamber of the lamp was full of silver coins.

In the old lady's kitchen Yashim accepted a glass of mint tea.

"There's never been anything like it in this house before," she complained. "Mattress on the floor, all split—and the cushions. Looks like the Tartars had been through."

Yashim poured the oil into her lamp and took Ozgem's lamp into the yard to shake out the money. The amount surprised him: more than sixty silver dollars, Maria Theresa thalers from the Viennese mint. He counted them. There were sixty-six in all.

"Does he pay you with these?" he asked, accepting tea in the kitchen.

"Them? I've never seen them before. Foreign, aren't they?"

"Maria Theresa thalers. One is worth about three hundred *kuruş*." He watched the amazement spread over her face.

"What shall we do? Put them back, efendi, before he finds out."

"He won't, hanum." Yashim bit his lip. "The fact is, Abdullah Ozgem's dead."

The look of terror that succeeded the amazement on her face told Yashim he'd phrased it wrongly. No doubt she suspected that he, Yashim, had killed Ozgem and come for his money.

"No, no. I didn't kill him—I'm with the *kadi*, as I said. I suggest you take care of the coins until we know who it all belongs to. He must have had family?"

It seemed that Ozgem's way of life had changed quite recently.

"At first I had him down as a student, efendi, whatever he said. Never much money—he'd give me five *kuruş* a week, for his board, same as the others. I don't know when he started wanting meat. Two months ago, maybe? He told me he'd got a better job, and they were paying him more. So I bought him meat. *He* bought new trousers, new everything, from that Castelar efendi, the Jew along the road here." She peered at the heap of coins. "And each one is three hundred *kuruş*?"

"He could have bought your whole house."

"I'm not selling," she said, surprised. Then her voice sank. "Poor Ozgem. He must have done something wrong to get so much money, mustn't he?"

62

"I'LL buy food."

Giancarlo nodded. "We may not need it," he said.

"Why not? You mean—Fabrizio?"

"He has his knife. Nobody watching. You heard him, Rafael. He knows he got us into this mess."

"What—what will you say to Birgit?"

"She doesn't have to know."

Rafael bit his lip. "I'll get some food. I'll give you an hour."

Giancarlo gave him a faint smile. "An hour's good. Thanks, Rafael."

He watched Rafael go down the road. A good boy, loyal and quiet. A real revolutionary. A Jew, as well. The Jews had nothing to lose by fighting the Pope.

The operation was, of course, a disaster. He had given it much thought since they arrived at the farm. Fabrizio was an amateur, a play actor, like so many of his southern compatriots. Rafael was too kind, too unimaginative. It was, Giancarlo had realized, the wrong team. Napoleon himself could have done nothing with them.

The wrong team—and perhaps the wrong time, too. The Pope could not last forever, but in the meantime he could make life very difficult. For Giancarlo's family, for instance. He needed to think about them, too— and the estate, and the men and women who lived on it; simple folk, who depended on the Tazzia family. They had responsibilities. Not standing— status didn't matter to Giancarlo, although his was a prominent family, it was true. And that would help, of course. People would speak for him.

His father was not well, as he'd last heard. Fabrizio and Rafael would not really understand, but in the end one could not shirk one's responsibilities, as a son, as a Tazzia.

He walked quickly down the street. It was the best way, he reflected. He should not have become involved at this time, and with this team. It was hardly fair to Birgit, either. No. He'd been a bit of a fool. At least he had been kind to Doherty, which could mean another friend in Rome, perhaps. Only a priest, but Giancarlo knew how the system worked. Patronage and favors, clients and protégés. Doherty could be a friend.

Lucky that Rafael was so trusting. Fabrizio already knew it was goodbye. Probably planned the same thing himself. Giancarlo grinned. Well, he wouldn't hold it against him. Just trust to luck they wouldn't be traveling to Italy in the same boat, God forbid.

There would be a boat, sometime in the next few days. In the meantime, he and Birgit could find another room, somewhere to lay up until the boat sailed. It wasn't like Rome here, you didn't need to show papers. He and Birgit could keep to their room until the ship was ready, and presto! A lot of time with Birgit, between the sheets.

He glanced up eagerly at the house. To Birgit then, and quickly. Rafael had given them an hour.

He pushed the door and stepped swiftly into the hall, which is where his nightmare began with a sudden, smashing blow to his face.

63

RAFAEL hurried through the market, stopping here and there to buy bread, cheese, and vegetables. Every now and then he glanced nervously over his shoulder.

A few days before, while everyone was getting ready for the assassination that never was, he had sensed that someone was following them. Admittedly he had seen no one, or at least no one he could point to; the others had scoffed at his fears.

"People watch us," Giancarlo had said. "We stick out, here. But as for being followed—that's in your head, Rafael. A persecution mania." And he had exchanged an amused glance with Fabrizio, meaning—what? That it was like a Jew, probably. Like a Jew to feel always hunted, everywhere.

Rafael glanced around again. Why not? He didn't need to feel that he was being followed to keep his eyes open. He might run into someone he knew—that friend of Palewski's, for instance, Yashim, who had shown them the ruined farmhouse. There would be questions, evasions, implications. Unforeseen complications. Better to buy his food and go, quietly.

On the other hand, he'd promised Giancarlo an hour, and so far he'd spent barely ten minutes gathering everything they'd need.

Rafael was drawn by the smell of roasting coffee to a small café that spilled out into a side street, close to the market. He did not mean to indulge himself. After all, Fabrizio was waiting, hungry, and it seemed disloyal to sit down, at peace, over a small aromatic cup filled with that rich and oily liquid, foaming at the brim. A little sugar in it, to calm him.

But Giancarlo was canoodling with his mistress, and Rafael needed to kill time.

He sat down on a stool, and the proprietor approached. But no sooner had Rafael made his order than he shot to his feet. Doherty! He had quite forgotten his promise to Fabrizio. What sort of wretch was he, to be thinking of his own comfort at a time like this!

Of course, it would take him more than an hour to find Doherty, speak to him, and get back. What of it? Giancarlo would be grateful for all the time he got—and it wasn't as if he'd be wasting their time, either.

Nonetheless, he waited for his coffee, because he did not know how to cancel his order without a fuss. He fidgeted with the cup when it finally came, then drank it off in a single gulp.

Giancarlo would not be pleased. After the hour with Birgit was up, Giancarlo would expect him back. He would have preferred to have the extra time in bed, with his girl. Rafael could see him pacing the apartment in a white fury . . .

Rafael laid the cup back on the saucer with trembling fingers. Thank God he had stopped to think first.

He took some money out of his purse and laid it on the table.

Well, it would take him ten minutes to reach the apartment if he walked slowly. Maybe the hour would be almost up—and surely Giancarlo would understand that early was better, far better, than late.

Then they could go together to the priest, if Giancarlo thought it was a good idea.

64

YASHIM wondered if he should return to Topkapi. Natasha would have had the news by now, crushing to her. He imagined her staring bleakly through the lattice, twisting her fingers.

At the last moment he changed his mind. Who was he, after all, to intrude on her disappointment? To assume that she felt for him anything as much as he felt for her? As if the flowering of that shy, scarred Russian girl into a fierce lover, a bold and independent agent of her destiny, was in his gift. She'd found the man in him, stirred him, given herself to him—but how could she know how much that meant; how could he guess what it meant for her?

"Do it." She gave him what was hers to give: he was not like those terrible men in Siberia who demanded it.

Natasha would come to him when she was ready: if she ever came at all.

He went home. She was everywhere: on the bed, as the rickrack slipped slowly up her thighs; lying warm on the divan, drawing the curve of her hip beneath the quilt; standing beside him at the stove, amused, curious—beautiful.

He dropped a cup on the floor and watched helplessly as it bounced and shivered into tiny fragments.

He swept up the china, splashed his face in a basin of water, and washed his hands. Perhaps, he thought, she would come. She would send him a message and he would fetch her here.

He sat quietly on the divan, and when he heard the tread on the stairs he almost blushed. But it was not—how could it have been?—Natasha. It was a *chaush*, with a note from the *kadi* informing him that an Italian had been arrested and jailed.

65

RAFAEL dragged his feet as slowly as he dared, and went into the house heavily, slamming the door.

Ghika did not appear, so he went upstairs and knocked.

When no one answered, he stood in an agony of indecision, before opening the door. "Ciao, Giancarlo! It's me! Birgit, hello! I'm back."

He was relieved to see that they were in their room, and that the door was closed. He went to sit on the divan, and then decided that it was macabre to sit waiting silently for his friends to complete their amours, so instead he went to the wine cupboard and jingled bottles. He didn't want wine himself, but Fabrizio had asked for some. He found a basket, and spent time carefully packing it with the food he had bought at market, and a couple of bottles.

"A corkscrew," he muttered, and went to find one.

Finally he sat on the divan and watched the shadows on the wall.

After a while he frowned, and stood up. What he had taken for shadows were dark patches on the wall, like thin paint. He did not think he had ever noticed them before, and he wondered if the apartment was damp. But what nonsense! It had not rained in weeks. First imagining he could reach Doherty and please Giancarlo at the same time, and now—imagining damp! It was certainly a great deal of stress, abducting people in a foreign city.

"Giancarlo! Giancarlo!" he waited. "Birgit?"

He was beginning to notice other things, not just the splashes on the walls. Like the shiny patch by the door, and the flies clustered thickly on the windowpane.

"Giancarlo!" Much louder now. The silence echoed in the room.

He crept to the door and listened. Not a word. Not a giggle.

Without hesitation he banged on the door. He felt rather frightened, but of what he could not say. There was no reply, so he turned the handle.

And peered inside.

In place of two satisfied lovers, what Rafael saw was an empty room. The smell of blood was in his nostrils before he could give it a name, or identify the sight. The mosquito net was tangled on the divan, in a mess of wound-up sheets and heavy stains, and a cloud of flies rose from a stain on the floor to buzz lazily around his head.

"Oh my God!" Rafael took a step back, and whipped around. There was nobody there. No Giancarlo. No Birgit.

He pushed open the door to his own room. Everything was in order, untouched.

His eyes went wildly around the room again. Now he saw the shadows as blood, and in the shadows, blood: across the walls, even on the windowpane. In the silence he could hear the buzzing in his ears.

Rafael stumbled to the door. He took the stairs three at a time, pursued by an eerie, meaning silence that fluttered at his back. He flung himself across the hall and wrenched open the door.

Outside he stood bent, taking in lungfuls of the warm Istanbul afternoon, his face dissolving into painful tears.

66

FOR Leandros Ghika the day had begun badly, and grew much worse. Worse, in fact, than he could have ever imagined.

His immediate impulse, on leaving his flat so abruptly, was to find somewhere to lie low for a few hours. Accordingly he went no farther than the second tavern he encountered, down toward the port, assuming that even a halfhearted search might reach as far as the first. He had money in his pockets for raki, and so he drank raki, touching it with water to make it cloud.

The man, Yashim, had caught him off balance, that was certain. He'd looked like nothing but he'd noticed far too much. First the blood on his slippers, then the knife: it was just Ghika's bad luck he'd seen it coming. He might have killed him—and then, if he'd kept his head, he could have dumped him in the upstairs room, the empty one that wasn't already full of blood, and who was to say?

He ground his teeth and sipped the raki, unable to draw his mind away from the might-have-been, the perfect crime that never was. Not that he was a killer, but if he'd ever needed to kill a man that was the time to do it. He could have cleaned his shoes, tucked away the jewelry properly, and gone out. Gone to the tarts, maybe, and worked up an alibi.

No one would have pinned it on him. They paid their rent, didn't they? He was a respectable landlord. Whoever had done that to the girl would have been copped for killing Yashim, in the end.

Maybe he'd have told them himself who did it.

A very ugly job. Shook him to his spine when he saw how it was, with the girl like that, spread-eagled. Spread-eagled on the bed—the way he'd have liked it with her, if she'd been a bit more . . . well, alive. Even dead he'd had a look, and that part upset him more than he'd expected it could. Put him right off, with the shock.

His hands had trembled as he took up all the stuff she wasn't going to miss and the killer hadn't bothered to pick up.

And on top of that shock to a respectable landlord, this Yashim bursting in and getting warm with his eyes on the slippers, and the knife. It wasn't fair. Not fair.

He mustn't overdo it. Sip it slow, stay sharp.

Easier said than done, though—hadn't it all gone wrong? Instead of the perfect murder, he had the perfect fuckup—this Yashim only winged, when he knew about the slippers and would probably take only a few moments to prove it about the jewels. It'd look like Ghika had killed her for them. Worth more than all the rent. Five hundred *kuruş*, easily. He could kiss that goodbye. Yashim'd probably just take the jewels himself.

He paid for his drink and went out. When he reached his own street he stayed in the shadows and watched. There was no one about. He was good at watching, and he gave it ten minutes.

Had he given it five, and made a dash for the money under the floorboards right then, he would have got away with it, as he constantly reminded himself later on.

After ten minutes, just as he had decided that the coast was clear, two watchmen with staves came up the street and passed within six feet of where he was standing. They went into the house, and they didn't come out. Ghika waited for an hour, then two. He was tired, and the raki had begun to give him a thirst.

Everything that happened to Ghika after that was a consequence of that first mistake. Had he waited just a few minutes less, and got his money out of its hiding place, he could have paid the tarts.

As it was, they knew him. They knew him and he knew them and he took one and bedded down with her in a stinking little hole where the stains on the mattress reminded him of the girl who was murdered and made him break into a sweat. He fucked the tart; it would have looked odd otherwise. But it looked odder when he suggested staying, sleeping even, so he could do it over again later on. Ghika, twice in one night? He had to order some raki at their price, and drink it, too, to convince her it was worth her while.

After that he tried to make the night last, stay awake, keep her going. He ordered more raki. It cost more after hours, she said, and he ordered it anyway, at fifteen *kuruş* the bottle, watching the puzzled frown on her ugly tart's face. Then she said it was time to do it and of course Ghika couldn't with the raki in him, and that screwed-up suspicious face peering down at him over her flat tits and sunken yellow belly. He remembered the lovely girl who was dead but whatever he said made the ugly one more angry and red so he took the rest of the bottle between his teeth and passed out.

Which was when she found out that he didn't have any money.

She'd called the pimp. Together they went through Ghika's pockets. For the liquor alone the bill amounted to twenty-five *kuruş*.

The pimp took Ghika's jacket and trousers, and the new slippers, and put them to account. The woman went to sleep. They would turn a profit, but it involved hassle. So the pimp and his chum carried Ghika through the streets and laid him facedown on the port road with an empty bottle tucked into each armpit, and left him there.

The imam who called the morning prayer found him exactly as he had been left, and not long afterward the night watchmen flung him on a hand truck, and took him to the nearest jail.

Ottoman justice was notoriously swift, but Ghika missed his appointment with the *kadi* that morning and went to the back of the queue. Swift as justice was, it was seldom quite as swift as the desire of anyone in an Ottoman holding jail to receive it. Ghika missed it because he was not awake to demand it; which turned out to be an advantage—if not to him, then to Yashim.

67

TOPHANE, on the Pera shore of the Bosphorus, was a tough area surrounding the old arsenal where the Ottoman navy built ships, and once imprisoned the galley slaves condemned to row in them; it was notorious for its grog shops and brothels and rowdy gangs of foreign sailors who stumbled through its narrow streets, searching for women and liquor and violence.

Embedded in the hillside, the ancient Tophane jail seemed as much a geological formation as a building raised by human hands: a vaulted cavern that exuded the scent of sweat and stale air, like an entrance to the underworld; sailors in liquor felt the chill and passed with averted faces, lowering their voices. The jail had been in continuous use since Byzantine times; parts of it had sunk below the level of the street; its grime-coated carapace was haphazardly punctured by iron grilles through which a feeble light, and less fresh air, percolated into the holes beneath.

When Yashim presented his letter from the *kadi*, a guard picked up a bunch of enormous keys. Beyond the first door, heavily barred in iron, torches flickered in sockets on the walls. The busy firelight glinted against the walls. They descended a few steps and followed a corridor of raw stone leading deeper into the building, where the fetid stench made Yashim's eyes water; but it was the sound that made his skin crawl. Groans and lamentations reverberated tonelessly through the vaults with a soughing, rhythmic quality, like wind in the trees or the rasp of waves on a shingle beach. Ceaseless, remorseless, the long, deep echo of centuries of oppression, injustice, and outraged innocence amplified and blended by the prison's dripping lungs.

The miasma grew thicker as they penetrated to the farther cells. The clatter of their footsteps, the clank of the gate, or the jangle of keys seemed to lose their spark and drift into the backwash of monotonous grumbling, like the remorseless grinding of teeth, that filled the vaults. The stink of unwashed bodies, latrines, and disease blew over them as the turnkey unlocked an iron door, leading Yashim into a vaulted chamber, where a line of squat pillars was divided by heavy iron grilles. Between the pillars Yashim saw white fingers gripping the bars as the inmates struggled for air. Yashim put his cloak to his face to breathe.

"I can't speak to him here. Fetch him to the guardhouse."

The turnkey grinned and shook his head. "Here or nowhere, efendi. Move back!" He rattled his stave along the bars of the gate. "Move back!"

Yashim went in, and the gate clanged shut behind him. The impression of crowding lessened somewhat, for most of the prisoners were at the bars, but the light from the corridor was dim and the piers cast huge shadows across the cell. He peered into the dark. Prisoners were lying on the floor, others propped up listlessly against the far wall. Someone was praying, kneeling on the ground; another man ran senselessly from one side of the cell to another, weeping.

Yashim pushed farther into the cell. A man sitting by the back wall raised his arm to shield his face. Yashim took a step closer.

"So they got you, did they?" he said.

Ghika lowered his hand and looked at him through red-rimmed eyes, but said nothing. He was thinking that of all the bad luck he had suffered in the past day, this was perhaps the worst of all.

"You went back," Yashim said.

Ghika shook his head. "I don't know what you're talking about."

Yashim considered him. It was hard to tell, but he thought he could detect the smell of liquor, sharp and sour.

"What are you in here for?"

Ghika averted his eyes. "Some bitch framed me, with the raki. Stole my clothes."

"I see. Lost your slippers, too? No, that's right. You left them at the house. With the jewels you stole, and the money in a hole in the floor."

Ghika groaned. Tears squeezed out easily from between his eyelids. This wasn't just bad luck, it was a nightmare. He could feel the executioner's sword on his neck already.

"You can keep it, efendi," he said. "It's yours—but I beg you, leave me be."

"Where's the Frank?"

Ghika turned his eyes to the far end of the vaults, where Yashim saw a muffled figure cradling his knees. "He's taken it badly," he said, with a certain gloomy relish. "How could I tell he didn't know?"

Yashim went over to Giancarlo, recognizing his fair hair. The face that looked up at him was covered in dried blood. Both his eyes were swollen; one was gummed shut, and his lip was split.

"Yashim!" he said thickly. "Thank God. It's not true, is it, what Ghika says?"

"I'm really sorry, Giancarlo." He squatted down and laid a hand on the man's arm. "Birgit is dead."

Giancarlo raised his puffy face again, and bared his teeth. "Dead? How? Why?"

Yashim told him.

Giancarlo seemed to wilt. He rocked back and forward, hugging his knees. "Ay! Ay! Ay! Is that—is that why I am here?" he asked at last. "Who would want—? You can't think it was me?"

"The judge may. When did you last see her, Giancarlo? After the baths, with Natasha?"

"The baths?"

"When Birgit came back from the baths with Natasha, were you there?"

"I don't remember."

It was impossible to read any expression in that battered face. "Where did you go? What happened to the three of you?"

Giancarlo began to sob.

Yashim laid a hand on his shoulder. "Giancarlo, the judge thinks that you killed her, or one of your friends. It doesn't look any better if you can't tell me where you were."

Yashim shook his arm. "Come on, man! Where were you all, while Birgit was dying in your own room? Why did you ever leave her alone?"

Prisoners were staring at him, shuffling closer.

Giancarlo's shoulders heaved.

"You must talk to me," Yashim said grimly, "or it's a judge who can't understand a word you say, and wants you hanged."

He waited. Then he stood up wearily, and picked his way back to Ghika.

"Five minutes," he said. "I'll give you five minutes to tell me everything. Lie to me, and the charge against you becomes murder and assault. I'll know if you're lying, Ghika, like I knew yesterday. Tell me the truth and I will even leave your money in its hole. Don't waste time," he added, because Ghika had begun to grovel, pawing his feet.

Ghika gabbled through it all, the girls coming back from the baths, Yashim in the hall, then silence; he had not heard a thing upstairs. No one came, and no one went. He thought it odd. He went upstairs in the morning to see if the girl needed anything—he glanced anxiously at Yashim, as if he was afraid his lie would be detected—and couldn't raise her. He'd gone inside.

"Why?"

"I—I just wanted to see if she was all right."

"Why shouldn't she have been?"

Ghika began to sweat. Yashim made to get up.

"No—no, efendi. I'm not lying, it's just, well . . ." He wiped his nose with the back of his hand, and sniffed. "I liked to look at her sometimes, efendi."

"Look at her? How?"

A flicker of a grin, bashful but unmistakable, passed over Ghika's

232 • JASON GOODWIN

face. "I saw her sometimes, twice, through the crack in the door. Taking her things off. She had such—"

"All right. You hoped to see her naked. So you went in."

"In, and stepped on that blood."

Everything else was as Yashim had suspected. Once Ghika had got over the shock of finding her, he'd stolen whatever he could see lying about, reasoning that whoever had murdered her might have done the same.

"Who did it?"

He looked at Yashim with big eyes. "I don't know, efendi. I honestly couldn't say."

Yashim stood up, and shouldered his way through the crowd. Giancarlo was still huddled over his knees, but he was shaking as if he had a fever.

"Who would kill Birgit?"

"As things stand it looks like you, or one of your friends. That's why you're here, Giancarlo. Where have you been?"

Giancarlo shook his head.

"You're thinking of protecting someone, is that it? All the way to the gallows? It's not like that here, Giancarlo. Executions are messy."

Arrests, too, he thought, looking at Giancarlo's battered face. Someone reached out from the dark and tugged at Yashim's cloak. "Efendi! Help me!"

Giancarlo turned his head aside.

"Who would kill her? Do you know?" Yashim paused. "Birgit's dead, and nothing is going to bring her back. But why should you protect her killer?"

"I am innocent, please. Efendi!" He felt another tug on his cloak. He was acting as a magnet in that hot, stuffy cell: a figure from outside, a breath of air and hope. Yashim did not glance around.

"I need your help, Giancarlo. For Birgit's sake."

"For pity's sake!" Another ragged voice whined at his elbow.

Giancarlo's lips moved, but the words were drowned by begging voices.

"A feather?"

Giancarlo gave a feeble nod. "La Piuma."

Yashim could make no sense of it. Someone shoved against him and he put out a hand to keep his balance: the floor was slick with damp. More people were drifting back from the bars to implore Yashim to listen.

Giancarlo would tell him almost nothing—and everyone else wanted to tell him everything.

"Come." He grabbed Giancarlo's arm and dragged him to his feet.

But it was getting harder to move. Dozens of men drifted around them, thrusting their hands toward Yashim, pawing at his shoulders, twisting his cloak in their fingers. Their murmurs and entreaties became a roar, hemming them in, gathering thickly between Yashim and the gate.

Clutching Giancarlo by the arm, Yashim pressed through the crowd and reached the gate.

The guard saw him and rattled his stick along the bars. "Get back! Stand back!"

But the crowd was too big, too blind, too pressing to move back. Yashim dragged Giancarlo in front of him, took hold of the bars, and braced his arms. Giancarlo stood in the little pocket Yashim had made. But the press was insistent. Yashim felt a body molding to his back. His turban slid forward. His arms shook.

"Get back, there! Away from the bars!"

A sudden pain made Yashim gasp, as the turnkey smashed his stick against the bars. The crowd wailed and roared. Giancarlo was braced against the gate, and Yashim was being squeezed, tighter and tighter. Quite suddenly his arms gave way and the weight of the throng drove him up against Giancarlo, who slammed into the bars.

Yashim was suffocated. All around men screamed and gasped. At Yashim's elbow a small man with a shaved head closed his eyes; Yashim saw his chin drop; in seconds he had slipped down under the throng, which jammed up to take his place. It was like watching a man drown.

Yashim had been close to death before, and he knew how it came in a wave of lassitude and longing. The screams and gasps had subsided to a ringing in his ears and he no longer fought for breath. The pain in his chest, and his smashed finger, had become something else: the glow of dying embers, or an abstract physical sensation that kept him anchored to the world. Everything was growing dark.

68

RAFAEL walked with giddy steps through the streets, his scalp creeping.

Whatever had happened at the flat, it was not the revolution. It was something dark, intimate and disturbed. But then it seemed to Rafael that the revolution had a tendency to darken as soon as words gave way to deeds. The blood congealing on the floor, and on the divan, and across the walls, had been splashed there by their revolutionary acts: of that, Rafael was certain.

The others thought of him as a Jew; he knew that, and avoided thinking about it. He was not, strictly speaking, Jewish. He attended a Christian school, and went to mass until, at the age of seventeen, he lost his faith. After that, it had been a short step to revolutionary ideas.

And yet, blood had been spilled on the ground—and Rafael, who had never seen blood before, knew that it cried for vengeance.

He walked on. Ahead of him, a column of children filed along the road behind an elderly mullah. They were walking two by two, holding hands and chattering merrily. A trip to a mosque, Rafael thought vaguely. He dropped back, disturbed by their gentle, happy prattle until the children streamed through iron gates into the courtyard of a little mosque.

His steps carried him past the railings, and he looked in. A dozen shaven-headed little boys, no more than seven or eight years old, all elbows and missing teeth, were making free of the small courtyard, racing around an old almond tree that had already begun to shed its leaves.

Rafael trailed slowly past a pillar and stopped by the railings. A boy was swinging on the lowest branch of the almond tree, and the old mullah had come out of the mosque to tell him off. The boy jumped to the ground, landed in a squat, and raced away. The mullah said something and turned and went inside.

The boy called to his friends and he began to play the mullah. He wagged his finger at them. He stroked his long beard. He felt a twinge in his back and began to hobble across the courtyard on an invisible stick, wagging his head.

The other boys laughed.

As quickly as the mullah had been assembled he was dissolved, and a new character took his place. Three or four boys lined up, the mullah—stick and beard and wagging finger all forgotten—gave a shout, and then they were off, pounding around the sides of the court, their little elbows pumping, heads up, feet flashing on the cobbles. They swept past Rafael watching at the railings. Once around was not enough! Again!

Another boy joined in, and they made the tiny circuit—but who had won? The argument collapsed almost as soon as it had begun. An armlock, a push, then everyone wanted to see what another little boy was looking at on the trunk of the tree. A lizard, maybe—Rafael couldn't see. All he could see was a knot of small heads, gravely inspecting the bark, voices low.

The mullah was back. He stood at the doorway and clapped his hands. The boys pulled away reluctantly from the tree, one by one, and began to form a line.

The little boy who had been a mullah, an athlete, and a zoologist was the last to drag himself away. As he finally went to join the others, he caught Rafael's eye.

Rafael smiled.

The little boy looked at him blankly. Then he slowly pointed two fingers, steadied them on his other arm, cocked his hammer thumb, and fired a shot—*pfui!*—that struck Rafael through the heart.

69

THE turnkey hoisted the torch from its bracket and brought it close to the bars above his head. It was worse than he'd thought—every man in the cell seemed to be pressing toward him in a horrible lump of criminal flesh.

It was the light—the glowing embers of the pain, as Yashim imagined it—that saved his life. For as the torch rose above their heads, Yashim glimpsed the outline of the massive piers, and the narrow ledge around them from which the vaults sprang.

Before the press could swallow him he made a final effort, reaching up as he felt his chest compressed. His fingers met an iron bar. The metal was rough and wet, but it afforded him a slight grip, and with a heave that almost wrenched his shoulder apart he managed to struggle an inch or so higher, above the heads of the crowd.

Two hands on the bar, he hauled again. Something like air entered his lungs: he no longer cared if it was fetid and dank. He sucked at it greedily. His eyesight cleared. The crowd surged against his legs, pinning them to the bars, but he was climbing, slithering out of that mass of suffocating men. His chest free, he breathed again, kicked with his legs like a swimmer surfacing in the water, and burst out, clinging to the top of the bars. Two shifts of his hold brought him to the ledge.

Now he could reach down and take Giancarlo's arm, wrist to wrist. The angle was wrong—Giancarlo had been squeezed into a sideways position, his back to Yashim, his other arm pinioned to the bars—and Yashim could feel the tendons in his neck about to burst as he hauled against the press of the crowd. But Giancarlo had his free hand on the bars and with another lunge he inched out of the scrum.

Fingers snaked around Yashim's ankles, grabbing at the folds of his cloak; he hooked an arm through the bars and resisted their pull, but somebody yanked at his leg and he almost toppled, losing his grip on Giancarlo, who swayed and crashed backward onto the heads of the crowd. Yashim reached out, but it was too late. Giancarlo squirmed for a moment on the shoulders of the men, and then began to sink, headfirst, a slow drowning in a sea of people.

Yet even as Giancarlo slithered beneath the frantic, howling heads, the crowd had begun to relax. It expanded, like a new breath. Perhaps, seeing Yashim rise by the bars, the people shoving from the back had begun to fall away: the surge weakened, the third line reeled back, the second staggered, and what was left of the first, crushed up against the bars, began to breathe.

Giancarlo was crawling on the floor, hacking for breath; bodies lay in two heaps, trampled and suffocated in that terrible small space, and men sprawled by the gate who, Yashim saw, would be meeting a different judge.

Yashim lowered himself slowly from the ledge. His legs shook and he could barely stand. At the far end of the corridor the turnkey was at the door, shouting for help; after a moment he went out, slamming the door behind him.

The light went with him, and with it new sounds arose in the dark: the wail of abandoned men, groans of pain, the rasp of breath. The walls absorbed them. Yashim could imagine, along the vaults, through the corridors, around and around the twisting stairs, the sounds being gradually, blandly, inexorably retuned to the soughing and sighing of this thousand-year-old prison.

For a long time he held the bars between his hands. Someone bumped into him: he shrank like a cat. At last he heard the tramp of feet, the key grated in the lock, and half a dozen men surged into the corridor.

A horrid fear arose in Yashim's mind—that the turnkey who had let him in would not come back, that his pleas would be dismissed and he would stay down here for days, months, never called out, never recognized, forgotten forever and lost to all his friends.

His hand raced to the pocket where he had tucked the *kadi*'s note, and when he felt its outline and the crack of the paper, he almost sobbed with relief. A light was thrust at him, and he blinked.

"There are five injured men, maybe more," he said slowly. "Open this gate."

For a moment he was afraid that the man had not heard him. He saw the key and heard it rattle in the lock. The jailers stood in a line, protecting the door and tapping their staves in their palms.

"Like a pack of rats." One of them chuckled.

Yashim swept through the gate and stabbed a finger toward the cell. "That man, there. Bring him out."

The jailer went inside. He took Giancarlo by the arm, and looked around at the bodies on the floor.

"I'm taking this man into my custody, at the *kadi*'s direction." Yashim waved the paper. "You will see that the cells are cleaned. The men need fresh water." It was too much to ask for air.

The turnkeys were too astonished to protest when Yashim pushed Giancarlo ahead of him and out the door. One of them followed with the keys, to lock them through.

The two men stood breathing heavily. The sun was sinking over the Prince's Islands, the first inklings of darkness creeping eastward across the Black Sea. Though it was not yet cold, Yashim shivered in the light evening breeze. Summer was over.

70

THE café owner swept the damp coffee grounds into a bucket, shook out his rag, and glanced again at the man huddled in the corner. It was the second time he'd been in that day, but compared with his first visit, he was almost another man. He might not have recognized him, even, except for his Frankish clothes. The café didn't see many Franks. If all Franks were like this one, an army of them wouldn't make him rich.

He dropped the coffee into the copper pot and set it on the coals. He always did that, letting the grounds warm up before he poured the kettle. He poured it now and stood stirring the pot with a long spoon.

After a while he took down a small china cup and spooned in the sugar the way the Frank wanted it, very sweet. The pot began to prickle. He raised it from the coals by its long handle and settled it back. Back and forth, back and forth. A lot of trouble for a stranger, but the café owner was a kindhearted man.

Kindhearted enough to stand patiently by while the man mimed his desire for paper and pen. The café owner even found a boy to act as messenger. The Catholic house? In Bebek; he could ask for directions when he got there.

The sad Frank opened his purse, and the café owner picked out the coins himself, so much for the refreshment, so much for the boy. The café owner supposed it was a matter of the heart, but perhaps it was family, when you needed a priest.

71

"GIANCARLO? What the devil's happened to you? Yashim?"

Palewski peered at them both.

"Marta!"

But she was already there. "I have put warm water in the room upstairs. You, follow me."

The young Italian! Always wasting her master's time, bringing him drink when he should work, with that pale voluptuous woman who drank like a man and had white hair, like death. And now he'd been in a fight. She gave him a salve for his bloody lip, and helped to sponge his swollen eye, though he yelped.

"Tsk, tsk. Perhaps next time you'll think twice, before you tangle with Istanbullu!"

Yashim was down first. He'd used Palewski's cologne, but it would take a trip to the baths to eradicate the underlying smell of jail.

"You smell like a Neapolitan tart, Yashim."

"Please, don't reminisce."

"As you know, it's not my style. Drink?"

But Yashim only wanted tea.

"I'll have one for you, then. Cupboard on the left."

Yashim passed him a brandy. "You were reminiscing just the other day, telling Natasha about Moscow."

"That was different."

"But what was it you said? About dispatches?"

"You won't catch me that easily, Yashim."

"No, no." Yashim shook his head wearily. "Something about betrayal."

"The end of the Russian campaign, when I rode with dispatches to Moscow. Staff job. Whole city in flames, you've heard about it. Spent half the night looking for the right man to give the letters to—until the seal broke. Wax pretty much slid off in that heat. Couldn't help seeing that they contained details of our strengths and the amiable suggestion that the bearer be shot. One scar I don't carry on the outside."

Yashim was silent, thinking.

"I can tell it again if you like, with more brio."

"No. That's all. I wonder if we're dealing with the same thing—running someone's head into a noose. Betrayal by letter. Well, here's our man."

Giancarlo came in slowly. His fair hair was clean and both eyes were open, but he looked haggard.

Palewski handed the young man a glass.

Giancarlo tipped back the brandy, and closed his eyes. "Birgit," he murmured. "I just can't understand it. She had no enemies. Only friends. Everyone liked her."

"Maybe it was her friends that got her killed?" Yashim paused. "Tell me about La Piuma."

"La Piuma?" Giancarlo took a deep breath. "It means—the feather. It's a code name."

"Code for what?"

"La Piuma is our commander. He gives us our orders and takes care of our needs. He sent us a warning in Italy, before we could be arrested. We received a note at the apartment we used in Rome, and it was raided moments after we'd left. Later he suggested we come here, to Istanbul."

"You know him well?"

"No." Giancarlo looked surprised. "I've never seen him. I don't know his real name, either. Of course not."

"Of course not?"

"Don't you know how a revolutionary cell operates? Two or three agents who can trust one another, work together. Each cell is a complete unit with no traceable connection to the organization. Even we don't know who our commander is. If we're taken and questioned, even under torture, we won't give anyone away because we can't."

"You can betray your friends. Your fellow members of the cell."

"And that's as far as it can go."

"Did Birgit betray you?"

"Birgit?" The question seemed to take him by surprise. "But she's not in the cell." A little color flushed into Giancarlo's bruised face. "I mean, she wasn't. Never."

"I see." Yashim's expression hardened. "And her killer would know that, would he? By some sort of secret sign, maybe?"

The knuckles on Giancarlo's hand whitened against the arm of his chair. "No—I mean—"

"She was with you, of course, but she couldn't betray you. She didn't know anything. She wasn't in the *cell.*"

"Oh my God."

There was a silence.

"Has La Piuma communicated since you arrived?"

Giancarlo thrust his hands in his pockets and put on such an obtuse expression that Yashim had an urge to go and find the *kadi*, and return him to jail.

"I see you can't betray La Piuma," Yashim explained patiently. "None of you know who he is. But while *you* can't betray *him*—do you see? He can betray *you*."

Giancarlo's eyes flickered from Yashim to Palewski, but he said nothing.

"My friend here, the ambassador, is an old hand at exile." Yashim stood up. "He pines for a nation that no longer exists—on the map. He has found an honorable way of fighting for his country, in ways you'd understand—charging the enemy on the battlefield, standing his ground while his comrades fall, believing in the promises of great men."

He held up his hand. "Forgive me, my friend, and let me speak.

"One word—one sentence—and he could go home. His estates, his horses, his houses, his hounds—he could have them all, if he would only recant. He could shoot duck again on the Podolian Lakes."

"Oh, Yashim." Palewski was frowning, waving his glass. Giancarlo looked uncomfortable.

"But he won't, because he believes in something. You believe in a place for your people? Palewski works for it every day. His dignity is Poland's, and he does it by the law, holding to the law—because it is justice, in the end, which defines the civilized man. Whatever it costs him, whatever he is forced to endure away from his home, there's a single belief that drives him on.

"One day, Giancarlo, he will win. I daresay he'll be dead, we'll all be dead. But no one will have died to protect Palewski. No one betrayed—or even misled. And no one, Giancarlo, will have been left to face death alone in the night, in a foreign city, for a cause that isn't theirs. For a man whose name they don't even know. For a secret message they couldn't even understand. The Baklava Club."

Giancarlo was slumped in the arms of his chair.

"What was La Piuma's message? I think I can guess. He told you to intercept Prince Czartoryski."

Giancarlo tossed his head aside as if he had been struck.

"Czartoryski is a friend of the ambassador. He is, if you don't realize this yet, the leader of the Polish cause, and the man the autocrats of Europe most fear. The Habsburgs are afraid of him, as is your friend, the Pope. And even the Russian tsar."

Giancarlo's expression was wild: "Then who in the name of Christ is La Piuma?"

"Anyone. Don't you see—he could be anyone, who writes notes in Latin, and knows that you're in Istanbul? Someone who'd do anything to destroy you, and Czartoryski, and anyone else who opposes the existing regimes."

"Who?"

But Yashim shook his head.

"You even killed the man who was following you, didn't you?"

Giancarlo was on his feet. "We didn't kill anyone!"

Yashim leveled a finger. "Then tell me in the name of God what you have done with the prince!"

They stood glaring at each other, Giancarlo turning pale and red by turns, Yashim crushing his fingers into a fist.

"Gentlemen—" Palewski began.

And then the door crashed open, and Natasha stood swaying, her hair disheveled, blood trickling from her lip.

She took a step into the room.

"Thank God!" she cried. "Yashim!"

72

YASHIM caught her as she took another step and stumbled into his arms. Her arms slid around his neck and her scent was on his lips and he swept her up and carried her to the armchair.

"Brandy!"

Palewski handed him the bottle.

"Natasha! Natasha." Yashim stroked the hair from her face. He glanced up. "Marta! Where's Marta!"

"I'll call her." Giancarlo ran out to the landing. "Marta!"

Yashim put the brandy to her lips. She gasped, and her head rolled back, and the corners of her mouth turned down.

"Oh, Yashim." She buried her face against his neck, her shoulders trembling and shaking. "Hold me! Tighter."

Yashim squeezed her, feeling her chest flutter. She lifted her face, with bloody lips searching for his and he kissed her, tasting the iron of her blood and the salt of her tears. "Natasha."

Then Marta was there, bringing hot towels, bathing the cuts on the Russian girl's face, rubbing her wrists with Palewski's cologne.

Yashim stood back, to give her room, and noticed Palewski looking at him curiously.

He knelt by the chair.

"What happened? Tell me."

"Oh! Oh!" Natasha took a deep breath. "I've been such a fool."

She put her fingers to the scratch on her cheek.

"I thought—you didn't come! I thought I had to try."

"Try what?"

She clasped her hands and twisted them. "When—you—left—" she began, hiccuping through her tears, "the valide—told me. She cannot write to the tsar."

Yashim took her hands in his. "I know. I'm so sorry."

"You—knew?" Her eyes blazed. "You knew? I didn't believe it when she said—"

She scrambled up in the armchair, snatching her hand away. "You knew—and you—you—" She dashed her knuckles into her eyes. She lifted her chin. "I thought more of you," she said, very clearly.

"I was waiting," Yashim began. "And then—"

"Then!" she cried imperiously. "Then! Your murders and your—" Her lips pressed together as she struggled to find words. "Deaths!"

She buried her face in her hands, and Yashim took her in his arms. This time she did not resist.

He murmured something Palewski could not hear, and she drew back her head.

"I thought I could still do something."

Yashim stroked her hair. "There's still a lot that can be done."

"No. I thought of one thing."

"What?"

"You will think I'm stupid. I was stupid. I thought he could help me. I—I went to him . . ."

Yashim knew what she was about to say. "The priest?"

"Oh, Yashim! He was about to leave and I—don't know—anyone! He is a friend of the Pope, I thought. For my father, I'd do anything now—and Doherty is going back to Rome."

She had calmed down now. She snuggled into Yashim's arms. "So I went to see him."

"Doherty—at his house?"

She nodded. "I didn't say anything to anyone. I thought I had to go, to see him before he left."

Yashim's mind was leaping. Doherty!

"Did he do this to you?"

"The Catholic house was empty—"

"How did you get there?"

"In a sedan." She sounded surprised. "From the palace, why not? There was no one except an old lady, an old nun. I went up and waited. Everything was packed, I mean, there was stuff packed in boxes, not everything. Old papers, manuscripts.

"I was determined to wait for him. I must have waited an hour before a boy came with a note. I took the note for him—what else could I do? It—it wasn't sealed and . . .

"And I think the boys, those Italians, are in some sort of trouble. It was from Rafael, the solemn one. He wanted Doherty to meet them at that old farmhouse where we had our picnic, Yashim, you remember? Where we swam."

Yashim stared at her. "But—that's it! Of course!" He sprang up. "Natasha, did Doherty get the note?"

"Yes. Yes, he got the note."

"I should have acted earlier." He dashed to the escritoire and began to write. "Palewski, get this to Midhat Pasha immediately, tell him I'm going to the ruined farm. The Baxi boy can take it, can't he? I'll need some support, as fast as he can bring it. Giancarlo—where is he?"

Giancarlo was not in the room. Yashim dashed onto the landing, to find Marta running up the stairs.

"Yashim efendi—the Italian boy! He's gone—"

"All right. Take this note, Marta. Give it to the Baxi boy and tell him to run like the wind. It's for Midhat Pasha."

"Yes, efendi. But the kyrie's gun was in the hall, and he took it, and ran!"

"The gun? Thank you, Marta. Get the note to the boy."

Palewski swung his legs painfully off the sofa. "Hold on, Yash. I can't let you go alone."

"It's no good, my old friend. We haven't time."

Natasha stood up. "I'll come," she said.

"Stay." But something in her expression made him hesitate. "It'll be dangerous, Natasha. I don't know what we'll find."

She stuck out her chin and gave a faint smile. "I'm Russian, Yashim."

Yashim nodded. He knew that she was strong. If anything went wrong he would need someone who could carry a report. And she had not finished her story, either.

"Very well, we'll go together. But you're under my orders. Palewski: just pray that we're in time."

73

THE moon rose as they scudded up the Golden Horn, silvering the water and the trees clustered thickly on the shoreline. Yashim lay back in the caïque, Natasha's head on his shoulder.

"I gave Doherty the note when he got back," Natasha was saying. "Once he'd read it, he was only interested in finding out if I had read it, too."

"And you told him you had?"

"Of course. I wanted to know if the boys were in trouble—I mean, after Birgit, and everything. And why were they at that farm? He went very pale. I'd never noticed his eyes before, but they were like the eyes of a snake, Yashim. I was frightened.

"He said: 'Why are you here?'

"'You are going back to Rome, Father. I want to ask your help.'

"'My help? For what?'

"'My father is among the last of the Decembrists still in exile. He is an old man, old beyond his years because he has worked in the mines, and he won't live long. My mother is dead, and I'm his only child. A word from the tsar would bring him home, to Saint Petersburg.'

"'But you have the valide in your pocket, don't you? Or has she changed her mind?'

"He said it so abruptly, Yashim. I'd thought of Doherty as a great talker, you know, convivial. Almost like a Russian. But he was different—abrupt, unsmiling. I'd seen the look in his eyes before, but not in him. It was like that man I told you about."

"Petovski?"

"The other one. Undressing me, even when I was begging for his help."

The domes of three mosques glittered in the moonlight. To their right, Yashim could see the dark mass of the shipyards. He squeezed her shoulder.

"I tried to tell him how circumstances had changed for the valide, and for me. I said there had been some outrage, something the Russians had done, and Midhat Pasha had told the valide she could no longer write to the tsar with the same familiarity.

"Doherty gave me a cunning look. 'She sent you here?'

"'No, no. It was my idea. Mine alone—that I could ask you for your help.'

"He took a step toward me. 'So nobody knows you are here?'

"'The woman downstairs,' I said. 'The nun, who keeps the house.'

"I suppose he realized then that I was afraid. 'A young communicant visits a priest. What of it?' He laughed. 'What do you offer in return?'

"'I—I have nothing, but my gratitude. My hope.'

"He was close to me. He put out his hand, as if he meant to take my arm, and I jerked back. I panicked. It—it made him angry.

"'What are you afraid of?' He grabbed me, held me. 'I smell a wantonness in you.' He sniffed at my hair: he was trembling. 'We must school it.'"

Natasha turned her head and looked out over the silver water.

"Once, Yashim, I would have believed him. I would have obeyed him, I know. But when I talked to you the other day—and when we, you know, were together . . . I think I found some courage. He tried to force me—but I got away."

Yashim searched for her hands.

"Do you think—do you think he—" She gulped. "Did he kill Birgit?"

Yashim hesitated. "Yes. Yes, I am afraid he did. He told us that he found her dead."

She squeezed his hand. He began to tell her what he had come to understand from piecing together the events of the past few days; the caïque sped up the dark waters and Yashim talked, glad to have her beside him, glad for this chance to explain, in part, the chain of errors and betrayals that had led them to enter this desperate race to the woods.

"I think La Piuma—that was the code name the Italians gave their controller—involved them somehow in the attempt on Palewski. That's the terrible weakness of their revolutionary system, which they think so impregnable. Machiavelli said that Western nations were easy to defeat, but complex and difficult to govern. He said the Ottoman sultan was harder to remove, but the system would always serve the usurper. Something like that may have happened with La Piuma. The Italians would have no way of knowing that it was Doherty who had started giving them orders."

"My God," Natasha whispered.

"Somehow they bungled their job, or took fright. I'm not quite sure. I think Doherty lost contact with them, or just lost patience. I hope to find that out. But that's why he killed Birgit. For information."

"But if she was dead she couldn't tell him anything."

"She couldn't anyway. She didn't know a thing."

Natasha shivered in the dark. "What will you do—when we get there?"

Yashim looked out over the water.

"Doherty got Rafael's note, didn't he? He'll be headed for the farm, if the boys are there. And Giancarlo, with his gun. He must have heard everything you said before he ran."

He turned his head and looked at her.

"I don't know what I'll do, Natasha. I just hope we are in time."

74

FROM the Eyüp stage they made their way cautiously to the edge of the woods. The moon was almost full and the shadows were crisp and dark. An owl hooted softly among the trees.

"Are we the first?"

Yashim shook his head. "Not sure. We must be very quiet, and watch. Don't forget Giancarlo has a gun."

He found the path without difficulty, but as they pushed deeper into the woods and the darkness gathered around them twigs snapped underfoot and branches snagged at their hair and clothes. Once a badger, disturbed in its rootlings, made off with a crash into the undergrowth.

"I'm afraid, Yashim."

"Yes." He regretted bringing Natasha. Close to the farm, the sense of menace had grown. He motioned to Natasha to stop, and held her close as he whispered into her ear:

"I want you to stay here, back off the path. There's a dip where you can hide. If anyone comes, just let them pass. Whatever you hear, stay put. Give me thirty minutes or so. If I don't come, get back to Eyüp and wait there for Midhat Pasha. Got that?"

"I want to come with you," she breathed, sliding her hand into the small of his back.

He traced the outline of her hip. Their foreheads touched. "Come into my dip," she said mischievously. "Do it to me again."

"Later. Now hide."

He had chosen the spot well. She sank like a hen pheasant, and he saw her white hand come out and stroke some ferns into place; but when she had stopped moving he couldn't have said if she was there or not.

Without Natasha, Yashim felt lighter and safer. He moved to the edge of the wood and saw the outline of the ruined farmhouse at the bottom of the hill, with the pool glittering just beyond. Everything was still, and only an army of cicadas in the grass kept up a raucous chorus in the moonlight.

The light, and the grassy hill, made it difficult to approach the house without being seen. Yashim descended in flits, darting between the bushes that were beginning to reclaim the abandoned land, until he reached the large cypress at the bottom and pressed up against its black trunk, with a view across tumbledown farm buildings to the house about twenty yards away.

Nothing stirred. The windows of the house were in inky shadow, and where the roof had fallen the moon lit up a cradle of broken rafters and tilted beams. There was not a light to be seen, and not a whisper to be heard over the sound of the cicadas. Yashim turned his back to the tree and scanned the empty hillside.

Perhaps he was too late, and Doherty had been and gone and left the farmhouse lifeless.

But Giancarlo had a gun.

Yashim looked up at the stars, watching a patch of inkiness slide across the sky. When the cloud began to envelop the moon, he dropped to a crouch and made a dash to the wall of the nearest outhouse, pressing himself into the shadows.

His hand closed on a loose stone on top of the collapsing wall. He lobbed it through the air, and heard it clatter on the ground on the far side of the farmhouse door.

Nothing moved.

The cicadas whirred and creaked. A gust of night air wafted through the valley, and silvery shadows raced across the grass. A shutter creaked and banged.

The place seemed more desolate and abandoned than ever. He remembered the secret valley the day they had found it, running down exhilarated across the grass; Natasha stooping to admire the wildflowers that she couldn't name, Birgit moving with a slow, simmering grace, her hem rustling across the grass. Doherty so genial, waving his stick, spouting scripture, ranting about dispossession and the loss of the good land. Everyone, it seemed, liberated to be the man or the woman they were. A sort of paradise.

"Imagine, Yashim!" Doherty had flung his arms wide, flushed with the good food and the cold champagne. "The return to Eden! Forever summer, the sun shines, the trees bear all manner of fruit. The rude habitation of the first man and the first woman—scarcely decayed. This, Yashim, is immortality!"

How different it seemed tonight. The old house watching the slope and the woods silent and withdrawn.

Yashim raised his head. Surely something had moved: his ears had caught a crack, above the drone of crickets in the long grass. He narrowed his eyes, and glimpsed something stepping out of the shadow of the trees. It seemed too long to be a man. Perhaps a deer, drawn to the lush pasture and the silence of the valley.

But it was not a deer. First one figure, then another, broke out of the deep shade and into the moonlight: two men, one behind the other, very close together.

Yashim strained his eyes, and then his heart stopped. The figure in front was not a man but a woman: he could see the tilt of her shoulders and the bulge where she held her skirts above the damp grass. She was making her way very slowly down the slope, and barely a pace behind her came the man.

He seemed to move more cautiously than the woman. Yashim heard a short bark and almost at once the woman paused, waited, then walked on. The man was wearing a wide-brimmed saturno, and the woman was Natasha.

No sooner had Yashim made them out than he heard a tiny rustle from the house, like someone shifting their balance.

75

DOHERTY made the most of the cover the girl afforded him, stooping slightly and careful to keep her always between him and the windowless house.

Yashim had no doubt that the boys were watching now: the shutter, banging in the wind, had fooled him momentarily. Three men—or two?—watching from the recesses of the windows. He wondered if Giancarlo was there, resting his gun on the ledge, squinting down the barrel. He would not be able to take a shot unless he was prepared to kill Natasha first.

The priest had a gun, too: Yashim had not expected that. But the Catholic house was bound to have arms for its own protection: the Catholics were not popular and it was all too easy for a mob to gather at its gate. Doherty would have known where to find it. He was using it now, lowered at Natasha's back, as they advanced slowly and deliberately down the grassy slope.

Yashim could only hope that he was invisible in the shadow of the wall. Doherty could not possibly guess the disposition of forces against him: but nor could Yashim. If only Giancarlo were to arrive now, late, and take Doherty out from behind: shoot him from the safety of the trees. But no: even that was not certain. He'd be likely to hit Natasha.

If Giancarlo was already in the house, would he try to shoot Yashim, too?

Yashim grimaced. Which of the Boutets had he snatched from the hall—the working gun, or the broken one?

254 • JASON GOODWIN

Natasha was making no effort to keep quiet. Once she stumbled, and gave a little cry: Doherty hissed at her, and Yashim saw him drop to a crouch, sheltering behind her. Natasha knew that Yashim was down at the farm, and she was giving him warning, making sure he noticed their approach.

If they tried for the front door, then they would pass scarcely ten yards from where he lay. But it was more likely that Doherty would seek the shelter of the outbuildings, as he had.

He dropped back silently along the wall. At the corner he almost stumbled over some fallen stones in the grass, but there was a narrow gap between his building and a small goat pen, deep in shade. He moved into it and waited.

He was not a moment too soon: Doherty had seen the advantage of the shadows, too. He could hear the sound of Natasha's stumbling feet, even the rasp of Doherty's breath, as they slipped in beside the wall where he had been hidden. Everything depended on the position they had adopted: Who was closer to him? Natasha, or the priest?

Then he heard Doherty whisper. "Stay down, girl."

It was now or never, before the priest had time to work out the lay of the land. Surprise was Yashim's sole advantage over an armed man with a hostage.

Yashim reached for a stone and flipped it over the wall: it landed on the far side of the outhouse. Natasha gave a gasp.

Yashim launched himself from his heels, swiveling around the corner of the outhouse. In a split second he recognized Doherty's broad back turned to him, and jumped.

Had Doherty been standing, Yashim would have gone for his legs, knocking him backward so that the gun flew up. Instead he sprang onto Doherty's shoulders, pressing his gun arm forward and downward as the priest flung out his hands to meet the ground.

Doherty was more powerful than Yashim had expected. He reared up. Yashim was flung aside, still clinging to Doherty's arm, wrenching the muzzle of his pistol away from Natasha but toward him.

His knees scrabbled against the ground. He flung his hand into the air. The barrel of Doherty's pistol rose a fraction, then dropped, and Yashim was staring into its muzzle.

Had Doherty been any good with a pistol, perhaps Yashim would have died then. Instead he heard a dry click as the trigger engaged—but no report. In a second he had recovered his balance. He rolled back into Doherty's legs. The priest folded over, sprawling across Yashim.

Yashim twisted beneath his weight. Doherty lunged forward: the gun had spun out of his hands and now lay a few feet away in the grass. As the priest scrambled toward it, Yashim reared and clawed at his legs, dodging his heavy boots.

Doherty rolled over, freed one leg, and delivered a crashing blow that snapped Yashim's neck back.

He grunted and shook his head. Doherty sprang to his feet, breathing heavily. He stood three feet away, his hands wrapped around the gun, his thumb firmly wedged against the hammer, and as the darkness cleared Yashim found himself for the second time looking down the barrel of a pistol. Doherty's grip was unsteady: the mouth of the barrel floated in the air.

Yashim reached for a stone, anything he could throw.

"They were falling apart, man!" Doherty gasped. "Turning to dust! And Agapios a blind man at that."

Yashim stared. "Dust?"

"The parchments belong to us!"

Doherty brought up his free hand to steady the pistol. "Forgive me, Lord."

They were the last words Yashim heard Doherty say. The priest had his aim, and Yashim saw him brace: and there was a spark, and then a crash, as the gun went off.

76

DOHERTY'S face splintered.

For a moment he stood still, and then keeled forward into the ground.

Giancarlo stepped forward, still pointing the gun at the space in the air where Doherty's head had been.

His mouth hung open in surprise.

Yashim got slowly to his feet. He took care not to alarm the man who had just saved his life—and might, for all he knew, decide to take it.

But Giancarlo made no move to reload. Instead he stared at the body of the priest, awkwardly slumped at Yashim's feet.

"I thought I would feel good," he said.

"Where's Natasha?"

Giancarlo pushed his hair behind his ear. "I saw her go into the house. Come."

At least she had not waited, Yashim thought.

He rubbed his neck. Doherty had been stronger and faster than he had expected. But also less experienced, which gave Yashim no cause for pride. He had not fought better than the priest. He had been clumsy and too slow: underestimating Doherty had been a fatal mistake. Doherty fought with a wild passion.

But Doherty had made a stupid error, not priming his gun. Stupid and surprising.

Yashim pressed his fingers to his neck, on either side, and rolled his head. Lights were still going off, and there was a steady ringing in his ears.

I thought I would feel good, Giancarlo had said. That was another illusion. It never felt good to kill. Yashim glanced down at the slumped figure of the priest, and felt nothing good at all. He didn't even feel relieved, just bruised and tired and disappointed. He leaned back against the wall, preparing himself for the next encounter: the solution to the whole unhappy riddle.

And he began to move only when he heard Natasha's scream.

77

THE first, irrational thought that flashed into his mind was that Giancarlo had shot her. But Giancarlo was there, in front of him.

Yashim tore around the corner of the shed, and raced toward the dark front door, almost colliding with someone stumbling out.

"Oh, Yashim!" She flung her arms around his neck.

"I heard you scream."

"There was someone—in the dark. I think he's dead."

Giancarlo had joined them in the moonlight. "What was it?"

"I don't know, Giancarlo. We need a lamp."

Giancarlo went in first. After the moonlight, they had to blink to let their eyes grow accustomed to the darkness. At the far end of the house the moonlight streamed through the broken roof, but here it was very dark.

Giancarlo bent down, searching for something. Yashim saw Giancarlo's silhouette rise against an empty window as he stood a lamp on the ledge.

"Matches!"

Giancarlo crouched to run his hands over the cobbled floor. Yashim drew Natasha to him, back to his chest, sliding his arms beneath her arms, leaning his tired head on her shoulder, inhaling the scent of her hair.

By the window a match fizzed, and Yashim saw Giancarlo's face, like a boy's, tongue held between his teeth, as he carefully ferried the bright light to the lamp. He heard the snap of the lever as he raised the mantle, and in a moment the darkness lifted, like a curtain, on the final act.

78

RAFAEL was lying on the floor. He was dead. The lamplight reflected gently in his open eyes.

He looked peaceful, even comfortable, like a boy lazing too long in bed.

Yashim held Natasha tight.

"Where's Czartoryski?" Giancarlo said.

Natasha unclasped Yashim's hands, and strode toward a bundle of hay that lay in the corner.

"Isn't that what this is all about?" she said.

"All what?" Yashim asked, woodenly. He took a step toward Rafael. "He's dead."

Giancarlo nodded slowly. "It was what it was all about." And he began to cry, silently, the great tears coursing down his cheeks.

Yashim sank to his knees by the corpse on the cobbled floor and with his thumb and forefinger he closed Rafael's eyes.

Giancarlo wiped his handsome face with both hands. He stepped into the doorway and seemed to hang there for a moment, one hand on the jamb, and then he walked out into the moonlight without another word.

79

NATASHA stirred the heap of straw with her foot.

"Nobody here," she said.

"Rafael," Yashim said. "The one who wrote the note."

Natasha looked up into the sagging rafters.

"I hope you don't feel you've wasted your time," Yashim said.

"My time?"

"In Istanbul." Yashim got up and came and stood by the pile of straw. "Perhaps they killed him after all."

She turned and looked at him curiously.

"Who?"

Yashim folded his arms, and looked at her.

"Czartoryski. The liberal prince. He might be dead."

She nodded, slowly. "Maybe, Yashim."

"Doherty wouldn't care. He died for his manuscripts. That's what he cared about. Getting his stolen parchments back to Rome." He ran his hands across his face.

Natasha stepped forward, took his wrists, and laid his hands on the sides of her face.

"He would have killed you for them."

"But he didn't have to." Yashim's fingers laced through her strong black hair and touched the hollow at the back of her neck. "It wasn't my affair. But it's how you brought him here, Natasha."

Her head swayed, and she closed her eyes. "When I saw his trunk, all packed with scrolls, and books . . ." Her neck rolled under his fingers. "He was terrified I'd tell."

"So you told him that I knew?"

Natasha arched her back. "That's it, just there. Mmmm."

"And on the path, when you heard him coming past . . . It was clever to make him take you hostage."

"People—" she faltered. "People are afraid of being shot."

Yashim nodded. She had staged her entrance very well.

"I did think La Piuma was Doherty," he said.

"I don't see why the Pope should have those documents, Yashim. They aren't his."

She bent upward and took his lip between her teeth, and kissed him. Yashim drew back.

"But why?"

"His job. To steal anything that made the Pope look like a ruler."

"That's not what I meant."

Natasha took a step back, and shook out her hair. "Don't talk to me anymore, Yashim. Come."

The questions buzzed between them like plucked strings of a guitar. She held out her hand. "I want you now. Here. In this dirty straw."

"No."

She frowned. "Now, Yashim."

Ghika had told the truth: Ghika, who watched everything, noticed everything. Ghika, of all people. After Natasha and Yashim left Birgit upstairs in the apartment, no one left and no one came. And Giancarlo wasn't there.

"When we made love," Yashim said thickly, "Birgit was already dead."

"Don't."

Doherty could not have killed Birgit. When Birgit died, Doherty had been talking to Palewski. Drinking his brandy.

"You told the Italians to shoot Czartoryski. But you weren't sure they had. So you killed Birgit when you got back from the baths. Before we— went home."

Natasha's head jerked.

"There are two Natashas, aren't there? That's what you said. Natasha who taught at school, and Natasha—the other one," Yashim said slowly.

She shook her head, letting her dark hair fall around her shoulders.

"But the boys had disappeared. You thought that by killing Birgit you could flush them out, finish them off. They'd be swept up and hanged. A judicial murder. But then you realized that Doherty was the perfect villain. So you went to see him, as you said. To discover his weakness. He didn't touch you, did he?"

"Shhh." She knelt down in the straw. "Nobody touches me except you. Come." She reached down for her skirt and began to pull at the hem, shifting her knees.

Yashim didn't move. She raised her chin.

"Do you remember about the tall one? Petovski's friend?"

"Of course I remember."

"Well, I stabbed him in the end. Last spring. He died. I didn't try to run away."

"No."

"So they sent me here, instead. Told me to be La Piuma. Protect my father."

"Natasha."

"Yes." She raised a hand toward him. "Come."

Giancarlo came running back to the house. Yashim had quite forgotten him. He was shouting. "Yashim! Yashim! There's—"

Something snapped outside. Not once but several times, very loud.

"What's that?" Yashim went to the doorway and looked out.

Ten yards away, Giancarlo lay sprawled on the grass with his hands flung over his head. He was not moving.

Natasha rustled in the dark behind him. She went to the window and leaned on the ledge. Presently a beautiful sprinkling of stars seemed to twinkle among the trees at the top of the slope. *Snap! Snap! Crack!*

Something whirred past Yashim in the darkness and smacked into the ground, with a sound of chipping stone.

"Get down!" He reeled back, away from the door.

Natasha was slow to react.

"Get down! Gunfire!"

She took a step backward, put her hand to her cheek, and sat down abruptly on the floor.

Yashim ran over and put his arms around her. "Someone's shooting. Are you—"

The question died on his lips. Her hand was clamped to her cheek, and through her fingers a welling black flood was spreading across her hand.

She looked at him with her big dark eyes, frightened and inquiring, and tried to speak. But only a jumble of sounds fell from her lips.

"Don't speak." He smoothed her hair. "You don't have to speak."

"Ya-Yachim."

He heard the blood in her voice. Nothing was clear to him, only a sudden bright light that flashed in at the window, illuminating the broken spars, the body of Rafael still warm on the floor, the woman in his arms.

A thunderclap sounded behind them, and the house shook.

"Ra—ch—ael. Fael."

"Rafael? You didn't need to—it's when I knew." His fingers searched her hair, to find that hollow spot on the back of her neck. He rubbed it, gently.

Natasha let her hand drop from her cheek. The side of her face had been shot away.

She reached up and placed her palm on his cheek.

"Uv. I—uv. You did it."

"Love?" He thought of Birgit and the boys and Doherty, who'd died.

Her fingers slipped back around his ear, pulling at it, drawing it around. "For you. Uv. Y-Ya-chim."

He looked down at her ruined face. Everything that was whole was still impossibly beautiful: her nose, her arched brows; a little scar on her lip that still cast a tiny shadow.

Her eyes welled up, and in her tears he saw the bright flash again, and the sparkling white trace that lit up the whole sky.

Yashim slipped his knee beneath her back, to hold her up, and cradled her head in his arms.

"Once there was a girl," he began. "She lived . . ."

"Stop."

Yashim looked down. She blinked.

There was a bang, and a sudden wind, and something fell from above in a flurry of old straw and crashed onto the floor. Natasha's fingers brushed Yashim's lips. Her eyes never left his face.

"A beautiful girl," Yashim whispered. "Who did terrible things for love."

"Father. You." Her head swayed. "Did you—?"

"Did I—?"

Her eyelids fluttered, and her chest convulsed.

"Before—and after, Natasha. I loved you." A tear rolled down his cheek. "I love you."

She closed her eyes. Yashim cradled her in his arms, holding her wounded face against his breast, staring at those dark brows, the tender bows of her eyelashes, the narrow bridge of her nose and the nostrils. She was alive, so alive against his leg and beneath his arms that he could imagine she was only sliding gently into sleep.

Once he thought crazily that her eyes were opening again. But it was only the light of the flames that licked across the broken roof.

He felt her shiver, for a moment, in his arms, and he rolled her head onto his chest and looked up at the lamp that was still glowing on the window ledge. A clump of burning sticks fell to the ground. Still Yashim did not move.

"The gunners have found their mark," he said aloud. "I don't know why."

And for some reason he thought of the old *kadi*, with his scrap of yellow paper.

"Of course," he murmured. He bent and kissed her brow. The clerk, with sixty-six pieces of silver! He'd sold the secret of Czartoryski's visit—and Midhat found out. The Italians didn't kill Abdullah Ozgem. Natasha didn't kill him. He was dead as soon as Midhat Pasha guessed.

Midhat, always so anxious not to be overheard, discovered there had been a leak right there, in the ministry—just as Yashim had warned him.

Midhat's reaction would be to stop the leak—and erase the evidence that it had ever occurred. He knew Yashim might uncover the trail. So he had Ozgem killed.

A plausible attitude to take, if the reputation of your ministry needed to be protected. Close down the whole operation. Czartoryski, the Italians—once they were gone, there was nothing, actually, to show that anything had happened. Czartoryski might never have arrived. Ozgem dead, a detail. The rest was anecdote.

There would have been a nest of foreign vipers in a farmhouse, plotting; but now wiped out. They'd murdered a girl. And Czartoryski nowhere to be found.

And outside, from among the trees, Midhat Pasha was finishing the job.

Yashim stroked Natasha's hair, and marveled at the chiseled beauty of her face as another rocket raced into the air.

She had tried to bring him home. Oh, she was a murderess, and a highly accomplished liar, and it probably didn't mean a thing but there, just for a moment, Yashim had glimpsed the longed-for place, and felt on his face the winds of home.

80

PALEWSKI, breathing heavily, staggered through the trees.

The gunners hardly saw him coming through the smoke.

"What the hell's going on? My friend's down there!"

Midhat turned his sad eyes on him. "That's the first I've heard of it, Your Excellency. Yashim, I believe, is still at Eyüp. This is an operation to clear out a nest of vipers and revolutionaries."

Palewski goggled at him. "You—imbecile! You've got Yashim, Czartoryski, and the Russian girl down there. Stop this bombardment at once! Send in your men."

"I do not believe in exposing men to unnecessary risk," the pasha replied. "My own son died at Shumla Pass because commanders took unnecessary risks."

"Your son? I don't believe this." Palewski simply stared. Midhat looked away.

"Stop the guns this minute, or you will have a Polish ambassador to account for, Midhat Pasha."

Palewski stepped away and began to walk, very slowly, downhill through the moonlight.

He could see the farmhouse at the bottom of the valley. Half its roof was gone, and from the other end bright orange flames were licking from beneath the tiles.

Palewski's attention was focused on a lamp that glowed in the window of the ruined farmhouse like a beacon, improbably small and hopelessly faint. It reminded him of the fire on his hearth, and Yashim dropping into his favorite armchair.

Palewski's chest hurt, but he didn't care. The grass under his feet was wet with dew: it made a swishing noise as he walked.

The light of the lamp was fading. The flames had taken hold of the roof, and their orange light lurched sickeningly at the window, now advancing, now backing into darkness. The lamp still burned, but against the leaping sheets of flame it dwindled.

He was halfway there. A rocket sizzled up, over his head. It blazed with a bright white flame, banishing the shadows around the farm. Palewski dropped his stick and began to run.

The blood from his wounds seeped through his shirt, but it was warm, and his feet flew over the grass, over the molehills and the tussocks, toward the lamp that burned and flickered in the window.

"Yashim! Yashim!"

The rocket dropped from the sky like a ballerina making a descent en pointe.

Palewski raised his hand to shield his eyes from the glare as it sank toward the farm. He seemed to be really flying now, as he had flown when his heavy brigade rode against the Russians at Borodino, the way his feet had flown as he rushed across the parquet to where Irina was waiting for him, long ago, and longer still, further back, down the long, great winding stairs at home, to his father standing in the hall . . .

He remembered those moments, and for Palewski they fused into a single, tiny flickering goal in the darkness beyond, a single moment that was, and would always be, the one small point at which a human heart can aim.

And the flash of the rocket lit up the smile on his face.

Epilogue

STEAM rose from the bath, in front of a crackling log fire. The shutters were drawn—with some difficulty, for they were old and slightly warped by sun and rain—and fresh candles twinkled in the pier glass.

Beside the bath, on a low inlay table, stood a tumbler of brandy and a book, taken at random from the shelves.

Prince Adam Czartoryski lay back in the bath and reflected that never, in these last twenty years, had he felt so well.

Respite from a diet of creamy sauces, salty stocks, and twelve elegant courses every night had done wonders for his digestion. He had lost some weight and livened up his musculature, taking cold dips in the pool. Apart from a mild anxiety that he might at any moment be called to his death, he had enjoyed a carefree week. For the first time in twenty years, he whistled in his bath.

The boy had it coming, anyway. When Czartoryski had stumbled on the old well, covered with a few rotten planks, the whole scheme had dropped into his mind complete and in an instant.

"I wonder," he had said, "since we have no food, if we shouldn't try drinking water from the well."

They'd gone to look. Czartoryski had peered over the edge and muttered that it looked dry. Fabrizio had peered, too, and Czartoryski pushed him in.

Tomorrow promised to be an interesting day—lunch with the sultan, and a discussion of his favorite schemes: a new European order, and a settlement for exiled Poles on the shores of the Bosphorus. A safe haven. It might be called something like Adampol, after him.

He took a sip of Palewski's brandy and picked up the book.

And as he peered a little closely at the letters—for his sight was not quite what it had been—he heard the front door bang, and light footsteps on the stairs, and a woman calling out in fear, or triumph. It was hard to tell.

"Kyrie! Yashim efendi! You—you are home!"

And he heard the murmur of men's voices, and the sound of their footsteps as they crossed the hall below.

GLOSSARY

Alhamdulillah—thank God

baglama—a Turkish stringed instrument

chaush—a page, errand boy

cicerone—a guide (Italian)

Circassian—i.e., from the Caucasus, the homeland of many harem
women

corek—a pastry

Decembrists—Russian mutineers of December 1825

divan—an Ottoman daybed

efendi—sir, gentleman

firman—an imperial order

Frank—a Christian from western Europe

gelato—ice cream in Italian

giaour—disparaging term for unbeliever, a Christian

gözde—a concubine, sleeping with the sultan

hamal—street porter

hammam—Turkish bath

hanum efendi—madam

imam—a Muslim teacher, attached to a mosque

inshallah—God willing

jezail—long-barreled musket

kadi—an Ottoman magistrate

kismet—fate

köçek—a transvestite male dancer

kuruş—Ottoman coin

lokum—Turkish delight, a sweet confectionary

medrese—a Muslim school that is often part of a mosque

milord—literally "my lord," a wealthy English traveler

mullah—a Muslim leader

Nasreddin—a foolish mullah, dispenser of folk wisdom

Nazarene—i.e., from Nazareth, a Christian

Nasdrovie—Russian toast

oka—a Turkish weight of about one pound

pasha—a title, minister of state

Patriarch—head of the Orthodox church

raki—aniseed-flavored alcohol

salaam alaikum—God be with you

saturno—a priest's hat

sipahi—Ottoman cavalryman

stambouline—Ottoman frock coat

Stambouliots—inhabitants of Istanbul, also Istanbullu

Sublime Porte—literally, High Gate, the name given to Ottoman
    government; shortened to the Porte

sufi—holy man

Sultan Abdülhamid—the valide's husband

Sultan Mahmut II—her son

Sultan Abdülmecid—her grandson and reigning sultan

ACKNOWLEDGMENTS

WH E N I let slip my initial anxiety that Yashim might not survive this novel, some of his admirers took to my website at www.jasongoodwin.info to protest: their humanitarian instincts, along with wise editorial advice from Julian Loose in London and Sarah Crichton in New York, turned the scales in Yashim's favor.

Kate, my wife, used her forensic erudition and a red pencil to heal narrative and psychological flaws in the story. Richard Goodwin encouraged our hero to reveal aspects of his physiology that had not been previously exposed. Sarah Chalfant and Charles Buchan at the Wylie Agency have been exemplary Yashimites, while my Estonian editor, Krista Kaer, arranged the world premiere of *The Baklava Club* in its Estonian translation; my thanks also to Juhan Habicht, my translator, and to Ott Sandrak and the Tallinn Headread festival.

Istanbul's role as a safe haven for European exiles and malcontents first struck me when I was researching *Lords of the Horizons: A History of the Ottoman Empire*, but with *The Baklava Club* already written, Professor Norman Stone reminded me of the many years Garibaldi himself spent in Constantinople. Thanks to him, and to Ömer Koç for friendship and hospitality. I am grateful to Edward Impey and Mark Murray-Flutter of the Royal Armouries for telling me about old guns, and to Enrico Basaglia for checking my blunders in matters Italian; while Emin Saatçi and John Scott—the editor of the world's finest magazine, *Cornucopia*—led me imaginatively through a duck shoot on the Çekmece lakes, formerly a wild region of marsh and water crossed by Sinan's beautiful bridge. Any subsequent errors are mine.

The female characters in this book seem to be mad, bad, or dangerous to know. My daughter, Anna, to whom this novel is dedicated, is quite unlike them. Except in her beauty. And her energy of spirit. This book is for her.

DORSET, 2014

A NOTE ABOUT THE AUTHOR

Jason Goodwin is the Edgar® Award–winning author of the Investigator Yashim series. The first four books—*The Janissary Tree*, *The Snake Stone*, *The Bellini Card*, and *An Evil Eye*—have been published to international acclaim. Goodwin studied Byzantine history at Cambridge and is the author of *Lords of the Horizons: A History of the Ottoman Empire*, among other award-winning nonfiction. He lives with his wife and children in England.